"*Daughters of Eve* is a rare find: a young adult novel that isn't afraid to engage with feminism in all of its complexity. I highly recommend it to all girls who are thinking about their place in the world."

Huntress

"Th ... e reason-
ably ... s one of
the ...

uthor of
Dope Sick

"Sh ... ind that
secr ... lutching
susp ... an Lois
Dur

ar Street

"I c ... reach a
new

iger Eyes

"Loi ... gobbled
up ... d scar-
ing ... e to be
daz

s series

"Lo ... ler the
cove

ay and
he Mall

"Lo

series

"Duncan is one of the smartest, funniest and most terrifying writers around — a writer that a generation of girls LOVED to tatters, while learning to never read her books without another friend to scream with handy."

— Lizzie Skurnick, author of *Shelf Discovery: The Teen Classics We Never Stopped Reading*

"In middle school and high school, I loved Lois Duncan's novels. I still do. I particularly remember *Killing Mr. Griffin*, which took my breath away. I couldn't quite believe a writer could DO that. I feel extremely grateful to Lois Duncan for taking unprecedented risks, challenging preconceptions and changing the young adult field forever."

— Erica S. Perl, author of *Vintage Veronica*

"**Haunting and suspenseful** — Duncan's writing captures everything fun about reading!"   — Suzanne Young, author of The Naughty List series and *A Need So Beautiful*

"*Killing Mr. Griffin* taught me a lot about writing. **Thrilling stuff**. It was one of the most requested and enjoyed books I taught with my students. I think it's influenced most of my writing since."

— Gail Giles, author of *Right Behind You* and *Shattering Glass*

"If ever a writer's work should be brought before each new generation of young readers, it is that of Lois Duncan. The grace with which she has led her life — a life that included a tragedy that would have brought most of us to our knees — is reflected in her writing, particularly (from my point of view) in *I Know What You Did Last Summer*. Her stories, like Lois herself, are ageless."

— Chris Crutcher, author of *Angry Management, Deadline* and *Staying Fat for Sarah Byrnes*

"Lois Duncan's thrillers have a **timeless quality** about them. They are good stories, very well told, that also happen to illuminate both the heroic and dark parts of growing up."

— Marc Talbert, author of *Dead Birds Singing, A Sunburned Prayer* and *Heart of a Jaguar*

How could anyone know for sure what went on in all the neat white houses that lined the streets of a pleasant and sleepy little town like Modesta? Behind each door there was a family, and every family held its own secrets....

Daughters

of Eve

by LOIS DUNCAN

LITTLE, BROWN AND COMPANY
New York   Boston

Copyright © 1979 by Lois Duncan

Author Q&A copyright © 2011 Hachette Book Group, Inc.

Little, Brown and Company

Hachette Book Group
237 Park Avenue, New York, NY 10017
Visit our website at www.lb-teens.com

Little, Brown and Company is a division of Hachette Book Group, Inc.
The Little, Brown name and logo are trademarks of Hachette Book Group, Inc.

The publisher is not responsible for websites (or their content) that are not owned by the publisher.

Revised Paperback Edition: October 2011
First published in hardcover in September 1979 by Little, Brown and Company

The characters and events portrayed in this book are fictitious. Any similarity to real persons, living or dead, is coincidental and not intended by the author.

Library of Congress Cataloging-in-Publication Data

Duncan, Lois, 1934–
Daughters of Eve.
Summary: A high school teacher uses the guise of feminist philosophy to manipulate the lives of a group of girls with chilling results.
[1. Feminism — Fiction. 2. Mystery and detective stories] I. Title
PZ7.D9117Dau 1985 [Fic] 79-14918
ISBN 978-0-316-19550-8 (hc) / ISBN 978-0-316-09897-7 (pb)

10 9 8 7 6 5 4 3 2 1

RRD-C

Printed in the United States of America

Title and chapter number art by Jennifer Heuer
Book design by Tracy Shaw

Also by Lois Duncan:

DON'T LOOK BEHIND YOU

DOWN A DARK HALL

I KNOW WHAT YOU DID LAST SUMMER

KILLING MR. GRIFFIN

LOCKED IN TIME

STRANGER WITH MY FACE

SUMMER OF FEAR

For my niece, Sheri Arquette

Chapter 1

The calendar placed the first day of fall on the twenty-third of September, and on the afternoon of Friday, the twenty-second, Kristy Grange walked slowly down Locust Street, her backpack heavy on her shoulders. Her head was bent forward beneath the additional weight of the last load of official summer sunshine.

It had been a long summer for Kristy — *a terrible summer*, she told herself resentfully — the kind of summer when anyone with any common sense left Modesta for somewhere else. The heat had begun in the early mornings. She'd woken up to it, feeling her body damp and sticky beneath the thin material of the oversize T-shirt she slept in, and by the time she was dressed in cutoffs and a tank, the droplets were already beginning to collect along her hairline and in the hollows under her arms and behind her knees. By noon, the walls of the Grange home had enclosed the sort of heat one might expect to find in an oven.

"I don't know why you won't let me turn on the air-conditioning," she'd complained to her mom. "Why do we have it if we don't use it? It's crazy."

"Your dad's the one who pays the utility bills, not you, Kristy," Mrs. Grange had said shortly. "You wait until four in the afternoon, and then you can turn it on and get the place cooled down for dinner."

Her mom worked all day in the women's section of an air-conditioned department store. A lot *she* knew about southern Michigan in the summertime. The truck her dad drove was also air-conditioned, and her brothers, Pete and Niles, spent the whole summer up at the lake sitting on lifeguard towers. As for nine-year-old Eric, he couldn't care less about the heat, or anything else, for that matter. Eric would go out and pedal his bicycle for miles under the blazing noonday sun, like a complete idiot, and come home with heat rash prickling scarlet all over him, and all their mom would say was, "You poor kid. Let's get you into a cool tub," and then to Kristy, "How could you let him do that? You're supposed to be taking care of him."

Yes, it'd been a gruesome summer, and the fall would be gruesome, too. It would cool down, of course; already the intensity of the afternoon sun was lessening. Even since school had started, Kristy could feel a marked difference. Two weeks ago she'd completed the mile walk from Modesta High School feeling as limp and exhausted as though she'd been running in a marathon. Now the sunlight on her head and the back of her neck felt lighter, and she no longer found it necessary to walk at the edge of the sidewalk in the shade of the maple trees.

But, summer or autumn, she was still Kristy Grange, the only girl trapped in a family of spoiled, conceited boys.

Her older brothers were standing in the front yard as she came up the walk. They'd been laughing about something, and their conversation broke off abruptly as Kristy approached.

"Well, here's our Little Miss Sunshine," Niles exclaimed in exaggerated welcome. "Our Cranky-Kristy, beaming and bright, bringing joy to all who know her!" He reached out and gave a lock of her hair a teasing tug. "You're going to crack your face someday with all that smiling, Sis."

Ignoring him, Kristy turned to her oldest brother.

"You drove off and left me! You know Dad said you're supposed to give me a ride home on days when you take the car."

"Couldn't find you," Peter said easily.

"You didn't look very hard. I always walk home the same way."

"You do?" Peter said. "Well, that's something!" He turned to Niles in simulated amazement. "Did you hear that? She comes home the same way *every* time!"

"Yeah — like this." Niles thrust out his lower jaw in a surprisingly good imitation of his sister's sullen expression.

"Oh — you can just — just — go to —" Kristy let the sentence fall away, unfinished. There was nothing to be gained by sparring with her brothers. At seventeen and eighteen, they were so filled with their own self-importance that it was impossible to communicate with them. She often wondered what their girlfriends saw in them. There must be something, because Niles went out with the cutest girls whenever he wanted to, and Peter had been going out with Madison Ellis, the most popular girl in the junior class, for over six months now.

"Our little sister wants us to 'go to,' Pete," Niles said. "Shall we honor her request?"

"By all means. Her slightest wish is our command." Peter gave Kristy a teasing swat on the back. "See you later! Oh — check the fridge door — Mom left a note for you."

"So what else is new?" Kristy snapped. She continued up the walk and went into the house.

As she let the screen door slam shut behind her, the engine of Peter's car churned to life in the driveway. She heard the crunch of gravel as he backed out into the street and the sudden shriek of burning rubber as he slammed down the accelerator.

"Go to — and stay there," she mumbled halfheartedly into the silence of the empty house.

Dropping her backpack on the coffee table, she bent to gather up the letters that'd been pushed through the mail slot in the door. She carried them out to the kitchen and tossed them onto the counter while she smoothed out her lunch bag and put it into a drawer. Her mother was undoubtedly the only woman in the world who made her children save their lunch bags for reuse. The note Peter had told her about was attached to the refrigerator with magnets. As she had known it would be, it was headed, "Things To Do List."

When Eric gets home, make him change his clothes
Clean up kitchen
Do laundry
Defrost hamburger meat
Put potatoes in oven at 5:00
Make salad

Well, Eric wasn't home yet, since the elementary school let out after the high school. "Clean up kitchen" could, in itself, take the whole afternoon. Kristy glanced around her in despair. The boys' cereal bowls from the morning sat out on the table with milk soured in their bottoms, and the egg plates were thick with yellow yolk dried onto them like cement. There was a pool of some unidentifiable liquid on the linoleum at the base of the refrigerator, and the lunch fixings were still on the counter where she herself had left them when Peter yelled that he was leaving and "anybody who wants a ride had better get out here." She'd dashed for the door with her hands still gummy with peanut butter, and the jelly jar had somehow overturned onto the stove top, where the purple glop had dripped into one of the burners.

Why couldn't their mom stay home and take care of things like some other mothers? Kristy asked herself bitterly as she surveyed the mess. She'd done that for a while after Eric was born, and it'd been great. But when Eric reached school age, she'd considered taking a part-time job, and their father had suggested she go for it. She got a job right away at JCPenney and quickly moved up to full-time. "We can use the extra income," Mrs. Grange had told them, and now with Peter planning to go to an out-of-state college and with Niles right behind him, it seemed doubtful that she'd ever be able to stop working. Kristy suspected she didn't really want to. Her mom actually liked her job. And why would anybody choose to stay home and do chores when there was a sixteen-year-old daughter to do them for her?

With a sigh of self-pity, Kristy shoved the stopper into the sink and turned on the hot water. She might as well put the egg plates in to soak before she rounded up the laundry. The upstairs hamper was always an adventure;

eight million smelly socks and a ton of jeans were to be expected, but once there had been a slithering, three-foot-long black snake of Eric's, and on another occasion she'd found a joint in one of Niles's pockets. That had been a worthwhile discovery — he'd been grounded for a week.

The mail lay dangerously close to the grape jelly. Kristy picked up the envelopes and rifled through them. It was mostly junk mail, with one formal letter addressed to "The Parents of a High School Senior" from a photo studio. And there was a square, white envelope —

Kristy stared at it. MS. KRISTY GRANGE was printed above the address in neatly rounded letters. Who in the world would be writing a letter to her? *Maybe it's just fancy junk mail,* Kristy speculated. But the envelope had the look of a formal invitation. Was she really being asked to something — maybe a party?

Placing the remainder of the mail on a clean spot near the counter's edge, Kristy began to open the envelope. She did it slowly, making the suspense last. Whatever it was, this envelope had to have something special inside.

For the first time since she'd gotten up that morning, Kristy Grange was smiling.

"It's a joke," Laura Snow said shakily. "It's got to be a joke."

"My goodness, honey, you look like you're about to fall over." Her mother leaned over her shoulder to read aloud the letter Laura clutched in her hand. "'We are pleased to inform you that you have been selected for membership in the Modesta chapter of Daughters of Eve.'"

"It's a joke," Laura said again.

"Now, why do you say that?" her mother asked her. "It looks real enough to me. What is this club anyway, some sort of sorority?"

"It's *only*" — Laura stressed the word sarcastically — "the most exclusive club at Modesta High. They have a membership of only ten girls, and each year they invite just enough new members to join to replace the graduating seniors. Erika Schneider's the president — you know who Erika is, don't you? She's the coolest girl in the Senior Honor Society. And there's Madison Ellis and Ann Whitten and Tammy Carncross." She shook her head firmly. "Somebody put my name on an invitation just to be funny."

"Laura, honey, what am I going to do with you?" Mrs. Snow regarded her daughter with affectionate exasperation. "Most girls would be squealing and jumping around, just ecstatic, and here you are, saying, 'It's a joke.' Why wouldn't they want you to join their club?"

"Oh, Mom, come on." How could she answer such a ridiculous question? All her mom had to do was look at her, just once, with her eyes wide open. If she did she might see her as she was: a massive lump with boobs that looked like twin watermelons and a butt that looked like twin something-elses. But her mom was blinded by something — love? Familiarity? Maybe the fact that she was overweight herself made bulk seem the norm.

"One reason they wouldn't want me is that I'm a junior," Laura told her as patiently as she could. "The policy is to take in the incoming sophomores. If I was a choice, it would've been last year."

"Well, evidently they missed you then and now they realize what a mistake they made." Her mother looked bewildered. "I don't understand you, honey. Don't you want to join? Clubs are such an important part of student life."

"Don't I want to join?" Tentatively, daringly, she let her imagination reach out and play at the edge of the impossible. She wanted to belong to Daughters of Eve the way she wanted to look like Madison Ellis — to be homecoming queen — to be a cheerleader — to be able to lose forty pounds overnight. She wanted it the way she wanted Peter Grange to fall in love with her. She wanted it the way, as a little girl, she had wanted to be a fairy princess so that she could wave her magic wand and fix all the cracks in her parents' splintering marriage; she wanted it with so much intensity that the mere thought made her dizzy.

Was it possible — could it really be possible? — was the invitation for real?

Slowly, Laura lowered her eyes to the envelope that lay in her lap. It was her name. It was her address. There was no mistake there. She looked at the card in her hand. *We are pleased to inform you . . .*

"I could go to the meeting," she said slowly. "The worst that could happen is that Erika would ask me what I was doing there. I could always say I walked into the wrong room by mistake when I was looking for a different meeting."

"Erika won't ask you what you're doing there. She'll be thrilled that you want to attend." Mrs. Snow smiled fondly at her daughter. "You're being so silly!"

"Daughters of Eve?" Bart Rheardon frowned thoughtfully. "I've never heard of it. Is it a religious organization?"

"It's a school club, Dad," Jane said. "I don't really know too much about it, except that some cool girls belong to it. It's a secret society. Nobody's allowed to say what they do at the meetings."

"I don't like the sound of that." Mr. Rheardon turned to his wife, who was engrossed in television.

"Ellie, have you ever heard of a group called Daughters of Eve?"

"What? Oh, sure," Mrs. Rheardon said, her eyes still glued to the screen, where a gorgeous doctor leaned worriedly over a pale and beautiful patient.

"Hey, turn that thing off. We're trying to talk about something." Mr. Rheardon brought his fist down hard on his knee. "Ellie, do you hear me?"

"Sure. Sure, honey. I'm sorry." His wife leaned forward quickly. She pressed the mute button on the remote, and then, after a quick glance at her husband's face, turned the TV off completely. Quite suddenly the room seemed double its former size and oddly empty.

Glancing back and forth between her parents, Jane felt the tiny muscle at the corner of her left eye tighten suddenly. It was the beginning of the tic she often got when she was nervous. *I shouldn't have shown Dad the invitation,* she told herself miserably. She should've known something unpleasant would come of it.

Still, when he'd come home that evening, he'd been in one of his good moods, laughing and teasing and reaching up playfully to slap his hand against the door frame in a joking attempt to pretend he was taller than the doorway and had forgotten to duck his head.

"What's new in your life, chicken?" he'd asked, ruffling the fine, light hair he'd referred to since her babyhood as "Janie's chicken fluff." And, on impulse, because it was such a happy surprise to see him this way on a Friday, Jane had brought out the invitation.

"I've been asked to join a club."

"That's nice. That's great, chicken." He'd laid the card on the end table and gone out to the kitchen to fix himself his martini. A moment later Jane had heard his voice raised in accusing anger. There was no gin?! What happened to the gin? No, of course he hadn't finished it all last night. It couldn't possibly have been used up that quickly. And, if it had been, why the hell hadn't Ellen bought more when she was out doing the grocery shopping? The liquor store was less than a half block down from the grocery store, and it was even on the same side of the street. Well, now he'd have to get back into his car and go out into the rush-hour traffic on a Friday, which was always one of the worst days at work....

After that, of course, nothing could go right. The gin, when he did arrive home with it, wasn't the brand he'd wanted. At dinner, the chops had been greasy and the beans were canned instead of frozen and the Jell-O hadn't been chilled long enough to hold its shape. The phone rang twice during the meal with women from the church wanting to discuss the potluck ("Don't you women have enough time to jabber during the day, Ellie?"), and the evening paper arrived with the sports section missing.

And now there was the invitation, "nice" and "great" when it had first been shown to him, suddenly a source of grave concern.

"What is this group, anyway?" Mr. Rheardon asked suspiciously, his voice unnaturally loud in the silence left in the wake of the television. "You say you know about it, Ellie? Where did you hear about it? Has Jane been telling you things she hasn't told me?"

"Of course not, dear," Ellen Rheardon said mildly. "Daughters of Eve is a national organization. There's a chapter here in Modesta that's been active for years. In fact, I was in it myself when I was in high school."

"You were? You never told me that." Mr. Rheardon leaned back in his chair and took a long swallow of his drink. "Well, tell us. What goes on at the meetings? What are all those secrets Jane was talking about?"

"I don't remember," Ellen said. "It's been so many years. They weren't anything big, just secret passwords and handshakes and things like that. We had projects and held bake sales to buy things for the school, and every once in a while we had a party." She paused. Suddenly her lips curved into a smile. "We had a club song. It was about being 'daughters of one mother, sisters to each other.' We formed a ring and held hands and sang it at the close of all our meetings."

"That sounds like a winner," Mr. Rheardon said. "Let's hear it."

"You mean, you want me to sing it?" His wife looked startled.

"Sure, sing it. We can use a little entertainment around here in the evenings other than those stupid TV shows."

"Oh, I can't," Ellen Rheardon said.

"What do you mean, you 'can't'? You've forgotten the words?"

"No, it's not that. It's just that we took an oath that we wouldn't sing the song anywhere except within the sisterhood. It was — sort of — sacred." Ellen gave a short, nervous giggle. "You know how kids are about symbols and ceremonies."

"But this is almost twenty years later! You're a grown woman, for god's sake, or at least you're supposed to be. You're a married woman whose husband is making a simple request, and you sit there and tell him —"

No, Jane cried silently, *no, no, no!* Her eye twitched again, hard. She could feel the whole left side of her face contorting with the muscular spasm. She dug her fingernails into the palms of her hands and tried to close her mind to her parents' voices.

"...really can't remember..." her mom was saying; and her dad: "You said you did a few minutes ago. Look, Ellie" — Bart Rheardon's voice was tight and hard —"I'm not about to be shut out of things in my own family. If you think that I'm going to let my daughter join the sort of organization that breaks up marriages by holding adult women to silly promises they made in childhood —"

"That's okay, Dad," Jane broke in quickly. "I don't want to join anyway."

"Sure you do. Why else did you haul out that damned invitation and shove it at me? You could hardly wait till I was in the door before you started raving about it. 'I've been asked to join a club!' you yelled, all excited."

"I've changed my mind."

"Well, I haven't changed mine. Your mother is going to sing for us. I mean it, Ellie. There's an issue at stake here. I'm going to hear that song from beginning to end if I have to —"

14

No, no, no! Silently screaming, Jane jumped to her feet. Her parents didn't seem to notice. Her mom sat scrunched back in her chair, her eyes wide and dark in the pale oval of her childishly unlined face. Her dad was flushed with anger, and a vein in his forehead was beginning to throb bright purple. One hand tightly clutched the martini glass, and the other was clenched into a fist.

"I don't want to join the stupid club!" Jane screamed at them. "I wouldn't join it if they paid me to!"

She whirled on her heel and ran from the room, up the stairs to the second-floor hall. She'd left the bedside lamp on in her room, and the soft pastels of peach and lime green beckoned to her from the half-open door at the end of the hallway. She burst through the doorway, slamming the door behind her, and threw herself facedown on the flowered spread.

It was always, *always* this way on Fridays. How could she have thought tonight would be any different? The "end-of-the-week letdown," her dad called it, when he called it anything, and her mom would say, "That's just the way men are, dear. You have to accept it. Your dad works hard, and he gets so wound up and tense. It makes him happy to have me taking care of things at home; otherwise he'd have even more to worry about."

But other people's fathers didn't get that wound up, did they? Did Ann Whitten's gentle, soft-spoken dad break character each Friday night to become a raging tyrant? Tammy Carncross's dad taught science at the school. Did he arrive home at the end of the week shouting for his gin bottle? Well, maybe they did. How could she know?

How could anyone know for sure what went on in all the neat white houses that lined the streets of a pleasant and sleepy little town like Modesta? Behind each door there was a family, and every family held its own secrets, clutched tightly away from the eyes of the rest of the world. You didn't dishonor your family by discussing problems with others — everything here in Modesta was very... polite.

I wish it were Monday, Jane thought wearily. *I wish I were back in school again. Walking down the hall. People laughing and shoving. Lockers clanging. Smelling chewing gum and tennis shoes and perfume and chalk dust....*

Jane pressed her hands against the sides of her face to control the twitching. From the room below there came a thud and a high-pitched cry.

A moment later, a thin, wavering voice began to sing.

Chapter 2

"The meeting will now come to order." Erika Schneider raised the small wooden gavel and brought it down on the tabletop with a sharp click. She nodded toward the partially open door. "Will somebody shut that, please? Thank you, Tammy. Now, everyone join hands and repeat the club pledge."

Hands reached out on all sides around the art-room table and closed around other hands, and a chorus of solemn voices rose softly to recite the words:

"I pledge myself to the spirit of sisterhood — and to the warmth of friendship. I promise to do my best — as a member of Daughters of Eve — to follow the code of loyalty, love and service — laid out for womankind since time's beginning — and to divulge to no one words spoken in confidence — within this sacred circle."

There was a moment of silence. Then the hands released each other, and there was a shuffle of bodies shifting position to sit back more comfortably in the hard, straight-backed chairs.

Erika glanced around the table, taking a silent roll call. Everyone was here, including the three new members. *An odd trio they are, too,* she thought as her eyes lingered momentarily upon their faces — Jane Rheardon, with the delicate, porcelain features and the incredible corn-silk hair; freckled, snub-nosed Kristy Grange; and Laura Snow. Erika still had reservations about Laura. The vote on her name had been close, and it'd been only because of Irene Stark's strong support of her that she'd been offered membership.

"We aren't selecting candidates for a beauty contest," Irene had said in that firm, decided way she had. "We're a school-sponsored service club, not a snobby sorority. We're extending an offer of sisterhood to people we feel would benefit from our supportive friendship. As your sponsor and adviser, it's my definite opinion that Laura Snow is one of those people."

Well, she probably is, Erika conceded silently. It was also true, of course, that beauty wasn't a criterion for membership. If it had been, Erika herself would've been an unlikely candidate. When she looked at herself in the mirror and saw a long, pointed nose and small, near-sighted eyes set close together in a narrow face, she was often reminded of a giant mosquito. When she put on her glasses, it really completed the picture, for the thick lenses exaggerated her eyes until they did, indeed, resemble insect eyes.

"I wish you'd let us get you contact lenses," her mom said repeatedly. "They'd make such a difference, Erika. Don't you want boys to ask you out?"

"Not particularly," Erika answered, and meant it. The senior boys at Modesta High were of little interest to her. The only one with even a smattering of intelligence was Gordon Pellet, and he was too lazy to do anything with it.

"Don't you ever want to get married?" was her mom's second question, delivered always with a soft little sigh of exasperation. "You'll never get married, Erika, if you don't start going out with boys." Erika seldom even bothered to answer. Marriage, for what it was worth, lay a million miles in the future, if it was there at all. First there was graduation with, she hoped, a science scholarship. Then there was college, and after that, med school. On the side there would be studying, which was something she enjoyed, and probably a series of mundane jobs to help cover expenses. When love came, if it did, there would be time enough to discard her glasses in favor of contacts, but she didn't intend to find romance among the boring, unambitious males who attended Modesta High.

No, Erika wasn't pretty, and she accepted that fact. Facial construction was something that God gave you. Being overweight was another thing entirely. She could think of no reason in the world for people to let themselves become unhealthy. To Erika, all it took was some discipline and exercise to stay in shape.

Still, what was done was done. The vote had gone through, just barely, and here sat Laura, looking eager and nervous and happy. She'd dressed for the occasion in a blue knit top that was pulled so tight across her chest that it looked as though it might split at any moment, and her head was squished down, giving her the illusion of extra chins that rested on her chest like a stack of saucers on a sky-blue tablecloth. On Laura's right sat Kristy Grange. There'd been no dissension over voting in Kristy; everyone at Modesta High knew the Grange boys, Niles and Peter. On her left was Jane Rheardon, a no-doubter. Besides her straight-A record from middle school, Jane was a legacy, her mother having been a member of the Modesta chapter back when it had first been established.

Erika drew a long breath and addressed herself to the three of them.

"It's my honor as president of the Modesta chapter of Daughters of Eve to welcome you — Jane, Laura and

Kristy — to our meeting and to extend a formal invitation to you to become members of our sisterhood. I'm Erika Schneider, and here on my left is our faculty sponsor, Irene Stark. She was sponsor of the Jefferson chapter in Chicago before she moved here the middle of last year, so she has a real background working with this organization. Do you want to say anything, Irene?"

"Well, I'll add my welcome to yours, Erika," Irene Stark said in a low, rich voice. "I want you girls to know how pleased we are to have you with us. You all know me as your art teacher, and, of course, I'm 'Ms. Stark' to you in class, but within our sisterhood I just want to be 'Irene.' I want you to feel free to come to me at any time with your problems, and to consider me a friend and, if you can, a sort of older sister." She turned to Erika with a smile. "Is there more I should be telling them, Madam President?"

"I think you covered it, Irene." Erika gently stressed the use of the given name. Of all the teachers with whom she'd had contact during her school years, Irene Stark was the only one who'd ever made her feel like a contemporary.

"Will the secretary please read the minutes of the last meeting?" Erika asked.

Ann Whitten got to her feet.

"The September eighteenth meeting of the Modesta chapter of Daughters of Eve was held in the high-school art room," she read carefully, frowning down at her own handwriting. "Seven members were present. The minutes of the final meeting in May were read and accepted, and the treasurer's report was given.

"As there was no old business, the president opened the meeting with the discussion of new members. Six names were suggested and voted upon. The girls elected to membership were Jane Rheardon, Kristy Grange and Laura Snow. It was decided that invitations be issued immediately so the member-elects could be initiated at the next meeting.

"As there was no other business, Tammy Carncross moved that the meeting be adjourned. Paula Brummell seconded the motion. The meeting was adjourned. Respectfully submitted, Ann Whitten, secretary."

Ann raised her face from her notes, looking flushed and a trifle embarrassed.

"I'm sorry that didn't sound very businesslike. I've never taken minutes before."

"They were fine," Erika said. "Are there any additions or corrections? Paula?"

"This isn't exactly an addition or correction," Paula Brummell said. "I just wanted to ask a question. Why is it we were only able to vote in three members? Is there some special reason why our number *has* to be kept to ten?"

"Is there, Irene?" Erika asked, turning to the teacher.

"I think the ruling is based on the size of the student body," Irene said. "The school in Chicago was quite a bit larger than Modesta High, so we were allowed seventeen members in our Jefferson chapter. The bylaws were formed at the national level, so we really don't have much to say about them."

"I think they're stupid," Paula said. "We wanted six girls as members, but we could only vote in three of them. What would be the problem with increasing our membership to thirteen?"

"Then the club wouldn't be as exclusive," said Holly Underwood. "Daughters of Eve has a reputation. We're not just any group that anybody can get into — we're *the* group. If we started taking in a bunch of extra people, it wouldn't mean as much to be a member."

"There's more to it than that," Irene said. "The importance of our group is the quality of sisterhood we offer each other, and that quality shows itself in what we do for the school. Each member's problems are the problems of all of us; we relate closely to each other with trust and loyalty and caring. When you expand membership, that personal element lessens. Pretty soon the group splits into subgroups who care more about themselves than about the membership as a whole."

"That makes sense," Erika said. "And now, I wonder if our prospective members have any questions before their initiation."

There was a pause. Then Kristy raised her hand.

"I've got sort of a problem about the meeting time," she said. "Is it always after school on Mondays?"

"It always has been," Erika told her. "Do you have a conflict?" Erika was surprised — she wasn't aware of Kristy being involved in any sports or other extracurricular activities. "Would another afternoon be better?"

Kristy hesitated, then shook her head. "No, not really, I guess. It's okay. I'll work things out."

"Do you have any questions, Laura?"

"No," Laura Snow said softly. Her eyes were glowing.

"Jane?"

Jane Rheardon gave a little start, as though her mind had been somewhere else. "I'm sorry, I missed the question."

"Do you have any questions about the club?" Erika asked patiently.

"No," Jane said. "I don't have any questions at all."

Something is wrong.

Wrong how?

I don't know. I can't put my finger on it.

Then it can't be very important.

It was a habit of Tammy Carncross's to have discussions with herself inside her head. Sometimes she felt there must really be two parts of her, two distinct personalities; one was the thinking part, and the other one

24

went strictly on emotions. As she sat now, silent, watching the initiation take place, the two voices within her head went back and forth at each other like bickering children, and Tammy longed to tell them, *Shut up! Be quiet. I'm trying to enjoy the ceremony.*

The shades in the art-room windows had been closed, and three white candles had been lit. Before them, Erika had placed an open Bible from which she read aloud:

"And Ruth said, 'Entreat me not to leave thee, or to return from following after thee: for whither thou goest, I will go; and where thou lodgest, I will lodge: thy people shall be my people, and thy God my God. Where thou diest, will I die, and there will I be buried: the Lord do so to me, and more also, if aught but death part thee and me.'"

It was a moving ceremony. At last year's initiation Tammy had found her eyes filling with tears at the beauty of the ancient words as they described the devotion of one woman to another and her decision to follow her friend to a strange and foreign land rather than let her journey there alone. They were no less beautiful now. The three new members stood with bent heads, and the light from the candles flickered softly upon their faces and threw leaping shadows on the far wall.

"Such is the spirit of sisterhood —"

Something is wrong.

You have no reason for thinking that.

I have this feeling —

At home they joked a lot about Tammy's "feelings." "Our oracle," her father called her, in the same fond way he called Tammy's older sister, Marnie, "our brain." It was a form of teasing, but there was just enough truth behind the nicknames to make them more than casual. Marnie had aced her way into a scholarship to Northwestern, the same college from which their father had graduated, and when Tammy had feelings, her family listened even when they laughed. Her mother liked to tell about a time when her younger daughter was three and had a "funny feeling" about the toilet in the ground-floor bathroom. "It feels mad at us," she'd announced with great earnestness. The next morning they had woken up to find that the toilet had backed up overnight and the entire first floor was inches deep in water, and Mrs. Carncross, who was a writer, had written the incident up as a short feature for the "Out of the Mouths of Babes" section of a national parenting magazine.

Tammy herself couldn't remember that occasion, because she had been too little, but over the years she'd come to accept her feelings as a natural extension of her thought process. When she took a school exam, she would think through each problem to a logical answer, and then, before writing it down, she would ask herself, *But what do I* feel? If the thought and the feeling weren't compatible, she would redo the problem.

Tammy also had feelings about people. These didn't come to her often, but when they did occur, they were rarely misleading. Two years ago she'd been one of the girls standing before the row of candles, listening to the biblical story of Ruth. Four girls were being initiated, and Tammy had known none of the others. Shy by nature, and awed by the solemnity of the occasion, she'd been standing with lowered eyes, with her full attention on the reading, when she'd become suddenly hyper-aware of the girl standing next to her and of another girl at the end of the row just outside the circle of light.

They will be my friends, Tammy had thought.

The knowledge had come to her with such certainty that her lips had curved involuntarily into a smile, and Marnie, who was then president, had paused in her reading and frowned at her reprovingly. "You were laughing during the Bible reading," she accused later, and Tammy had said, "No, I wasn't, Marn. I was just feeling happy."

It hadn't happened overnight. The bonds between them had grown slowly. But now, in their senior year, Ann Whitten and Kelly Johnson were her closest friends.

Today, with the same intensity of feeling, Tammy knew that something was very wrong. There was an alien presence in the room. It moved like a shadow between her eyes and the flickering candles, and though the room was warm, actually quite hot with the windows covered and the people within it gathered so close together, Tammy shivered.

What is it —?

And then she saw it, thick and dark, dripping from one of the candles like melted wax. The word flashed through her mind like a high-pitched scream — *BLOOD!*

Did nobody else see it? Evidently not. Or perhaps they simply didn't want to see.

Erika had laid the Bible aside now and was explaining the meaning of the pledge. "It shows us in the Bible that Eve was the universal mother, so we are all, in a sense, her daughters, and by acknowledging this we claim each other as sisters. Just as Ruth was willing to sacrifice her personal comfort, her ties to home and her chance for remarriage in order to be supportive of Naomi when she was lonely and in need, so do we, within this sisterhood, promise to make the same sacrifices for each other. Do you so vow?"

Three voices — softly —"I do."

"Then let us welcome our three new sisters into the light!"

Someone switched on the overhead lights. The room leaped into brilliance.

The candle shafts gleamed white and pure.

Tammy closed her eyes and pressed her hands against the lids. It hadn't been real; there was no blood. Her mind had been playing a trick on her. But there in her self-created darkness, the bleeding taper reappeared, etched against the inside of her lids, and a terrible warning kept shrilling through her brain.

She felt a hand on her shoulder.

"Is something wrong, Tammy?" Irene Stark asked her worriedly. "Are you feeling sick?"

Tammy lowered her hands from her face and blinked at the brightness. The other girls were all out of their seats now, gathered in a noisy, welcoming group around the new ones. The room was filled with laughter and happy chatter and hugs.

"Are you sick?" Irene asked again, and Tammy nodded.

"It's so hot in here," she said weakly. "I think I'd better go out — where it's not so hot." She got up from her seat, crossed the room and opened the door. The air from the hallway felt cool against her face.

"Hey, Tammy, where are you going?" Kelly Johnson called out to her, but she didn't answer. Halfway down the hall she broke into a run. She reached the door at the end and hurled herself against it, pushing it wide, and a moment later she was outside, running through the golden sweetness of the September afternoon.

Chapter 3

Ann Whitten recognized the sound of the pickup truck and smiled to herself in the darkness before it came around the bend. *Half an hour late, as always,* she thought without rancor, and used her foot to give a little shove to set the porch swing to rhythmic creaking. She focused her eyes on the curve of the road and waited for the lights to appear like two great cat eyes slashing through the black. When they did she was only mildly surprised to see that one of them had a drooping lid.

Dave gets one thing working and something else goes wrong, she thought with a sigh as the truck came groaning into the driveway and pulled to a stop behind her father's sedan. It gave a roar and a gasp and went sputtering into silence; the cat eyes blinked once and went out.

The door of the cab opened and slammed closed, and a moment later Dave was coming across the lawn, the white splash of his shirt catching the light from the living-room windows. As he mounted the porch steps and turned to press the doorbell, Ann said, "Boo!"

He gave a start, and she laughed with satisfaction. "Did I scare you?"

"Gave me a heart attack, that's all." Dave crossed the porch and groped his way to the swing. "Got room there for a friend?"

"I might. It depends who it is."

"Somebody with straw in his hair okay?"

"Oh — him." Ann pretended to be mulling the situation over. "I'll have to give this some thought. Am I really that sort of girl?"

Dave took the teasing good-naturedly. "Well, while you're thinking, move over and let a tired man sit down."

The swing creaked as he settled himself beside her and then grew quiet as the motion stopped. Dave's arm came around her shoulders and drew her against him, and with the ease of long familiarity Ann laid her head back against it and raised her face for his kiss.

"Mmmmmm," she said contentedly. "You smell like toothpaste and shampoo. You don't have straw in your hair at all. You must have just washed it."

"That's what took me so long," Dave said. "I couldn't come over here fresh from feeding the pigs, now, could I?"

"I guess you could have," Ann said, "but I'm glad you didn't. Hey, did you know one of your headlights isn't working right?"

"Yeah, I realized it when I started out tonight, but it was either drive with it that way or stay home. I'll do something about it tomorrow. That is, if I have time. Man, the days go by too fast! How was school?"

"Okay," Ann said. "I showed Irene — Ms. Stark — my sketches from this summer."

"What did she say about them?"

"She liked them," Ann said. "Especially the one of you on the tractor, and that last one I did with the fence in the foreground with all the crows lined up along it and the pasture behind it and then the house. She said that had good perspective. She wanted to know what kind of art training I've had."

"So you told her 'none'?"

"Well, none except the regular school classes. But I've done a lot of work on my own, you know. I told her I've got a closet full of sketchbooks that go back to elementary school, and that I've been working in watercolor for a couple of years now. I said I'd bring some of the paintings in to show her."

"That's good. Maybe she'll give you an A."

"She kept the sketches," Ann said.

She wanted to tell him more, to describe the way Irene had sat there studying the drawings, her dark brows drawn together and that strong, intense face taut with concentration. There had been other students in the room waiting to talk with her, but for that moment Ann had felt that only she existed in Irene's world.

"These are strong," Irene had said. "Especially the one with the tractor. I like the lines of the man's shoulders. I'm glad you didn't try to fill in the face."

"The face doesn't matter," Ann said.

"Of course it doesn't. You caught the man's spirit in the arch of the body. The features of the face would have detracted rather than added."

She'd understood it so quickly, and yet Dave's reaction to the same drawing had been bewilderment. "When are you going to finish it?" he'd asked. To Dave, "a really good painting" was *The Valley of the Good Shepherd*, a brightly colored representation of Christ in flowing robes surrounded by a collection of adoring sheep, which his mother had removed from an outdated calendar and taped to her kitchen wall.

"Ms. Stark kept my sketches," Ann said again now, and left it at that.

"So what else did you do today?" Dave asked her. The question was more than ritual. His unfeigned interest in the details of her days was to Ann one of his most endearing qualities. "You had a club meeting this afternoon, didn't you? Were your minutes professional enough?"

"Well, nobody booed." Ann paused. "But something weird did happen after the initiation ceremony. Tammy ran out of the room."

"Why'd she do that?"

"I don't know. I didn't see it happen. I was busy welcoming the new members, but Kelly saw her from across the room and tried to go after her. By the time she got out to the hall, Tammy was gone."

"Maybe she wasn't feeling well," Dave said reasonably.

"It wasn't that. We called her as soon as the meeting was over. She was home by then, and she sounded really freaked out. She said, 'Something's going to go wrong this semester, and I don't want anything to do with it.' She's going to drop out of Daughters of Eve!"

"I didn't think she could," Dave said. "I thought you told me nobody ever did that. Once you're in, you're in for life."

"Well, Tammy says she's quitting, and once she makes her mind up about something, she usually goes through with it. I don't understand it. We have so much fun in that group, and all our friends are there. She'll miss out on everything! It'll ruin her senior year."

"Do you know what she meant about something going 'wrong'?" Dave asked, a note of worry in his voice. "People don't just get ideas like that out of the sky."

"Tammy does," Ann said with a nervous little laugh. "She gets these premonitions, and, weird as it sounds, sometimes they turn out to be right. I remember one time..." She let the sentence fall away, uncompleted.

"One time what?"

"We were sitting in a booth down at Foster's," Ann said slowly, "Tammy and Kelly and I, and this guy came in and ordered a Coke. We'd never seen him before, and Tammy told us something about him — and it turned out to be true."

"Maybe she was just remembering something she'd heard somewhere."

"No — that wasn't it."

It had happened over a year ago. It was the end of the summer, and the man had been red-faced and sweating, with his blond hair plastered to his head. He was dressed in boots and overalls, and he was obviously a local farmer who'd come into town on an errand during lunch. He stood at the counter, swigging a Coke in great thirsty gulps, the muscles in his arms and shoulders standing out in corded lumps beneath the damp material of his cotton shirt.

"Why would anybody wear a long-sleeved shirt on a day like this?" Kelly wondered.

"To keep from getting burned when he's out in the fields, I guess." Ann glanced across at Tammy. "Hey, what's with you? You're staring at that guy like you know him."

"I feel like I do," Tammy told her. "He's going to be — important — I think — to one of us."

"You've got to be kidding!" Kelly exclaimed, and Ann said, jokingly, "To you, Tam?"

"No," Tammy said. "To you."

They had all laughed then. The mere idea of fastidious, artistic Ann Whitten becoming involved with a farmer was ridiculous. Even Tammy hadn't quite believed it. She'd told Ann later, "I get these feelings, but I can't always trust them. That was one time when I thought I was freaking out."

Yet she'd been right. The impossible had happened; here Ann sat now with her head on the "farmer's" shoulder, as contented as a cat who'd waited all day to settle on the comfort of a warm lap.

One of the living-room lights went off, and a moment later the front door opened.

"Annie," Ann's mother said through the screen, "did Dave ever get here?"

"I'm here, Mrs. Whitten," Dave said. "The chores ran late tonight. We're just sitting here talking about our days. Want to come and join us?"

"No, thanks," Mrs. Whitten said. "Dad and I are going to turn in early. I just wanted to check that you'd gotten here and Ann wasn't sitting out there by herself worrying over you. Remember, it's a school night."

"I'll remember," Dave said. "I'll be leaving in a few minutes. My day begins pretty early, too, you know."

"Night, Mom," Ann said. "See you in the morning."

"All right, dear. Good night."

The door closed, and Ann felt Dave's arm tighten around her.

"Your parents are pretty cool about it," he said softly. "About my being over here so much, I mean."

"They like you," Ann said. "You know that. Dad really respects you, taking over the running of the farm after your father died. He says that with all you hear these days about the 'irresponsibility of youth,' it's great to see someone your age who's not afraid of hard work."

"You know, on the way over here I was remembering how we met. At first I didn't think you'd go out with me," Dave said. "When Holly introduced us at her brother's wedding, you gave me a long, weird look that made me feel like my suit coat was buttoned wrong or there was corn stuck between my teeth or something. I thought, great, here goes nothing; this girl is used to cool guys who are going somewhere. At least, as cool as you can find in Modesta."

"It wasn't that," Ann said. "I just — thought I'd seen you somewhere before. Then you smiled, and I thought, nobody has eyes that blue — that absolute, clear, pure blue like pictures you see of the Mediterranean."

"I almost didn't go to the wedding. I hadn't seen Gary Underwood since high school."

"I almost didn't go either. It was such a pretty day, I was going to go sketching down by Pointer's Bridge.

37

Then Holly called and asked if I'd help serve punch at the reception, and there I was, stuck." Ann laughed. "Is that fate or what?"

"Fate for you, maybe; luck for me. For one David Brewer, it was the luckiest day in his life."

He bent his head to kiss her, and it was a long kiss, not a light one as the other kiss had been. Dave's arms locked around her and pulled her tight against his chest, and Ann could feel the pounding of his heart so clear and strong it might've been her own. Her mouth went soft beneath his, and her eyes closed, and she let herself be drawn into the kiss as she had, on that first day, been drawn into the blue of his eyes.

When it was over, he didn't release her, but kept holding her tightly against him. He was breathing hard, like a man who had come running a long way.

"I love you," he whispered. "You know that, Annie? I love you so much I could almost die."

"I know," Ann whispered back. "I love you, too."

"Enough to marry me?"

She was silent for a moment. Then she said quietly, "I think I do."

"You mean that?" He loosened his hold and drew away from her just enough to look down into her face. His own was lost in shadows, but she knew it so well that she could see it in the darkness.

"Don't tell me that unless you mean it, Ann. I couldn't

stand it if I thought you were saying yes, and then it turned out I was wrong."

"I love you," Ann said. "I'm sure of that. It's just — marriage…we're so young. I need to get used to the idea."

"Well, so do I when it comes down to it. We've both got time for thinking. You won't graduate until next May."

"A June wedding?" A series of pictures flashed before her. Modesta Community Church with its windows wide and the scent of lilacs pouring through them with the June sunshine. Tammy and Kelly in identical pink bridesmaid dresses. Holly Underwood at the organ. Herself in the white satin wedding gown that had hung for twenty years in a plastic bag in the back of her mother's closet, waiting for a second use. Her father tall beside her, and at the aisle's end, Dave, huge and handsome in a dark suit, his blue eyes shining with pride and happiness as he watched her come slowly toward him.

June was a time for weddings, for new beginnings. In May the life she'd known for twelve long years would be over. No longer would her days be regulated by a schedule of classes, club meetings and school-centered social activities. Her friends who were fellow seniors would be zooming off in all directions. Tammy would be leaving to follow her sister Marnie to college, and Kelly to attend business school in Adrian, Michigan, while Erika would undoubtedly pick up a scholarship and be off and flying. Life would be opening wide for all of them, and for herself — what? A waitressing job at Brummell's Café on Main Street? A position as a salesclerk at the Dollar Tree? A clothing store? There'd been a time when she'd dreamed of attending art school somewhere, but her father's forced retirement because of a heart condition had made that financially impossible.

June — a time of beginnings — and why not marriage? Wasn't that what her mother had done the June she was eighteen? Her parents would be pleased. Her mother had always hoped that Ann would marry somebody from Modesta after high school and settle down close by, and Dave's farm would provide a good life, a clean, solid life — and whom would she ever want to marry if not Dave?

"It's a really nice house," he was saying now. "And there's even that little side bedroom where you could set up your painting stuff."

"Have my own little studio?" She was touched by his thoughtfulness.

"Why not? There's plenty of room. And you'll have my mom to talk to when I'm out in the fields, or you could pack us up a picnic and come down and meet me at lunchtime, and we could sit by the creek and eat, and you could do your sketching."

"Like we did this past summer." It had been a beautiful

summer of blue skies and sunshine, and even the heat hadn't mattered, because the creek that ran along the edge of the fields at the south end of Dave's land had been clear and cold and the grassy banks had been dappled with shade from the willows.

"And at night we'd have dinner together," Ann said dreamily. "In the winter we could eat by the fireplace and listen to the wind whistling around the corners of the house, and it wouldn't matter because we'd be inside together, and when the evening was over neither of us would have to drive home."

"We'd be home," Dave said. "So is it 'yes,' my gentle Annie?"

It was his own pet name for her, based on an old folk song both of them loved, and the tenderness with which he used it touched her deeply.

"It's 'yes,'" Ann said, and at that moment, in some far corner of her mind, she heard the voice of Tammy Carncross raised in warning.

Something's going to go wrong this semester!

With Dave's arms warm around her, Ann called back silently, *For somebody else, maybe, Tammy, but not for me!*

Chapter 4

It was Friday, the sixth day of October.

"I hate to say no to you, Kristy, but I have to," Mrs. Grange said firmly. "I know you're disappointed and I'm sorry, but what you're asking is impossible at this particular time in our lives."

"It's not impossible! Other girls get to do what they want to after school!" Kristy glared across the table at her mom. "Why do I have to be different from everybody else?"

Immediately she wished she hadn't asked that. It was the question that her parents always waited for, and both of them had their mouths open with the answer before the last words had reached their ears. Miserably she glanced around the table for support, knowing as she did so that there would be none. Eric was shoveling food into his mouth as though he hadn't eaten for weeks, and Peter was off somewhere in outer space. Only Niles was paying attention to the conversation, and he was leaning back in his chair, grinning. Niles loved arguments.

"Because your family —" both her parents began simultaneously.

"I'm sorry," her mom said, and her dad continued, "Because your family isn't like 'everybody else's.' It's a luxury to have four kids these days, and with the economy like it is, it takes two wage earners working overtime to keep it going."

And whose fault is it we have this "luxurious family"? Kristy wanted to yell at them. *Nobody forced you to keep on having babies! You could've stopped after me — three kids are plenty!* With an effort that almost choked her, she swallowed the accusation and struggled to bring her anger under control. From experience she knew that shouting would get her nowhere, and her only hope was to reach them with calm reason.

"You don't understand how important this is," she said carefully. "It's not just some random old club I've been asked to join. It's Daughters of Eve, a national organization. There are chapters all over the country, not just here in Modesta. Wherever I go for the rest of my life, I'll have sisters."

"What are you looking for, Sis, quantity or quality?"

43

Niles asked impishly. "If that tub of lard you brought home from school with you this afternoon is an example of the 'daughters,' I'd say Mother Eve should have stopped a while ago."

"Laura Snow is one of the nicest girls ever," Kristy said defensively. "She can't help being overweight. It runs in the family."

"I bet that's the only thing that 'runs,'" Niles said. "Laura looks like she can hardly waddle."

"Oh, come off it, Niles," Peter said lightly, zeroing in on the conversation for the first time. "Laura's not so bad if you like them well-padded. She's got a couple of good points in her favor."

"Good points!" Niles burst into laughter. "Nice one!"

"Boys, stop that," their mother scolded. "That's not the kind of language I want to hear at the dinner table. Kristy, I'm sure this is a fine club. That's not the issue. The problem is that you're needed at home in the afternoons."

"That's right," Mr. Grange said firmly. "Your mother's only human. She can't hold down a full-time job, do all the housework, and get dinner on the table at a decent hour without some help. Besides that, we can't have Eric coming home to an empty house. He's only nine, and he needs some supervision."

"It's only one afternoon a week," Kristy protested.

"That's one afternoon too many if last Monday was any indication," her dad said. "When we got home, this place was a disaster — breakfast dishes not even rinsed and put in the dishwasher, dinner not started — and Eric and his friends had burst one of the sofa cushions jumping on it in the living room. Your mom and I don't need to face that sort of mess at the end of a long, hard day."

"Besides, it wouldn't be just 'one afternoon a week,'" Mrs. Grange said. "I know what school clubs are like. There'll be after-school projects and parties, bake sales and poster-making and decorating the gym for dances and lord knows what all else. Please don't pressure us, Kristy. It just can't be managed."

"That's not fair!" Kristy cried. "Why can't the boys do some of the work around this place? All they do is mess it up, and I'm stuck with all the —"

"Sis, suck it up," Peter said briskly. "Niles and I aren't about to go into training to become housewives. We're getting ready for college, and I need to save all my energy for when I'm on the court. Coach said so."

"There'll be no more discussion, Kristy. Your family is the priority. The subject is closed." Mr. Grange laid his knife and fork side by side on his plate and wiped his mouth with his napkin. "What's for dessert?"

Laura Snow lay back in the bathtub, letting the water grow tepid around her as she relived the events of the day. It had been, without doubt, one of the happiest days of Laura's life. Actually, since the arrival of the magical invitation two weeks before, all of her days had been happy, but this particular day had been filled with one sparkling moment after another.

First there had been the invitation to Holly Underwood's seventeenth birthday party a week from Saturday. It was the first party Laura had been invited to since she started high school. Then, between first and second period, Ann Whitten had beckoned to her in the hall and drawn her aside for a whispered disclosure.

"Dave and I are engaged!" she told her ecstatically. "We haven't told anybody yet except our parents, but I wanted my sisters in Daughters of Eve to know about it. Laura, I'm so happy!" She gave Laura a quick hug and ran off down the hall, calling, "Ms. Stark? Can you wait a minute? There's something I want to tell you!" and Laura carried the glow of the wonderful secret around with her for the rest of the day, incredulous that she had been among the ones chosen to share in it.

At noon she carried her lunch to the cafeteria and found herself at a table with Erika Schneider and Paula Brummell. They laughed and chattered and included Laura in their conversation as though she were truly one of them, a friend and a sister, and on her way back to class, Paula asked her if she'd like to be on the Community Services committee to investigate the needs at a Modesta nursing home.

"Kelly and I are going out there next Tuesday," Paula

said. "Then we'll make up a list of suggestions for things the club can do to help out, and we'll present it at the next meeting. Do you think you could go with us?"

"Yeah, I'd really like to," Laura said, and Paula exclaimed, "Oh, great!" with real enthusiasm in her voice, and said, "I'll call you tonight about the details."

But the crowning event of the day, the one she'd saved in her mind until last to savor at the end of her reverie, had occurred when she walked home from school with Kristy Grange. It was strange, when she stopped to think about it, that they hadn't walked home together before, because they lived within two blocks of each other, but somehow this had never happened, and today when Kristy had called, "Hey, wait for me!" Laura had thought at first that she had meant somebody else.

But a moment later Kristy caught up with her and fell into step beside her as though they made this walk together all the time. Within minutes, they were chatting easily and naturally, just like old friends.

When they reached her gate, Laura said impulsively, "Do you want to come in for a while?" and felt her heart sink as Kristy shook her head.

But then she realized she wasn't really being rejected.

"I've got to get home to babysit my kid brother," Kristy told her. "Why don't you come to my place? You can keep me company while I shovel a path through the kitchen."

"Shovel a path?" Laura repeated in bewilderment.

"Have you ever seen the mess three boys can leave in the mornings?" Kristy grimaced. "If you haven't, I've got quite an experience in store for you. Come on."

So they walked the short distance from the Snow home to the Granges'. Peter was sitting at the kitchen table, eating a bowl of chocolate ice cream.

As the girls came in, he glanced up and said, "Hi."

"Hi, yourself," Kristy said. "Laura, this is my brother Peter. The one with his head in the refrigerator is my second brother, Niles. And my third brother, Eric, will be charging in here pretty soon now, and at that point you'll probably decide you want to go home."

"I know Laura from algebra class," Niles said without turning around. "Hi, Laura."

"Hi," Laura said, but she couldn't tear her eyes off of Peter. In all the daydreams she'd had about him, she'd missed this scene — Peter in his own home kitchen, greeting her casually with the wave of a sticky spoon.

The empty ice-cream carton lay on the counter, oozing brown liquid from its open end. Kristy picked it up and put it into the garbage can.

"It looks like the human disposal here has managed to put away what was left of the ice cream, but we have some Coke, and I hope we've still got some cookies. Sit down, Laura, and I'll see what snacks I can dig up for us."

"That's all right," Laura said. "I really don't want anything."

"Of course you do," Peter said pleasantly. "You haven't lived till you've had some of my sister's cookies, fresh from the package. She opens the cellophane with a flick of her nimble wrist. So sit down and tell me all about yourself. What's a nice girl like you doing with a nerd like Kristy?"

And for the next few minutes, until he'd finished his ice cream, she'd sat at the table across from Peter Grange, and they'd talked. Now, in the rapidly cooling water of the bath, Laura tried to recall exactly what they'd said to each other, but no words came back to her — only Peter's face: that handsome, movie-star face, with the dark hair curling over the forehead and the brown eyes smiling out at her from beneath the heavy lashes. He had freckles on his nose. She hadn't realized that before. They didn't show up at a distance, but when you sat directly in front of him, you could see them spattered lightly under his summer tan.

Then, too quickly, it was over. Niles said, "Hey, Pete, we told the guys we'd meet them back at the gym to shoot some baskets," and Peter said, "Okay, okay, don't pee your pants."

He'd shoved the bowl into the center of the table and gotten lazily to his feet.

"Great ice cream, Kristy. You cook better every day. So long, Laura. See you around."

"See you around." Laura repeated the words softly to herself, trying to remember the exact inflection of Peter's

49

voice. Was it as casual as it seemed, or maybe it could've been a question? "See you around?" Could it have been meant that way —"Will I see you, Laura?" If so, she should've answered in some encouraging manner. "I hope so," she should've said, or, "That would be great." What had she said? She couldn't remember. Something nothingish. Maybe she hadn't answered at all, since he'd said it when he was already halfway to the door.

Not that it mattered, because, of course, it hadn't been a question. Everybody knew that Peter dated Madison Ellis, and no boy who went out with Madison could possibly be interested in a fat nobody like Laura Snow.

There was a rap at the bathroom door, and her mother's voice called in to her, "Laura? You haven't drowned in there, have you, honey?"

"No," Laura said. "I'm just about ready to get out."

"That's good, because you had a phone call. I took the number and said you'd call back when you were out of the tub."

"Who was it?" Laura was surprised to hear her voice emerging in a hoarse whisper. It wouldn't carry through the door. She drew a long breath and tried again. "Who was it, Mom?"

For a moment her heart stopped beating.

"It was somebody named Paula," her mother told her. "She wanted to talk about going to the nursing home."

Laura let her breath out in a sigh.

*   *   *

The living room was dark except for the muted glow of the lamp on the end table. At the edge of this circle of light there lay a shattered ashtray. The coffee table had been overturned; the shelves of the bookcase by the door had been swept clean, and books lay scattered about in the shadows like bodies on a deserted battlefield.

"Is it over?" Jane asked.

The figure stretched on the sofa raised her head.

"It's over," Ellen Rheardon said. "What are you doing down here? I thought you were sleeping."

"I was," Jane said from her position in the doorway. She glanced nervously around the quiet room. "Where is he?"

"I don't know. Gone out somewhere to cool off, I guess."

"Are you all right?" Jane came into the room and crossed over to stand looking down at her mother. "Your mouth is bleeding. Do you want me to get some ice?"

"I've got some in this towel," her mother told her. "It'll keep down the swelling. I'll look all right by Sunday."

"What's Sunday?"

"You know — the church potluck."

"That's right. I forgot." For a moment Jane continued to stand there beside her; then she drew away and sat down in her father's armchair. She leaned back against the headrest and caught the faint odor of lemon-scented hair tonic and pipe tobacco, and for an instant she thought she was going to throw up.

She drew a deep breath.

"Mom," she said quietly, "when are you going to leave him?"

"I don't know," her mother said in a flat, emotionless voice. "I've asked myself that a lot of times, and I never have an answer. Next week? Next month? Ten years from now? And then what happens? Where would I go? What would I have without your dad?"

"You'd have — yourself."

"Myself? What's that?" Mrs. Rheardon said wearily. "Face it, Jane, I don't have any self except what your dad's given me. I married him when I was eighteen years old, and I thought I'd hit the jackpot. A handsome man — a college graduate — a lawyer, for heaven's sake — what more could any girl ask for? I was so much in love my head was swimming. We settled here in my own home-town, and he took the job with the bank. We built this house, and it was all so wonderful, and somehow it got out of hand. I started irritating him. He should have married somebody smarter, somebody more like himself, and then he'd be happier."

"Mom, don't," Jane said. "It's not your fault. There's something wrong with Dad. Normal people don't act this way. What set him off tonight? Your watching TV?

Some book he couldn't find when he wanted it? I'll bet you can't even remember, it was so minor."

"What does it matter what it was?" her mother asked her. "So it's one thing — so it's another — it's Friday night and he's tired. He works hard all week, Jane, and he's under a lot of pressure. He comes home, and he feels he has to let off steam, get it out of his system —"

"You're defending him," Jane said incredulously. "My god, Mom, how can you lie there with blood smeared all over your chin and defend somebody who hit you in the face?!"

"He didn't mean to," her mother said.

"Of course he meant to!"

"In his heart, he didn't. It was his temper that got away from him. He'll be sorry tomorrow, just see if he isn't — the way he was sorry a couple of weeks ago about how he acted about Daughters of Eve. He apologized for that, didn't he, and he said you could join? He begged you to join. He had tears in his eyes, and he said, 'Janie, I'm sorry. You go out and buy yourself a new outfit for that initiation, and I don't care how much it costs.'"

"And he brought you flowers."

"Yellow roses. My favorites. That's what I carried in my bridal bouquet — yellow roses."

"So you had your flowers, but you couldn't go anywhere because your face was so banged up you couldn't leave the house." Jane shook her head in bewilderment.

"So you forgave him. And tonight it happened again, and tomorrow you'll forgive him, and maybe he'll bring you a necklace, and if the swelling goes down you'll wear it to the potluck, and everybody will 'oooh' and 'ahhh' and say, 'Isn't that the most romantic thing,' and you and Dad will be holding hands and smiling at each other, and —"

"Jane, hush." Her mother pulled herself painfully into a sitting position. Her face looked distorted, as though it were being reflected in a carnival mirror. Staring at her, Jane saw that the lip was worse than she'd thought it was, for it had been pierced by a tooth. Her mother's eyes were sunken hollows in the depths of her pale face, and they held no light.

"You don't understand your father," Ellen Rheardon said slowly. "He had a hard childhood. People raised the way he was — well, they're a little different from the rest of us."

"Mom," Jane said softly, "someday he's going to kill you. He'll be sorry afterward, I'm sure."

"You asked when I'm leaving. It will be before that, I promise." Her mother lifted the wet towel and pressed it against her cheek. "After you graduate from high school. It won't be so hard then. I'll find an apartment — get a job of some kind. I'm just not ready yet. Right now, it's more than I can handle. Can you understand that?"

"No," Jane said, and she felt her left eye twitch.

Chapter 5

"So Kelly will get the raffle tickets printed for the drawing at homecoming," Erika Schneider said. "We'll distribute those at the next meeting so we can all get busy selling them. Now, if there's no further old business, we do have something new to discuss. Tammy's resigned her membership."

"Resigned membership!" Irene Stark leaned forward in surprise. "Tammy?"

"That's right. I got the note yesterday." Erika held up a sheet of paper. "It says that 'after deep consideration,' she's 'decided to drop her membership.' She doesn't give any reason."

"I don't believe it," Irene said. "From what I've been told, Tammy's sister used to be president of Daughters of Eve when she was a student here. Do any of you girls know what's going on? Ann? Kelly? You seem to be especially close to her."

"She got upset about something during the initiation ceremony," Kelly Johnson said. "She wouldn't say what it was. Ann and I both tried to talk to her."

"She acted really strange," Holly Underwood said. "I noticed at the end of the initiation when the lights went on, she was sitting with her eyes closed. Then, suddenly, she jumped up and left the room without even welcoming the new members."

"I thought she looked ill," Irene said. "In fact, she told me herself she wasn't feeling well. I think we should table this resignation, Erika. Perhaps Tammy will change her mind."

Kristy Grange raised her hand.

Erika acknowledged her. "Kristy?"

"I'm going to have to resign, too," Kristy said apologetically. "It kills me to do it, but my parents are making me."

"What is this, a mass exodus?" Irene regarded her with bewilderment. "You're going to leave two weeks after you join us?"

"I shouldn't have joined," Kristy said unhappily. "It's just that all my life I wanted to have sisters, and suddenly I had a chance for some, and I grabbed it. I should've known it wouldn't work out. My parents need me at home."

"To do what?" Holly asked.

"I've got a bunch of chores to do, and my kid brother would wreck the place if I wasn't there to keep an eye on him. He basically did that last week. My parents will hit the roof tonight when they find out I came to the meeting today, but I wanted to explain it. I didn't want you to think I *wanted* to quit."

"This is incredible," Irene said. "Do you mean that you're expected to give up all your after-school time to be a housemaid and babysitter? Is this something you're getting paid for?"

"No," Kristy said. "Dad thinks I owe it because I'm the daughter in the family. The boys don't do anything. They just wander in and out when they feel like it and mess things up. Remember how it was when you were over last week, Laura?"

"You mean it's like that all the time?" Laura asked in surprise.

"You don't know the half of it. You should see the place when the guys have their friends over. It's just since Mom's been working longer hours. Dad says we need the extra money if the boys are going to college out of state."

"I should think your brothers would be the ones to donate their time to that cause," Irene said. "Is there some reason they can't take over for one afternoon a week and allow you some outside activities?"

"Irene, you don't know Peter," Madison Ellis broke in. "There's no way he would stoop to babysitting. I can just imagine poor Kristy trying to convince him. Pete would explode!"

"It sounds to me as though it's Kristy who ought to be doing the exploding," Irene said.

"I think it's sick," said Kelly. "Why should it be the *girl* who gives up everything while the boys get off? At our house we divide up the chores and everybody takes a turn at doing everything."

"Including your dad?" Paula asked her.

"Well, not him, of course, but the rest of us."

"Meaning you and your mom and your sister?" Paula shook her head. "It's not the same, Kelly. You don't have brothers, so you can't compare the situations. Take a look at my house. Mom gets up and goes to work at the same time my Dad does, and she's on her feet all day while he sits at a desk. By nighttime she's beat, and I help with the housework, and she does the dinner and I load the dishwasher. Dad sits and watches the news. You know what my brother Tom does? He carries out the garbage. Big deal!"

"Is it that way in all your homes?" Irene asked incredulously. "Ann?"

"Well — yes," Ann said slowly. "I never thought anything about it, though. My mom's a housewife. That's what housewives do, isn't it?"

"Your dad's retired," Madison reminded her. "He's got as much time around the house as your mom does."

"Dad isn't well. Besides, Mom likes to cook. I'd hate to think what it would be like to eat a meal Dad made." Ann strove for a touch of levity. "Everybody's got their own talents."

"I'd hate to think that the depth of one's talents is reflected by who does the best job waxing the floor." Irene shook her head in amazement. "Honestly, girls, this whole town is stuck in a time warp. This is the way women talked and felt fifty years ago. Haven't the words 'Women's Lib' ever made their way to Modesta?"

"Modesta is a small town — we're not as modern as the rest of the world," Erika said. "It's just not the way things are done here. Back when my brother, Boyd, was a baby, Dad started a college fund for him. Dad never went to college himself, and he wanted to be sure Boyd had the chance. Okay, great. But did he start one for me when I came along two years later? Of course not. I'm a girl. I'm not supposed to need college in order to be a housewife and maybe just work part-time in a store."

"Some housewife you'll make, with a garage full of rats," Paula said, laughing.

"Who's got rats?" Holly asked.

"Erika does. Whole cages full. What are you going to do with them, Erika?" Paula prodded good-naturedly. "Come on — you're among your sisters. Open up."

"They're part of a project I'm working on for the science fair," Erika told them. "I've got all this data I'm collecting, and I'll be making the presentation to Mr. Carncross in December. If he selects my project to represent the school, I'll go on to the state competition and get a crack at a science scholarship."

"Good for you," Irene said approvingly. "The world needs more female scientists. In fact, it needs more females in all areas of advanced achievement." There was amusement in her voice. "Do you know that at one time it was widely believed that a woman's brain was smaller in capacity than a man's?"

"That's ridiculous," Kelly said. "Look at our group here. We've got the school's top achievers all in one package. Erika's vice president of the Honor Society, Ann's an artist, Holly's a musician —"

"And none of you are going to have an easy time of it, I'm afraid. Who reviews the arts?" Irene challenged them.

"Who? Well, art reviewers," Kelly said.

"Male or female?"

"I don't know," Kelly admitted. "I never thought about it."

"The art critics with major art journals are almost all men," Irene said, "and male artists receive almost all the space in art reviews. In fact, there are only a few women represented by major art galleries."

"Maybe the women who could be contributing to the art world are busy doing other things," Ann said.

"That's very likely. What do you suppose those things could be?"

"Having babies," Kristy offered. "And working at places like JCPenney."

"Is that what you meant, Irene?" Erika asked. "Or did you mean they weren't getting recognition for their art because they were women? That would be a completely different thing."

"Who's to say for sure?" Irene said. "One thing that has been proven is that women painters and sculptors in juried shows do a great deal better than in invitational shows. In juried shows the names are concealed, so the judges don't know the sex of the artist. In invitationals, the artists are known."

"Does it work that way with music, too?" Holly asked, frowning.

"It's possible," Irene said. "I heard that the major American symphony orchestras with the most women in them are the ones that audition their instrumentalists behind a concealing screen."

"That's so wrong!" exclaimed Madison. "How sexist can people get?!"

"It can go beyond the arts," Irene said. "What percentage of the teachers in this school are women?"

"Almost all of them," Kelly said. "Tammy's dad is

the only man, isn't he, except for Coach Ferrara and Mr. Muncy, who teaches the shop classes? And Mr. Carncross teaches science. That's probably considered a masculine subject."

"I don't see why you say that," Erika said irritably. "How can one subject be any more 'masculine' than another? Science is science — period."

"What about shop?" Kelly said. "You don't consider that a boy's subject?"

"I don't know why it should be," Erika said.

"Then why aren't any girls taking it?"

"The point I wanted to make," Irene broke in quietly, "is that, despite the large number of women teaching at Modesta High, Mr. Shelby, the principal, is a man."

There was a moment's silence.

Then Paula said, "That's true, isn't it? And the principal at the middle school is a man, too."

"According to a survey I read, despite progress, women are still a relatively small percentage of secondary-school principals," Irene said. "Do you want to know how that comes to be? I'll tell you a story. This is about a friend of mine back at Jefferson High in Chicago. This woman had a master's degree in education with a minor in her subject specialty, and she'd been teaching at Jefferson for eight years. She asked the principal about the possibility of moving into an administrative position, and he told her she couldn't be considered unless she had a PhD.

"Well, my friend took him at his word and went back to school in the evenings and got her doctorate. The year she got it, the position of assistant principal opened up at Jefferson. My friend was overwhelmingly qualified, and was assured there was no serious competition. Then, suddenly, she received notice that the position had been filled. Can you guess by whom?"

"By someone from another school?" Erika hazarded.

"No," Irene said, "by the boys' PE instructor. This man, Robert Morrell, had only a master's degree and had been at Jefferson five years."

"But how could that be?" Kelly asked incredulously. "I thought you said it took a PhD to get moved up like that?"

"That's what my friend was told."

"But, this guy, Morrell —"

"Was a man." Irene completed the statement for her. "The principal said he thought Morrell was simply more suitable for the job. But trustworthy sources said the principal really thought a man would be more authoritative when it came to dealing with students and parents on an administrative level — and that he wanted to reward Morrell for coaching that year's winning football team. He thought that triumph deserved recognition."

"More recognition than getting a doctorate?" Kelly murmured.

"Ironic, isn't it? And here's another twist." Irene's normally calm voice had taken on an edge, and her dark eyes were smoldering. "My friend had been quite closely — involved — with Morrell. They were in the habit of spending much of their time together, and she'd been doing a lot of his paperwork for him, filling out grade sheets and so forth. He'd known she was applying for the assistant principal position. He'd never told her that he was also."

"I hope she gave him his walking papers," Madison said tersely.

"She did. And, in another way, she got her own. Some of my friend's students were very angry about what had happened and staged a demonstration in front of the principal's office. The principal held my friend responsible. She was forced to resign."

"Do you mean they fired her?" Laura asked.

"She was offered that alternative. Either she could hand in her resignation on her own and come out of the situation with a chance to teach somewhere else, or she would be fired, which would've meant an end to her teaching career. She resigned and accepted a position in a rural community in another state at a great reduction in salary."

"I never thought things like that actually happened."

Kelly's brown eyes were huge and solemn. "My mom has always said she doesn't feel like she's discriminated against, but then she's never tried to get a job."

"If she ever does, it'll be an eye-opener for her," Irene said. "Men in this town may feel a woman's place should be in the home, but when the middle-aged housewife gets forced into the workplace because of some emergency situation, the employer doesn't excuse her lack of experience. Discrimination is a reality. We have to face it, and we have to fight it."

"But how?" Kristy asked worriedly. "I'm not a servant. I've got as much right to do things I want to do as Niles and Peter. I've tried to get that across to my parents, but they won't listen."

"What if you went on strike?" Paula asked her. "What if you just told them that you're not going to come home on Monday afternoons?"

"Dad would ground me."

"So what else is new?" Paula said. "It sounds like you're pretty much grounded anyway."

"Would he hit you?" Jane Rheardon asked. It was the first time she'd spoken since the meeting had begun, and her voice rang out thin and unnaturally shrill.

Kristy turned to her in surprise.

"No, of course not. Why would you ask that?"

"You said he'd be angry," Jane said defensively.

"Okay, so he'll be angry. He gets angry about things

lots of times, but that doesn't mean he goes totally insane. The worst he'll do is ground me, or maybe I'll have to miss dinner. I can pick up a burger at Foster's on my way home."

"You'd have to be prepared to stick by your ultimatum," Irene said. "If you back down, you'll have done more harm than good. Your parents have to be convinced that you mean what you say."

"I'll convince them." Kristy's face was pale and determined beneath its sprinkling of freckles. "I'm not going to be walked over anymore."

"That's right," Erika said. "Remember, you've got sisters behind you."

"Hear! Hear!" cried Madison, her eyes sparkling, and suddenly the room was filled with applause.

They were so innocent, the lot of them, so totally naive. Irene's eyes moved in amazement from one young face to another. They might have sprung from the pen of Louisa May Alcott, products of an earlier era when men spoke and the women in their lives leaped to obey.

Perhaps it was fate that she had come here to this improbable hamlet that *did* seem stuck in a time warp. These girls needed her in a way the ones at Jefferson hadn't. Those had been city teens, tougher, more aggressive, able to recognize injustice and react to it. They had understood the situation immediately.

66

All she had to do was to repeat the conversation to them.

"I didn't tell you I applied because I wanted to surprise you," Bob had told her. Smiling. So pleased with himself. "I thought I'd wait and see how things turned out. You can't be mad, Renie. After all, it's for us."

"For us?" She had forced out the words.

"Well, sure. I love you, honey. I want to take care of you. How do you think I'd feel, getting married to a woman who earned more than I did?"

Even now, almost a full year later, she couldn't think back on that scene without feeling sick with anger. Rage rose within her, and a sour taste flooded her mouth. "I love you, honey" — the meaningless words were tossed out so easily! And she'd allowed herself to think he might be different!

He was exactly like the rest of them, shallow and arrogant, ready to crush her into nothing in the name of "love."

The newspapers had implied that she had incited the riot. That wasn't true. She'd only told her girls what had happened, and they'd risen on their own. How proud she'd been of them, all those fine young women, showing their love and loyalty in the only way possible!

Some of them had cried when she left.

"We'll never forget you," they had told her.

Irene, herself, had been too furious to cry.

But here, in Modesta, there was a chance for a new beginning. Here, she was truly needed.

"...will form our circle," Erika was saying, "and all join hands."

Irene rose to her feet with the others. She felt Erika's strong, fine-boned hand close upon hers on one side and Laura's smooth, plump one on the other. The circle of vulnerable young faces swam before her eyes, blending one into another, to form a ring of light, and her heart lifted from its depression with a strange sense of pride.

These are my girls! These are my lovely children! No one will hurt them! No one will hold them down!

"Daughters of one mother — sisters to each other —"

The light, sweet voices rose all around her, and Irene joined them with her own.

Chapter 6

During the second week of October the weather turned. It happened quickly; people who drifted off to sleep beneath cotton sheets got up in the night to hunt for blankets, and in the morning the air held a chill and the indescribable tang of autumn. All across Modesta, homeowners scrambled to switch out screen doors for storm ones, and people sorted through summer clothing to pack it away in storage closets. Laura Snow's mother served hot cereal for breakfast ("With raisins, honey, to give you energy"), and Madison Ellis reluctantly zipped a hoodie over her sleeveless T-shirt.

Erika Schneider brought her rat cages in from the garage and installed them in her room.

"Your mom's going to freak out," Paula Brummell

said. Paula, who lived next door, was Erika's closest friend and had come over to help with the moving. Between them the two girls had managed to carry the four heavy cages in through the back door and up the stairs into Erika's small bedroom, where they were now piled in layers separated by plywood sheeting. Within their confines, the plump white rats scurried anxiously about, peering through the chicken-wire siding at their new surroundings with sharp, pink eyes.

"Probably," Erika agreed without concern. "She freaked out last winter. She refused to come into my room for four whole months. She'd leave the sheets in the hall outside the door and yell in to me to come get them."

"Won't she try to get you to move them out?" Paula asked.

"Sure, but after a while she'll give up. I can't move them out, and that's all there is to it. They'd die in the garage when the winter cold sets in, and I might as well get them in here now so I don't risk losing them." Erika bent to look in at the rats on the lowest tier. "Are you guys all right in there? I'm sorry we had to jolt you around so much."

"Ugh," Paula said. "I don't see how you stand them. Doesn't it give you the creeps to sleep in the room with them?"

"Nope," Erika said. "I'm used to them. Besides, they're working for me. Every day they're putting me one step closer to that scholarship."

"You're really counting on winning it, aren't you?" Paula regarded her friend with respect. "You're not worried about the competition?"

"There isn't any on the local level," Erika said matter-of-factly. "I've checked it out. It's me against Gordon Pellet, and he didn't even decide to enter until last week. What can he throw together before December? It'll be stiffer at the state level, but I feel pretty confident about that, too. What I've got is something special."

"What is it?" Paula asked. "You've been working with those things for over a year now, but you've never explained to me exactly what you're doing."

"I didn't want to talk about it," Erika said. "I knew if I told people they'd think I was nuts. I wanted to test it first and see if I could back up my theory with statistics. It's amazing — I mean, really amazing."

"What is it?"

"You promise you won't tell? Especially not Mr. Carncross. I want to spring it on him right before the competition. This will knock him dead."

"I promise," Paula said. "I give my word as a Daughter of Eve."

"Okay." Erika gestured toward the top cage. "Do you see those ones?" She drew a deep breath. "They're alcoholics."

"They're what?" Paula asked blankly.

"You heard me right. The rats are alcoholics. They're genetic alcoholics. Their parents were alcoholics, and their grandparents and their great-grandparents. These poor slobs stay drunk all the time. See how sluggish they are?"

"You mean you feed them alcohol?" Paula asked skeptically.

"They feed themselves alcohol. The desire is bred into them. See those bottles?" Erika pointed at a row of four glass bottles, hung upside down across the far end of the cage. "See that guy going over to drink? He'll choose the one at the far end. There — see? I told you. They all choose that one. I have to refill it a couple of times a day. Know what's in it?"

"It's not water?"

"It's half water, half vodka. The bottle next to it is twenty-five percent vodka. They'll go to that one if the end one is empty. The third bottle contains ten percent vodka, and the fourth is pure water. If there's anything in the other bottles, they won't touch the water. What they have there is a self-service bar, and they operate it themselves."

"What about the ones in this cage?" Paula asked, indicating the one on the second tier. "They seem livelier. Are they alcoholics, too?"

"Watch and see," Erika said. The two girls sat silent for a moment, intent on the performance of the animals. Then Erika asked, "Well?"

"They're drinking from the water bottle. That is, unless you've changed the order."

"No, that's straight water, all right. This is my control group. They can't stand alcohol. I think they'd die of thirst before they'd take a swig of half-and-half. What I'm proving, Paula" — Erika's eyes were shining with excitement —"is that the tendency toward alcoholism is not only genetically inherited, but it's a chronic disorder."

"You mean somebody with an alcoholic father or mother has a better chance of being alcoholic than the average person and will stay an alcoholic forever?" Paula frowned, trying to understand. "I thought that had already been proven. Didn't Mr. Carncross say something about it in class?"

"Yes," Erika said, "well, part of it. This experiment reinforces the theory that alcoholism is hereditary, but he said researchers question the idea that alcoholism is a chronic disorder that can only be treated with lifelong abstinence. They believe that for alcoholics, relapse is *not* inevitable. But groups like Alcoholics Anonymous teach that alcoholism is a disease and that alcoholics will always relapse if they have the opportunity.

"So I'm challenging the researchers. My theory is that the compulsive desire for alcohol is not psychological, but physical. It's in the genes. You can pass it down from generation to generation, like curly hair or brown eyes, and it's a permanent and chronic disease. That's what I'm proving with my experiment."

"But how —" Paula began.

"I ran through a lot of rats the month I started," Erika told her. "I had them in a cage with my bottles, and almost all of them drank the water, but there were a couple who liked the water with the ten percent vodka. I put those in a separate cage and bred them, and out of a couple of litters there were a few who liked the ten percent stuff and a couple who went for the twenty-five percent. I got rid of the water drinkers and bred the heavier drinkers to each other. I kept doing that until — behold — my alcoholic generation!"

Erica went on, "Then I wanted to see what would happen if I tried to rehabilitate them. This part's the key. I divided the alcoholic rats into three groups. One group I kept as alcoholics. The second group I forced to quit drinking cold turkey by only giving them water with no other choice. The third group I forced to quit, but once they had been drink-free for a number of months, I introduced the choice between water or alcohol by giving them two separate bottles — they all went right back to the alcohol."

"That's incredible," Paula said.

"Exactly!" Erika gestured toward the second cage. "Those are the descendants of the nondrinkers. I've kept records on all of them. And those two sectioned cages are for breeding. I'm so excited about it, Paula — the way it's all working out — it's revolutionary! It'll blow their minds!"

"How do you think Mr. Carncross will take it?" Paula asked. "Won't he be annoyed if you prove the stuff he's been telling us in class is wrong?"

"No, I don't think so," Erika said. "He's a pretty cool guy. Besides, that's what the field of science is all about — breaking through old beliefs and proving new things. That's why it's so challenging, and why it means so much to me to win that scholarship."

"You'll win it," Paula said with certainty. "How could you not?"

"I've got to admit, that's what I think, too. And you can see why I can't risk the health of these guys by keeping them out in a cold garage?"

"Of course!"

"Though with the amount of booze this one batch gulps down, they probably wouldn't feel the cold." Erika burst into laughter, and Paula laughed with her, caught up by the contagious excitement.

Erika's eyes, behind the thick lenses of her glasses, were sparkling, and her narrow face was aglow with accomplishment. Looking at her across the stack of cages, Paula thought with surprise, *She's kind of pretty!*

It was the first time, during all the years of their friendship, that this thought had occurred to her.

"Hey, Maddie, it's nice you could make it," Peter Grange said sarcastically. "I've been sitting here waiting for you for a good twenty minutes. You're lucky I didn't pick up somebody else and take off on you."

"Don't call me 'Maddie'. You know I hate that nickname." Madison Ellis dumped her backpack in through the car's open window on the passenger's side. "I told you I had to talk to Ms. Stark awhile. You didn't have to wait if you didn't want to."

"I thought that dumb club only met on Mondays," Peter grumbled. "That's what Kristy keeps telling us. But you seem to be involved in it twenty-four hours a day."

Madison pulled the car door open and got in, shoving her backpack onto the floor of the car.

"She's right, the meetings are only once a week," she said. "You can't do everything during those, though. Like tomorrow, we're going door-to-door selling raffle tickets to benefit the school athletic fund. The homecoming queen does the drawing, you know, so it's only a couple of weeks away. That's what I had to talk to Irene about. I'm in charge of assigning the girls to their districts."

"You'd better not assign Kristy to one," Peter told her. "She's in enough trouble at home without taking off for a whole day on the weekend. You should talk to her, Madison. She's acting weird lately. I think she's lost it."

Madison pulled the door closed and leaned back, smiling at him.

"I did talk to her," she said. "I congratulated her. I think she's great, sticking up for herself the way she is. Frankly, I didn't think she had it in her."

"She's nuts," Peter said. "What does she think she's going to accomplish, anyway? So she abandons ship every Monday afternoon — she'll just end up grounded every weekend. She's not gaining anything except keeping our parents riled up all the time, and her chores are doubled on Tuesdays, and it makes Mom a worried wreck wondering what Eric's doing with nobody around to watch him."

"You or Niles could watch him," Madison suggested.

"No way." Peter gave the key a vicious twist and started the engine. "Basketball season's just around the corner, and we'll be practicing. Besides, babysitting is a girl's job, and all of Kristy's bitching about it isn't going to change that. She's making a big show out of this independence thing, but she won't last. Tomorrow, there's this birthday party she wants to go to, and Dad's not going to let her. A few more rounds of that kind of thing, and she's going to back down."

"I'm sorry she won't be going to Holly's party," Madison said. "We'll miss her."

"What do you mean — 'we'?" Peter turned to look at her with surprise. "You're not going to that party."

"Of course I am," Madison told him, equally surprised. "I got the invitation over a week ago. I told you about it, Pete; it's a slumber party for Holly's seventeenth birthday. It's going to be fun."

"You didn't tell me it was on a Saturday."

"Yes, I did," Madison said. "You just didn't listen. You're never interested in hearing about anything I'm doing unless you're part of it. This is just an all-girls' night with the Daughters of Eve. I wish Kristy were going to be there."

"Well, don't worry about it," Peter said, "because you're not going to be there either. We're going to the movies just like we always do on Saturdays. That's our date night — or are you too busy being a 'Daughter of Eve' to remember that?"

"I didn't think it mattered all that much," Madison said. "Geez, Pete, a movie's a movie. We can go tonight instead, can't we? What's the difference?"

"The difference is that I don't want to go tonight," Peter said. "I have other things I want to do tonight."

"Like what?"

"Like — I don't know. Like going bowling with the guys, maybe."

"You made that up just now."

"So what if I did? Is it any different for me to want to go bowling than for you to want to go to a slumber party?"

"You're being ridiculous," Madison said. "The party's a one-time thing, and the bowling can be anytime. What's with you anyway, Peter? You're really bothering me."

"Look who's talking!" Peter exclaimed angrily. "It's you who's doing the bothering, Maddie, and I'm not going to take it. We're supposed to be a couple. What do you think that means? That I sit around on Saturday night and watch sitcoms with my parents while you're out giggling with a bunch of girlfriends?"

"I thought it meant we cared about each other," Madison said. "I thought we were supposed to relate to each other, not own each other. I do my best to make you happy, Pete —"

"Like shit, you do!" Peter exploded. "You put out just

about as much effort as an ice cube. It's a joke. All the guys at school would give their right arms to change places with me. 'There's lucky Pete, out with the hottest-looking chick in town. Man, he must really be getting some, huh?' Yeah, right!"

"I didn't mean 'make you happy' that way," Madison said coldly. "I told you from the beginning that I wasn't going that far with anyone yet. I have a modeling career ahead of me, and I'm not going to take any chances screwing it up."

"Come on, it's not like you'll get pregnant," Peter said. "There are tons of ways to prevent it."

"Yeah, I know. And I've picked the best way. The only one that's absolutely foolproof." Her voice shook slightly. "If that's all you want, then you've wasted six months of your precious time, because you're not getting it. There are girls in the world who will give you what you want under pressure, but I'm not one of them. If you don't want to go out with me on those terms, then say so."

There was a moment of silence. When Peter spoke again his voice was tight and controlled. "Are you going out with me Saturday night?"

"I told you, no. I'm going to Holly's party. We can go out tonight instead."

"No way."

"Then maybe you'd better let me out of the car," Madison said. "I don't think there's anything else we need to talk about. Besides, you'll need the rest of the day to figure out a new plan."

"That's cool." Peter gave the wheel a twist and brought the car over to the side of the road, where the tires grated against the curbing for a ten-foot stretch before the vehicle came to a stop. He turned to glare at the girl beside him. His handsome face was dark with fury.

"I suppose you expect me to come around and open the door for you, Your Majesty?"

"I think I can handle it." Madison reached down to gather up her backpack. "Have a wonderful time at the movie. Bring a blanket to snuggle with at the theater."

As usual, she'd managed to get in the final word, slamming the door before any further retort could be made. In outraged frustration, Peter sat gripping the steering wheel as he watched her walk away with her long, model's stride, her legs flashing straight and slim beneath the provocative flare of her short skirt. After several paces she gave her head a toss, flipping the long, blond hair across her shoulders in a gesture that sent Peter jerking backward as though the shining strands had struck him in the face.

"Bitch," he whispered under his breath. "Bring a blanket, huh? I sure as hell think I can manage a new date."

He had driven only three blocks farther when he saw a heavyset figure plodding along the sidewalk and slowed the car to pick up Laura Snow.

*　　*　　*

"Mom and Dad, I have something I want to talk to you about," Tammy said. "I've done something I guess was pretty dumb."

"Dumb how, Tam?" Mr. Carncross raised his eyes from the pile of student papers he was grading to focus his attention on his daughter.

In the chair across from him, his wife was engrossed in proofreading a manuscript. She, too, glanced up, quickly alert to the note of distress in the girl's voice.

"What is it, honey?" she asked.

"It's dumb because I didn't think it out. I just did it on impulse." Tammy drew a deep breath. "Brace yourselves — you'll never believe this. I dropped out of Daughters of Eve."

"You're right, I'll never believe it," her mother responded. "What happened? That club's been a huge part of your life for the past two years."

"That's why it's so dumb. I don't know what happened." Tammy laughed nervously. "I was sitting there during the initiation ceremony when all of a sudden I got this — this really weird picture — in my mind. It was so real that at first I thought I was actually seeing it, but, of course, I wasn't. It was just my mind doing one of those things it does sometimes. But it scared me. I got up and ran out.

"The next day I wrote Erika a note and told her I was resigning."

81

"And now you're sorry?" her father asked.

"All my best friends are in Daughters of Eve," Tammy said miserably. "Now I'm an outsider. I hadn't realized before how tightly we were all connected to each other."

"Surely the mere fact that you've dropped out of a club won't cause you to lose the friendship of the girls," Mrs. Carncross said reasonably. "There's a lot of life beyond the activities of a club. You're still Tammy, even if you're no longer a member of Daughters of Eve."

"Holly Underwood is having her birthday party tomorrow," Tammy said. "I wasn't invited."

"You can't read into that, dear," her mother said. "Nobody can include everybody she knows every time she gives a party. Holly's a junior, isn't she? She's not even in your class."

"But everybody else is going, even the new girls. Kristy Grange and Jane Rheardon are only sophomores." Tammy fought to keep her voice steady. "Even Laura Snow was invited. You can't understand why that's a big deal, Mom, because you've never met Laura, but Dad can tell you. She isn't the type of girl who gets asked to many parties."

"I'm afraid you're right there," Mr. Carncross said. "I have Laura in my second-period general science class. She's a bit overweight, and kids can be pretty cruel sometimes."

"It's worse than that," Tammy said. "She's sort of — pathetic — you know? She's got that 'please, somebody, like me' look all the time. There's no way Holly would even have considered inviting her to anything last year, but now that she's part of the sisterhood, she's included in everything."

"How did she get into the sisterhood if she's that unappealing?" Mrs. Carncross asked. "Members have to be voted in, don't they, like in a sorority? In fact, it is a sort of sorority, isn't it, when it comes to that?"

"We don't think of it that way," Tammy said defensively. "It's a club."

"But you do vote on members?"

"Yes," Tammy admitted.

"So how did this Laura get invited to join?"

"Irene — Ms. Stark — our adviser wanted her," Tammy said. "We all discussed it, and Irene explained that Laura is the kind of girl who needs sisters who can help her feel better about herself. Daughters of Eve isn't just for beauty queens."

"That's a nice idea," Mrs. Carncross said slowly. "Ms. Stark is a new sponsor, isn't she? You girls must think a lot of her to respect her views so much."

"Everybody worships Irene," Tammy said.

"Why do you feel that way?" her father asked her.

"You know what she's like, Dad. You've met her."

"Of course, at faculty meetings, but I don't really feel like I know her," Mr. Carncross said. "The principal seems impressed with her teaching ability. Actually, I've found her pretty aloof and standoffish. I've heard several students express the same opinion."

"I bet they were boys. They don't know her the way

the girls do," Tammy told him. "Irene's never aloof with us. Everybody thinks of her as sort of an older sister."

"Like Marnie?" her father suggested.

"No, not exactly. Irene is — I can't describe it. Even the girls who voted against Laura felt guilty for doing it and were sort of glad when she made it in."

"What did Irene have to say about your resignation?" Mrs. Carncross asked.

"She said she was sorry and that she wished I'd reconsider. Ann told me that when Erika announced I was resigning, Irene said to table it for a while and see if I'd change my mind."

"Well, now that you've reconsidered, what do you think?"

"I don't know." Tammy regarded her parents helplessly. "That day at the meeting the feeling was so strong. And then, afterward, when Irene came up to speak to me — I had to get out, something awful was going to happen! But nothing has. Everybody seems to be having a good time just like always. I think back now, and I don't see how I could have reacted the way I did over something that was just a picture in my mind."

"What was it you saw, Tam?" her father asked her gently.

"A bleeding candle. That's pretty dumb, isn't it? It doesn't mean anything. One of the candles of sisterhood had blood running down the side of it. Does that sound crazy?"

"It doesn't sound crazy, dear," her mother said. "We've all accepted for a long time the fact that you do seem to have a greater sensitivity than most people. You've startled us at times with some of these odd visions that materialize and predictions that really come true. The thing is, though, there are other times when they turn out to be false alarms. Right?"

"Yes," Tammy said. "There have been times like that."

"Don't you think this could've been one of them?"

"Yes." She wanted to believe it so much that she said it again, trying to convince herself. "Yes, it could've been. Like I said, nothing has happened."

"You can't let these feelings of yours control your life, honey," her mother said. "You have to use your common sense. What sort of awful thing is going to happen at a club meeting in the middle of the afternoon?"

"The roof might fall in on us, I guess." Tammy giggled, faced with the absurdity of the statement. "You think I should go back, then?"

"I certainly do, dear, if it's making you so unhappy. If anyone brings out a bleeding candle you can always leave." Her mother was teasing her.

Tammy turned to her father.

"You think so, too, Dad?"

"I think the decision should be yours, Tam," Mr. Carncross said quietly. Unlike his wife, he wasn't smiling.

Chapter 7

"Is something bugging you tonight? You're awfully quiet." Mr. Grange glanced across the top of his paper at the woman on the sofa. "You hardly talked during dinner. Do you have one of your headaches?"

"No. I'm sorry. I've just been thinking."

Edna Grange was a small woman with a short, flat nose like her daughter's and a tired, soft face. As a girl, she, like Kristy, had always looked younger than her years. Now, at thirty-seven, she looked closer to her mid-forties. Sometimes in the mornings as she hurriedly applied makeup before leaving for work, she had the odd feeling that she was decorating the face of a stranger.

Now she became aware of that stranger's voice, dull and apathetic. "I'm sorry." Why in the world had she said that? What was it she was apologizing for? "I've been thinking," she repeated.

"What?" Her husband, who'd returned his attention to the paper, looked up again in surprise. "What did you say?"

"I was thinking about tonight — that party at the Underwoods'. We should've let Kristy go."

"Oh, Edna, don't tell me we're back on that again," Mr. Grange said irritably. "What are you trying to do, encourage her in this rebellion? It's been a whole week now since she made that defiant announcement of hers, and she's just as stubborn as she was in the beginning."

"But is it going to help anything to keep her home every evening?" his wife asked. "Like you say, it's been a week. What are we accomplishing?"

"She can reverse things anytime she wants to. All she has to do is give up that club and start helping out around here the way she's supposed to."

"She does help, George. A lot, really," Mrs. Grange said. "It's not as if she was asking for every afternoon free. One day a week doesn't seem unreasonable when you think about all the freedom the boys have."

"Don't you remember our first talk about this subject? It won't be one afternoon. You made that point yourself. These school sororities take up all kinds of time other than just for meetings."

"We could probably work around them somehow. Maybe most of them would take place on evenings or weekends, or maybe there wouldn't really be all that many. I was upset that evening. I overreacted."

"My god, Edna, what's gotten into you?" her husband asked in bewilderment. "You're the one suffering because of Kristy's defiance. You come home Mondays to a wall-to-wall mess and have to start putting together some sort of supper, and you've told me yourself you worry all afternoon about what sort of trouble Eric's got himself into at home by himself. All I've tried to do is back you up on this and get Kristy to come around and shape up."

"I know."

She did know that he was trying to help her, to get things under control again so she wouldn't be overburdened. That first night, she'd been grateful for his support. And that evening a few days later, when Kristy had stood before them, her jaw set, her freckles standing out in a pattern of dark dots against her pale face, grounding her had seemed to be the only alternative.

"I'm not giving up my membership," Kristy had stated flatly. "I'm attending Monday meetings. I'm sorry to upset you, Mom, but that's just the way it's going to be."

You couldn't let a child say something like that, could you?

Or — could you?

I never said anything like that to my parents, Edna Grange thought. *I never said anything like that to anybody.* How could she have the nerve? That bothered her almost as much as the proclamation itself, because it was so out

88

of character. Kristy had never been a defiant child. Niles, yes — Niles had always defied authority; they had come to accept that as part of his personality. And Peter, being the first and so uncommonly beautiful, had been able to get his way by smiling at them. Kristy sulked and grumbled; that was her method of dealing with adversity. But during the past week, Kristy hadn't been sulking. She'd come straight home from school four days in the week, picked things up and done the laundry with a seemingly pleasant attitude; she sat with them at the dinner table, cleaned up the kitchen and retired without a complaint to her bedroom with an armload of schoolbooks. And on Monday afternoon, she didn't come home till dinner.

It was driving George crazy, but Edna herself was beginning to be amused by it. To see Kristy, funny, meek little Kristy, holding her own like this was such a new experience, you had to pause and give the situation another mental run-through.

"I'm beginning to wonder if she might not have a legitimate gripe," Mrs. Grange said now, letting the words slide tentatively into the space between them. "She did try to talk to us about her side of this, and we wouldn't listen to her. Maybe taking this stand was the only way she could find to get through to us."

"She's gotten through, all right," George Grange said. "She's got me so mad I'm ready to disown her. She knows perfectly well what the situation is around here, and she has her responsibilities as part of this family."

"And the boys don't?"

"What do you mean by that?"

"What Kristy said was true, George; Peter and Niles don't lift a hand to help out. She was right when she said that it isn't fair. It's not fair."

"What's unfair about it?" Mr. Grange asked impatiently. "Pete and Niles are boys. You can't expect them to put on aprons and flit around polishing the furniture. I didn't do that when I was a boy, and god help anybody who suggested it to me."

"They wouldn't have to do anything like that," Mrs. Grange said. "They could simply take turns staying home on Monday afternoons to keep an eye on Eric and pick up the house a little. And it wouldn't be impossible for them to put a meal together either. Plenty of professional chefs are men, aren't they?"

"Sure, and what else are they?"

"Come on, there's nothing especially feminine about chopping up salad greens. Besides, when you think about it, the whole reason I'm working so many extra hours is to add to *their* college funds."

"Look, it's been a long week. We're both tired. This is a silly argument." Her husband's voice had settled into that solid, reasonable tone that she knew so well and liked so little. It made her feel diminished somehow, childish, as though nothing she said was of any value — yet at the same time it contained affection. There'd never been a moment in the duration of their marriage that she'd doubted George's love for her, and that, in a way, made everything harder. You couldn't resent someone who loved you, could you? Not unless there was something wrong with your value system.

Yet tonight she did resent him. There was no other word for the way she was feeling as she sat listening to that familiar, self-assured voice.

"Men are men, and women are women," George Grange was saying firmly. "Both have their places in the world. When you try to shift things around and change those places, you get yourself a lot of mixed-up people who don't know what they are.

"I went to a bar in Vegas, Eddie, back when I was in the service. You know what they had there? Guys dressed up like women. I mean, they looked just like women, with boobs and their hair all puffed up on top of their heads, and there was one of them who sang like a woman. He sang 'Over the Rainbow,' and, my god, he sounded exactly like Judy Garland in *The Wizard of Oz*. I thought right then, if there's ever a time when I have sons and one of them turns out like that…well, can you imagine how their parents must feel?"

"You think their parents were responsible?" Despite herself, she was affected by the picture he had drawn for her. "From what I've read, some people think it's genetic, just like being left-handed or having freckles."

"Maybe so, but if those guys had been raised right they wouldn't have been out there flaunting themselves that way, like they were proud of being freaks. We're lucky to have two real men in Pete and Niles. Let's be grateful, huh? Let's enjoy them for what they are."

As always happened when they argued, she'd gotten nowhere. Everything George said was logical to himself. She couldn't refute it. She knew she was blessed to have married such a good and stable man, and she shouldn't focus on his faults. When she thought back on the era between her high-school graduation and her marriage, it returned to her, not as a series of individual days, but as a great, gray cloud of time in which she hung motionless, suspended between childhood and adulthood. Waiting for George to get out of the army, she'd lived at home with her parents. She'd made herself as useful as possible, helping her mother with the gardening and canning, and babysitting for neighbors in the evenings. She'd read a lot, and taken long walks along the edge of the creek, and written George letters once and sometimes twice a day, and marked off on a calendar she kept beside her bed the slow passage of the days and weeks and months that would bring her finally to a moment of self-identity when she would become Mrs. George Grange.

"How about some coffee?" her husband said now. His eyes were back on the newspaper.

"It's on, and the cups are in the drying rack."

"I didn't ask you where it was. I said, how about some?"

"I know. I'm sorry." Edna Grange got to her feet and went into the kitchen and poured his coffee. She put milk and sugar in it, gave it a stir, and carried the mug into the living room and set it on a TV tray beside his chair.

Then she went upstairs and stood outside her daughter's closed bedroom door. From behind it she could hear Kristy's radio playing softly; it was bluegrass, rich and earthy with a strong melody line, a far cry from the hard rock that usually blared from the stereo in the boys' room. Edna herself played bluegrass on those few occasions when she was alone in the house and there was no one to scoff at her taste.

She reached out her hand and rapped lightly.

"Who is it?"

"It's Mom." She turned the knob and opened the door.

Kristy was sitting in bed, reading. She glanced up quickly, her face apprehensive.

"You want something, Mom?"

"Get dressed," Edna Grange said. "And pack up some overnight stuff. I'm driving you over to Holly's party."

"It's me, honey. May I come in?"

"Sure, Mom," Laura said. "The door's not locked."

She was seated at the dressing table, and in the mirror she watched the bedroom door open and her mother's cumbersome bulk appear.

Mrs. Snow's eyes also focused upon the mirror images, and she gave a little gasp of delight.

"Honey, you look just beautiful!"

"Do you like my hair this way?" Laura asked nervously,

fingering the cluster of curls she'd worked over so laboriously for most of the afternoon and had now fastened to the top of her head.

"It's lovely," her mother told her. "You look just like a movie star. Are you wearing mascara? Is that why your eyes look so shiny? I wish I had a camera with me this very minute to take your picture."

"I've got some eye makeup on," Laura said. "I've got foundation, too. I read this magazine article about how to apply a couple of different shades and blend them together. It's supposed to make your face look narrow."

"You little silly!" Mrs. Snow came into the room and stood behind her daughter, stooping so that their faces showed side by side in the reflecting glass. "Two peas in a pod. That's what Papa used to call us when you were little."

"He did?" Laura stared without expression at the undeniable likeness. Even with the darker shade of foundation along the sides of her face and under the chin, the contours didn't seem to be greatly diminished. "About Papa — I've been meaning to ask you — am I supposed to go see him this Christmas?"

"At Christmas?" her mother said vaguely. "My goodness, honey, I don't know. Why worry about something like that right now?"

"Christmas is only two months away," Laura said. "That's pretty close. And doesn't the custody agreement say that I'm supposed to spend vacations with him? I didn't last summer."

"You had that terrible virus. They were afraid for you to expose the baby."

"It was only a summer cold," Laura said. "It didn't last very long."

"You really want to leave your mama all alone during the holidays?"

There was no answer for such a question.

"It's just that I haven't seen Papa for such a long time. It's been over a year now." She dropped the subject. "You really do like my hair?"

"It's as good as Mrs. Brummell could do at the salon," Mrs. Snow said admiringly, reaching a finger to touch the curls. "Do you know what would be fun for you to do tonight? You could do the hair of all the girls at the party. That's what we always used to do at slumber parties when I was a girl. We'd sit up all night giggling and talking and giving each other makeovers."

"It's not a slumber party, Mom."

"It's not?" Mrs. Snow said in surprise. "I thought it said that on the invitation."

"It did," Laura told her, "but Holly decided to change it. She told me yesterday. It's going to go pretty late, but we won't be sleeping over. They don't have enough beds, or something."

"Then you'll want me to pick you up?"

"No, just take your pill like always and go to sleep. Mr. Underwood is going to drive us all home when the party's over." Laura shoved her chair back slowly so as to allow her mother an opportunity to move out from behind it. "In fact, I've got a ride over, too, with one of the girls. She's going to pick me up out in front in a couple of minutes. So you don't have to do a thing except wish me a nice time."

"You'll have one, I know," her mother said confidently. "I just wish there were going to be boys there to see how pretty you look."

Laura turned to press a kiss on the smooth, pink cheek and then, impulsively, threw her arms around her mother's plump shoulders in a spontaneous hug.

I wish that I could tell her, she thought regretfully. *She'd be so happy for me.*

But she'd promised.

"I don't want a bunch of people talking about us," Peter had told her. "That club of yours is a bunch of gossip fiends. That's one reason I broke it off with Madison; she was always telling everybody everything we did together. I like my privacy, you know?"

"I know," Laura had answered breathlessly. "I'm kind of a private person, too."

She'd pleaded sick when she called Holly to back out of the slumber party. It had been a lie then, but now it was close to the truth. Her face felt feverish and her stomach churned with nauseous growling sounds, and her heart was beating so hard that she was afraid she might faint. There were other worries, too — that the Daughters of Eve might call tonight to ask how she was; that her mother might wait up for her and see she'd lied about who was bringing her home — but if those things happened, she'd have to deal with them later.

Right now the important thing was to get herself over to the corner of Locust and Second streets for her date with Peter Grange.

Ann Whitten's cell phone rang just as she was going out the door.

For a moment she was tempted not to answer it. They were late already because Kelly had to wait for her father to come home with the car. Now she was parked in the driveway with the engine running, beeping the horn in a "hurry, get out here" manner, and over at the Under-woods' they were probably waiting on them to start din-ner and growing more impatient by the minute.

Still, there was always the possibility that the phone call was important. Her parents had gone into town to an early movie, and with her father's health the way it was, something could've happened.

"Hang on a sec!" she yelled to Kelly, and pulled her phone out of her bag and answered without looking at the screen.

"Hello?"

For a moment there was only silence. Then Dave's voice asked huskily, "Annie?"

"Yes, it's me." He must have switched the position of the mouthpiece, because suddenly she could hear his breathing, harsh and ragged, and a cord of fear twisted somewhere deep in her stomach. "Dave, is something wrong?"

"Yes." There was silence again, and then a strange, choking sound, and she realized to her horror that he was crying.

"What is it?" Ann demanded. "What's happened? Dave, are you okay?"

"Mom's dead."

Ann's hand tightened convulsively on the receiver.

"What? Dave, she can't be! I was over there this afternoon. She was teaching me to make chocolate cake from scratch not using a cake mix. She was just fine."

The words were ridiculous, and she knew it even as she spoke them, yet the reality was impossible. Mrs. Brewer had been all right — a little tired, maybe, but she'd been chatty enough, even joking a little about the collection of odd recipes she was planning to give Ann as a wedding present. There was one cake you made with diet soda and another with a can of tomato soup.

"She didn't eat much at dinner," Dave said. "She said she was going to lie down for a while before she did the kitchen, and I told her to leave the dishes and I'd rinse and load them when I got back from the evening chores. When I came in a few minutes ago, she was lying on the bed, and I thought she was sleeping. I went over to lay a blanket on her, and I saw she wasn't breathing."

"Oh my god, Dave, that's horrible!" Her heart wrenched for him. And as though she were there beside him, she saw the blue-eyed man bending worriedly over the still figure on the bed, reaching in stunned disbelief to touch the closed eyelids, speaking a name and hearing nothing in answer but silence.

"Maybe she's just unconscious," she whispered. "A little stroke or something. You called 911, right?"

"Someone should be here any minute now. They called for an ambulance out of Adrian, but it won't help, Annie."

"You're sure." It was a statement rather than a question.

"Can you come?"

"Of course. Kelly can drive me. She's here now, parked out in the driveway. We were just leaving for Holly's."

"Oh, yeah — the party. I forgot. That's why I wasn't going to see you tonight." He paused, fumbling, trying to put the pieces of life together to make some sort of pattern, yet unable to focus. "If you think you should go there first —"

"Dave, don't be crazy. How could I even begin to think about a stupid party now? You want me with you, don't you?"

"Yes, I want you." His voice broke. "Annie, please come now. Hurry. I need you so much."

"I'm on my way. Just hang on. I love you."

"I love — you — too." He was weeping unashamedly now, and she was also as she flipped her phone shut and hurried toward Kelly's car.

Chapter 8

The November 6 meeting of the Modesta chapter of Daughters of Eve was called to order by the president, Erika Schneider. The pledge was repeated. The secretary, Ann Whitten, read the minutes from the previous meeting, and Madison Ellis presented the treasurer's report.

"Ninety-three dollars and seventy cents," she read. "And a couple of people I know had better get themselves in gear and turn in their November dues so we can buy nice material for the nursing-home curtains."

Irene Stark observed her with satisfaction. When she'd taken on the sponsorship of the group at the beginning of the school year, she hadn't been sure she was going to take to her. Madison had the sort of striking beauty that came across as not quite real: The hair, the skin, the figure were all so perfect that she might have stepped straight out of a TV show.

It had come as a heartening surprise to discover that beneath that surface the girl was made of steel wire.

"I broke up with Pete," she'd announced to Irene one Monday morning between classes. "If there's one thing I don't need, it's a male chauvinist pig trying to run my life for me. He was telling me what I could and couldn't do with my spare time, like he was my dad or something!"

If only they all had Madison's strength and self-confidence, Irene thought now, surveying the array of young faces before her. If only they were all able to stand up for themselves and demand of life the things they deserved. Here was Ann Whitten, as talented an artist as had ever come through one of her classes, blithely preparing to destroy the possibility of any sort of art career by settling down at eighteen to marry a farmer. Here was bright, levelheaded Kelly Johnson, who might make a fine lawyer someday, setting her life's goal to be an administrative assistant. She'd spend a lifetime brewing coffee and typing letters for some demanding male boss with half the native intelligence she had.

And Tammy Carncross. What had happened to Tammy? Tammy with her dreamy eyes and sweet, expressive face was a little shy, but liked by everybody. What had caused her to act so strangely at the initiation meeting? That was a worry, and so was Jane Rheardon, sitting quiet and withdrawn with her chair pulled a little away from the rest of the circle, one of them and yet not one of them, a sister and yet strangely unreachable. Jane needed friends to talk to. Well, they were here. Why was she unable to open up to them?

And then there was Laura Snow. Laura was involved with someone. Attuned as she was to the emotions of her girls, Irene could pinpoint the very weekend it had started, for Laura had come to school the next week with an odd sort of glow about her, a dreamy, drifting look that Irene had seen on the faces of girls before. *My dear,* she'd thought, *poor girl, you have to get a grip on things.* There were girls who could handle sexual relationships during their teen years, and there were others who were not emotionally equipped for them. Laura definitely fell into the latter category.

Especially disturbing to Irene was the fact that she couldn't figure out who the boyfriend was. Laura continued to walk through the halls by herself or with girlfriends, and at lunch she sat at a table with Erika and Paula. No boy hovered by her locker or carried her books to classes, and when school was out she waited alone at the south door of the building for Kristy Grange, who walked home in the same direction. Still, Laura had the unmistakable aura of a girl in love, and Irene was finally forced to come to the conclusion that he wasn't a student at Modesta. This opened the door to all sorts of distressing possibilities. There were men in the world who made a game out of seducing young girls, especially those as vulnerable and inexperienced as Laura.

On Irene's first teaching day at Modesta, she'd spotted Laura alone at a table in the school cafeteria, hunched over a wedge of chocolate cake, her jaws moving rhythmically, her eyes glued to the wall as though it were a movie screen portraying a situation far more intriguing than the bustle of activity around her. The girl's stolid acceptance of her loneliness had struck Irene as pathetic, and it had jolted her back in place and time to another girl alone in a crowd of her contemporaries, defiantly pretending that she didn't care.

That girl had been Irene herself. She hadn't had a weight problem; for her there had been the simple fact that, by the standards of her day, she was ugly. In an era when pale daintiness was considered the essence of femininity, Irene's dark complexion and black hair had set her apart. Heavy brows, a strong-boned face, and a shadow of dark fuzz across the upper lip had completed the unappetizing picture. Like Laura, she'd moved alone through a social scene of teen couples, holding herself aloof in an attempt to convince her classmates that such idiotic behavior was beyond her comprehension.

On the day that she overheard her father remark quite matter-of-factly to her mother that "We'd better get her all the education we can, because god knows she's never going to find a husband," Irene had decided to kill herself. This decision had lasted for the length of time it had taken her to lock herself in the bathroom and extract the razor blades from her father's old-fashioned shaving kit. At that point there had flashed through her mind a vision of her mother, whom she loved, gazing down on her daughter's body on the blood-drenched tiles and being carried off, shrieking, to a sanitarium. A wispy little person of a sensitive nature, Mrs. Stark had a history of emotional breakdowns.

So Irene had put back the blades, unlocked the door and kept on living. The following year her parents had separated, and her mother's final breakdown had occurred. For cold comfort, Irene had the knowledge that she herself wasn't responsible. She accepted her college tuition from her father and never again acknowledged his existence.

In college, for the first time in her life, she fell in love. The man was a dreamy, bespectacled art professor, married, with children in high school. Their romance lasted several months before the professor's wife paid a visit to Irene in her dorm room. She didn't rant or weep; she simply sat on Irene's lumpy bed with her legs demurely crossed at the ankles and explained that her husband was going through what she called "his midlife crisis."

"He feels youth slipping away," she explained, "and

he compensates by cultivating young female students." Irene, it seemed, was one of a number of those who came and went as semester followed semester.

"You're better than that, aren't you, dear?" the woman asked her.

Numbly, Irene nodded. Then she asked a question of her own.

"Why do you stay with him?"

"I'm used to it," the woman told her. "Besides, what else is there for me to do? I've got five kids. I've never worked. I'm stuck." She leaned forward in a conspiratorial manner and took Irene's hand. "Don't ever get stuck, dear. Take it from somebody who knows what it's all about. You have that first baby, and they've got you. You're a sharp girl, I can tell that. I used to be sharp once, too, can you believe it? But I let myself get buried, and I could never dig my way out again."

"I'm an education major," Irene said. "I'm minoring in art."

"You want to teach painting?"

"I want to help kids with talent learn to express themselves."

"If that's what you want, go for it," the woman said. "Don't let them stop you."

"Nobody's trying to stop me," Irene told her wryly. "I'm not exactly the type men stand in line for."

"Don't underestimate yourself. It's not always a pretty

face that hooks them. Sometimes it's the challenge of trying to keep a strong woman down." The professor's wife uncrossed her ankles and got to her feet. "Well, good luck, dear. I've enjoyed our talk. I must say, my husband's taste is improving."

"Thank you," Irene said politely. "It was nice meeting you."

After her guest left, she got out her English class notebook and wrote down the entire conversation in as much detail as she could remember, because she knew that later she wouldn't be able to believe it had actually occurred.

I should have that notebook now, she thought, *to share with them — with Laura, especially, and with Ann.* If they could read that dialogue, they might begin to realize what they were doing to themselves. They would learn, of course; all women did eventually. If only they could be saved from gleaning that knowledge too late!

It was Erika's voice that snapped her out of her reverie.

"May we have the report on the sale of the raffle tickets?"

"They're going really well," Kelly said, consulting her notes. "I had five hundred printed, and we've already sold almost half of them with the rest of this week still to go before the drawing. If anybody wants extras, I've got some with me."

106

"I need some," Tammy said.

"That's right, Tam, you didn't get any, did you?" Kelly took a packet of tickets from the box in her lap and passed it to her friend across the table. "We're charging less this year so people will buy more of them. We decided the price we asked last year was too high."

"What are the prizes?" Tammy asked.

"We've got some really good stuff. There's a charcoal grill from Williams, and Paula's dad has donated dinner for two at the café, and Steinmetz Photography is giving a free portrait session. There's a lot of small stuff, too. Most of the places we asked came through with donations."

"Does the club do this every year?" Kristy asked.

"They started a few years ago when my sister was a junior," Tammy told her. "All the school-sponsored organizations take on one project a year to benefit the school, and that year Daughters of Eve decided to raise money for the athletic fund. The raffle idea was so successful that we've done it ever since. The drawing takes place during intermission at the homecoming dance."

"Why did you choose the athletic fund?" Irene asked her.

"I don't know. It wasn't anyone here who did it. Those girls have all graduated." Tammy frowned, trying to recall the circumstances of the decision. "I think Marnie said something once about the principal suggesting it. The football team needed uniforms."

"And what do they need this year?"

"I'm not into athletics. Paula probably knows." Tammy passed on the question. "What's on the want list?"

"Everything," Paula said. "Wrestling mats, baseball gear, warm-up suits for the basketball guys; you name it, they need it. Coach Ferrara's counting the days till homecoming so he can cash in."

"What about the girls' teams?" Irene asked. "Do they have everything they need?"

"There aren't many girls' teams," Kelly said. "It's just basketball, and they haven't done very well. I'm sorry, Paula; I know you're on the team. I didn't say that to put you down, but it's a fact."

"Sure, it's a fact," Paula said irritably. "What do you expect? We never get a chance to practice. The boys use the gym every afternoon until six o'clock, and then they lock the place up."

"Really?" Kelly said, surprised. "When do you practice then?"

"Saturdays, and whenever the guys decide to take a day off and bother to let us know. We can get the gym before school in the mornings if we want it but it's impossible. By the time you shower and change, you're late to first period and then you're exhausted the rest of the day."

"Why are practices set up like that?" Irene asked.

"It's just the rule."

"Why do the boys get the gym every single afternoon?"

"Well, they're the champs," Paula said. "They've been in either first or second place in the regional tournament for three years now."

"And why do you think that is?"

"Because they're good. They really are."

"They're good because they practice?"

There was a moment's silence. Then Paula said, "That's a lot of it, I guess."

"If the women's team had the same opportunity for practice, how do you think you would perform?"

"We'd be great," Paula said. "We've got some good players, it's just that we don't play together enough to know what we're doing. Coach says that when there are two teams wanting to use the same facilities, the one that's doing the best job and bringing honor to the school should get first crack at them."

"It's a vicious circle," Holly said. "Why aren't there any sports except basketball open to girls here, anyway? We don't even have a softball team. Do the guys need to use the baseball field? Is that the reason?"

"Don't ask me," Paula said. "I don't organize the sports program. Modesta High's a small school. We don't have enough money for everything. That's the reason Mr. Shelby asked us to support the athletic fund."

"The point is, from what you say, it doesn't sound as though you girls are getting much benefit from this fund," Irene said. "Wrestling mats and warm-up suits for the boys aren't going to help much in getting a softball team established for you or in getting you half-time use of the gym for basketball practice."

"What do we do?" Kelly said. "Start a petition?"

"That's one possibility. It's been known to work. I read an article the other day about a junior-high girl in Lyndhurst, Ohio, who wanted to be involved in an interscholastic sports program. The principal told her there wasn't enough interest for the school to implement the program, so she circulated petitions. Over half the girls in the school signed them, and the sports program has now been started."

"I don't think that would work here," Ann Whitten said doubtfully. "Mr. Shelby hates petitions. Remember that time Brad Tully started one about setting aside a smoking area? Mr. Shelby called a special assembly just to tell everybody that he'd heard that it was going around and that if it was ever turned in to him he'd burn it without even looking at it."

"That was because of the issue," Tammy said. "My dad didn't like the smoking-area idea either. I don't know that they'd feel the same way about something like this."

"We could try it," Kristy Grange suggested. "What is there to lose? It might work out. Like all of you were telling me about that thing with my parents, there comes a time when you have to stand up for yourself."

"Is Pete still having fits about that?" Madison asked with a laugh.

"He and Niles are so pissed off they don't even speak to me," Kristy said. "Not that I miss their voices all that much. It's nice, actually. The problem is that my dad's mad at my mom because she's started sticking up for me. I feel kind of guilty about that."

"What about Mondays?" Madison asked her. "Does your mom have the guys staying home?"

"They won't do it, and Dad's backing them up on that, so Mom's hired a woman from down the street to come in and pick up the place and get dinner started. Mom's paying her every week out of her paycheck before she puts it in the college savings account."

"So Pete and Niles are really paying the housekeeper out of their own college fund! Ha! That's awesome!" Madison's crow of delight was so contagious that it brought answering smiles from the faces all around her. "I never would've thought your mom would come through for you like that. I mean, she's really nice and all, but she's so conservative."

"It seems like there have been a lot of women in this little pocket of the country who have been sleeping," Irene Stark said quietly. "It's like they got stuck in the beginning of the twentieth century and haven't noticed how much things have changed." The low, strong voice broke through the chatter and brought sudden silence as the girls turned to stare at their sponsor, startled by the intensity of her expression. "Like Kristy's mother, these are nice women, quiet, gentle women, who have grown from being dutiful daughters to being dutiful wives and mothers. They've laid themselves down for men to walk on, because all their lives they've been led to believe that this is what women are supposed to do. Back in seventeen seventy-six, when patriots were demanding a Declaration of Independence, John Adams's wife, Abigail, wrote to him in Philadelphia, saying, 'Do not put such unlimited power into the hands of husbands. Remember, all men would be tyrants if they could.' Adams wrote back to her, calling her 'saucy' and saying, 'Depend upon it, we know better than to repeal our masculine systems.' Times may have changed in many ways, but apparently, here in Modesta things have not. The men who live here seem to feel exactly the same way. They're afraid to let the whip slip out of their hands."

"Not all men," Ann said, frowning. "Dave isn't like that, and neither is my dad."

"My dad isn't either," Tammy said. "He lets my mom have her own career."

"He lets her?" Irene repeated the words, putting them in the form of a question. "The very fact you phrase the statement that way makes my point. Why should he have to 'let' your mother have a career, as though he's offering her some special privilege? Would you ever think of saying, 'My mother lets my father teach science'?"

"Men are supposed to have jobs," Tammy said. "They have to support their families. With women there's usually a choice. When a woman decides to work it's because she wants to —"

"That's not true," Paula broke in. "Maybe your mom works because she likes to. She's a writer. That's like a hobby, something she can do on her own time when she feels like it. My mom works at the salon because we need the cash, and when she's through with that she comes home to clean and do laundry and make dinner. Dad sits there on the sofa watching TV, acting like Mom's long day doing people's hair wasn't anything and the stuff she's doing at home is her recreation."

"What about the rest of your mothers?" Irene asked. "How many of them hold jobs outside of the home?" Kristy Grange raised her hand, as did Madison. Holly raised hers halfway.

"My mother gives piano lessons part-time. Does that count?"

"Do you think it counts?" Irene asked her.

"Well, sure. It's work, isn't it?"

"Does your father think it counts? If someone were to suddenly ask him, 'Does your wife work?' would he say, 'Yes'?"

"I don't know. Probably not," Holly admitted. "It's

not what you'd call a career. It's just a couple of hours a day, and she uses the money for extras like presents for people and my music lessons and stuff like that. How'd we get onto this subject, anyway?"

"Straight from Abigail Adams," Madison said. "Irene was saying men want to hang on to the whip, and Ann said, 'Not all men.' How can you know that, Ann? Dave isn't your husband yet. You haven't had anything to disagree about. When you do, maybe you'll see another side of him."

"No way," Ann said crisply. "You're just bitter."

"Admitted. Pete's a shit — sorry about that, Kristy — but I can get him back if I want him. I'm in the driver's seat. That's the way it should be."

"Dave and I don't have a driver's seat," Ann said. Her normally gentle face was flushed with irritation. "We love each other. When people love each other, nobody has a whip. That makes it sound like you're going to hit somebody. No man hits a woman unless he's some kind of lunatic, and in that case —"

"Shut up!" The thin, shrill voice interrupted her in mid-sentence. All faces turned toward the girl who had come so abruptly to her feet.

Jane Rheardon stood, clutching at the edge of the table as though for support, her eyes wild and anguished. The left side of her face jerked uncontrollably.

"Shut up, all of you!" she shouted at them. "You don't

know what you're talking about! You don't know anything at all!"

"What is it, Jane? All I said —" Ann regarded her with startled bewilderment.

"I know what you said, and you don't know anything about it. Men do hit women, they do it all the time, and women put up with it because there's nothing else to do! I'm right, aren't I, Irene? It does happen!"

"Yes, Jane, I'm afraid it does," Irene said quietly.

"You can't know what it's like — hearing it happen — with him yelling and swearing and her crying and furniture knocking over — and afterward, it's even worse, because we have to hide it! We're just the *nicest* family! *Every*body thinks so!"

With a choking sob she sank back into her chair and brought her hands up to cover her face. Rising quickly, Irene went over to her and put an arm around the slim shoulders. Her own face was dark with anger.

"So that's the way it is," she said. "I knew there was something. Poor Janie — poor little Janie. But at least you've told us. It will be better now. You're not alone anymore. You've got your sisters."

Chapter 9

Peter, we need to talk.

Such a simple statement, composed of five easy words. There was nothing there to trip up the tongue or to cause the speaker to stop for a breath halfway through it. Why, then, was it so impossible for her to say?

Laura had been repeating the line over and over in her mind from the moment that Peter's car had pulled to the curb at their usual meeting place at Locust and Second streets. She'd rehearsed it at home before that, sitting silent at the dinner table, staring down into her plate while her mother bustled about pouring more milk and getting the rolls out of the oven.

Peter, we need to talk.

In her daydream, the words had rung out clear and bell-like, and Peter, his face suddenly sweetly vulnerable, had turned and said hesitantly, *I was just going to say the same thing to you. I didn't know how to start. I was afraid you might laugh.*

Laugh, Pete?

Well, you never know. I don't want to scare you off or anything, but...but...

Gently. Encouragingly. *Yes?*

I...just want you to know...there's never been a girl in my life who mattered...really mattered...until now. Even Madison...she was just a way of filling the time...waiting... until the real thing came along....

In her mind, the lines had written themselves, falling so easily and naturally into place, but now in the car with Peter really beside her, she couldn't speak the initial sentence that would begin the flow.

Instead, she heard herself asking, "Where are we going now?"

"Where do you think? To an exotic island in the Caribbean where coconut palms sway in the breeze and dancing girls in grass skirts line the shore."

"No, really," Laura said. "You're headed down to Pointer's Creek Road, aren't you?"

"Well, sure," Peter said. "Where else can we park where there won't be any streetlights?" He paused and then turned to glance sideways at her as a thought occurred to him. "Hey, you're not on the rag, are you? If you are, you should've told me before."

"What?" Laura asked in bewilderment.

"It's not your time of the month?"

"Oh, no — no." Under cover of darkness, Laura felt her face growing hot with embarrassment and was astonished by her own reaction. She and Peter had already gone all the way. There shouldn't be anything so intimate that they couldn't talk about it, but…

"It's not that," Laura said hastily. "It's just that it seems so early. It's barely ten o'clock."

"That other movie wasn't any good," Peter told her. "I saw it before when it was playing at the Cedars. I'd have gone to sleep if I'd had to sit through it as a double feature."

"We could've gone somewhere else for a little while. To the coffee shop or the diner, maybe. Isn't that where the crowd usually goes on weekends?"

"I'm hungry for something, for sure, but it's not burgers." He reached across and put a hand on her knee.

Laura shivered slightly and slid closer to him, straining against the seat belt, tilting her head so that it rested against his shoulder. Four weeks ago, if she could've pictured herself in this situation she would have died of joy. It had come to pass so quickly that she kept having to stop and ask herself if it might not be a dream, something from which she might awake as she had from so many other dreams, to find her mother bending over her, shaking the covers and saying, "Wake up, you little sleepyhead, it's time for breakfast!"

Even now there were times when she wondered about its reality. In the halls at school, Peter passed her as though she were a stranger. In the cafeteria, he sat at a table with a group of his friends while Laura ate with Erika and Paula. When he spoke to her at all, it was just casually, to a friend of his sister's —"Hey, Laura, how's it going?" — with a quick, impersonal smile and his eyes sliding past her to focus elsewhere.

How astonished they would be, the girls at school, the teachers, everybody, if they had any idea that this disinterest was a facade to conceal the fact that Peter Grange and Laura Snow were going out!

"This is nobody's business but ours," Peter had told her the first night they had been together. "We've got a good thing going here, and we don't want a lot of outside pressure messing it up. That Daughters of Eve bunch would turn on you if they thought you were going out with me after I broke it off with Madison."

"You're probably right," Laura had agreed in a daze. "Still, it's not like I had anything to do with what happened between the two of you. You wouldn't have gone back to her anyway, would you? It's over and finished?"

"Of course it is," Peter said. "But Madison may not think so. She's a spoiled bitch, used to getting her way about everything. She'd freak out if she knew I'd found somebody else so soon."

This made sense when he said it. Madison would,

indeed, have been angry, and the other girls in the group would have been, too. They had taken the oath of loyalty to support the members of the sisterhood in all situations, and as Kristy herself had put it, even though Peter was her brother, he was "on the club's official shit list."

"He's a chauvinist pig," she'd said. "He thinks girls are second-class citizens. I never could see how Madison put up with him as long as she did."

"I'm a sucker for charm," Madison admitted ruefully. "For a while there I thought he was something pretty special." Then she'd laughed. "Oh, well, there are tons of guys out there. At least I've got my sisters for moral support. Maybe you guys can toss me some of your leftovers."

They all had laughed at that, and Laura, turning away, had stared out through the art-room window at the blue autumn sky with guilt rising thick within her, the biblical words of Ruth painfully sharp in her mind —

Whither thou goest, I will go ... thy people shall be my people....

"My people" are the Daughters of Eve, she thought, *and I'm deceiving them. But I can't help it. I love Peter — I love him more than Madison ever did! I've loved him from the first time I ever saw him, and I'll keep on loving him till the day I die.*

Now, close beside him in the moving car, she at last brought the preplanned words to the surface, forcing them out with a little gasping breath.

"...We have to talk."

"You say something?" Peter asked her.

"I said...we have to talk about something," Laura said more loudly. "This thing...about being secret...it's not working, Pete. I mean, we can't ever go anywhere this way."

"We're going somewhere now," Peter said lightly.

"You know what I mean."

"We just came from watching a movie. That's 'somewhere,' isn't it? At the prices they charge, it better be."

"That's all we ever do, though — go to movies. And out to Pointer's Creek."

"You don't like that? You don't like being alone with me? You'd rather go to coffee shops and sit around with a bunch of other people chattering all around us?" He sounded hurt. "If that's the way you feel, I'll take you home now. I don't want to force a girl to do something she hates just for my sake."

"That's not it at all," Laura exclaimed, clutching at his arm. "I love being alone with you. It's just that I want to be with you other times, too. I don't care if the Daughters of Eve get mad at me. They'll get over it, and if they don't — well, they'll just have to kick me out of the club. When you were going out with Madison, you went everywhere together. You walked her to classes and waited for her by her locker and took her to parties."

"And so, what happened?" Peter said. "We broke up, that's what. Too much togetherness can do that."

"The homecoming dance is this Saturday. Can we at least go to that together?"

"Saturday is pretty far away," Peter said. "Who knows what we'll feel like doing Saturday? Let's hang out and play it by ear, okay?"

"But I need to know. I have to get a dress." She hated the note of pleading that had crept into her voice, but she had to make him understand how important this was to her. "Girls like to plan ahead. They need time to get ready."

"Don't push me, Laura. I don't like being nagged, okay?" He tightened his hand on her knee, giving it a quick squeeze. "There are better ways to get a guy to do things than by nagging. A sweet, loving girl can get just about anything she wants as long as she doesn't keep annoying a guy."

"I just think it would be so much fun," Laura said, "to go to a dance."

"Maybe it would, maybe it wouldn't. I'll think about it." He slowed the car. "You call it. You want to go to the creek or not? If you don't, just say so. I'll take you home."

"Do you — love me?" She asked the question in a whisper.

"Speak up. I can't hear you."

"I said — yes. I want to go to the creek." He was here with her now, wasn't he, not with some other girl? The question was ridiculous. Of course he loved her.

*   *   *

Holly Underwood sat with her eyes closed, listening to her mother at the piano building Debussy's castle, note by silver note, to the height of the stars. The room was filled with the ocean, with foam and froth and circling gulls and salt winds whipping icy spray against palace walls.

The winds grew steadily stronger, as Holly had known they would. The waves leaped and splashed, and the gulls began to scream their warning. Still the shining notes continued to pile one upon another to form spires and towers. At the window of one of these stood a princess with a face like a flower, her eyes focused dreamily on the horizon as she waited for the ship that would bring the prince she was to marry.

But she lingered too long in the starlight. The waters beneath the castle opened, and the waves came rolling green and wild through the marble halls and up the stairs and into the chamber where the princess stood. She opened her lips to cry out, but the salt water filled her mouth and her nose and her eyes and lifted the strands of her golden hair and sent them swirling around her like a cape. Then, with one great roar, the sea came crashing in over her, and the palace sank forever beneath the waves.

In the silence that followed, Holly drew a long breath and opened her eyes. Her mother turned from the piano with a sigh.

"I've gotten so out of practice."

"Considering how little you play these days, I thought it was fabulous."

"It's a vicious circle. I don't play much anymore because I can't stand to hear myself, and the lack of practice makes it worse than ever." Mrs. Underwood lifted her hands from the keys and flexed her fingers. "Piano-hands, my teacher used to call them, wide and strong with a lot of stretch to them. You've got them, too, but don't ever let them stiffen up like mine."

Holly looked down at her own hands. They were as her mother described them, broad and muscular with stubby, square-tipped fingers. Once at a Halloween carnival when she'd thrust her hands through the opening in a screen to have her palm read, the unseen fortune-teller had taken her for a boy.

"A beautiful, dark-haired woman will enter your life," she'd told her, and when Holly had asked, "To do what?" the fortune-teller had gasped, apologized, and started a whole new fortune in which the "dark woman" was replaced by a "dark man."

"Gary has piano hands, too, doesn't he?" Holly said. "But he's never played."

"Gary has the hands, but not the ear. What a waste!" Her mother smiled at her. "The music in this family has come down through its women. My mother played beautifully, and her mother also. In fact, this piano used to be your grandmother's. I picture her sometimes as she must have been as a young girl practicing her scales on it."

"Is she the one who taught you?" Holly asked her.

"She gave me the basics, the same way I did you. Then, later, I had lessons. All little girls had piano lessons in those days. I had so many friends who hated them, but they had to keep plugging away anyway until they were twelve. That was the breaking point, where you got to decide whether to quit or continue."

"And you continued," Holly said. "If music meant so much to you, why didn't you ever do anything with it?"

"Like what?" her mother asked her.

"Like — I don't know — play with a symphony orchestra — play concerts — make records."

"I did win a contest once," Mrs. Underwood said. "It was sponsored by some music-appreciation group — Friends of the Arts, I think it was. My music teacher sponsored me, and I got a medal. It was a huge, awful gilt thing, and I wore it to bed at night, pinned to my pajamas."

"You didn't answer my question," Holly persisted. "Why didn't you go on? If you were good enough to win contests, why are you giving beginner lessons out here in the sticks?"

"Because 'the sticks,' as you call it, is where we live," Mrs. Underwood said reasonably. "It's where your dad has his business. Besides, I haven't had the training to be a concert pianist, and I certainly don't have the time to put in the necessary practice."

"You would've had the time if you hadn't gotten married."

"I don't know about that. I'd have had to be doing something to earn a living."

"That's the whole point, Mom. You could've earned a living with your music." Holly leaned forward eagerly. "Isn't that the greatest thing that can happen to somebody, to be able to support herself doing something she loves? Think about what it would be like to get up in the morning and go straight to the piano and not have to do anything except the thing you wanted to do?"

"Life isn't like that," her mother said. "Nobody lives like that, dear. If I'd done that with my life, you and Gary wouldn't be here now. The two greatest moments in my life were when my babies were born, and I certainly wouldn't have placed you in a day-care center while I practiced piano eight hours a day."

"I don't want children," Holly said.

"You'll feel differently after you're married."

"I might not get married."

"Of course you will. The right boy will come along, and you'll fall in love just like everybody else. I guarantee it." Her mother regarded her with amusement. "You'll play Debussy for your own daughter, and if you're lucky, she'll understand and love it, and you'll have something special to share. That's what music is — something lovely to share with somebody you care about."

Holly looked down at her hands, the great, ugly, beautiful hands that had been her bane and her joy since she'd first realized what they were and what they could do.

"Mom, if I were a boy — and I had the talent, the musical gift that has come down through our women — if I were a boy, Mom, what then? Would you still be telling me the best thing I can do with my life is to stay here in Modesta and have babies?"

"That's a ridiculous question," Mrs. Underwood said impatiently. "It's the fact that men can't have babies that makes it necessary for them to fill their lives with other things."

"Where are you going, chicken?"

"Out."

"That's no answer," Bart Rheardon said. "You don't just put on your coat and walk out the door without a 'hey' or a 'hi' to anybody. When I say, 'Where are you going?' I want to know."

"To meet some friends at the coffee shop," Jane said.

"What friends?"

"It wouldn't mean anything if I told you. You don't know them."

"Somebody from that club, I'll bet. From Daughters of Eve, right? I'll tell you, chicken, I don't like the way these girls are taking you over. It starts out to be a once-a-week, after-school thing, and all of a sudden you're a regular groupie."

"You've got the wrong word, Dad. A groupie is somebody who trails around after a rock band." Jane adjusted the collar of her jacket. "I'm going to meet my girlfriends for some food. Is that a crime? If there's something wrong with it, just tell me, and I'll reconsider. I sure wouldn't want to do anything you didn't think was right."

"Cut the sarcasm," Mr. Rheardon said sharply. "This is part of what I'm objecting to. You never used to talk to us this way. It's just lately, since you've started running around with this particular group of girls, that you've been shooting your mouth off and acting like you've always got a chip on your shoulder. Who the hell are these kids, anyway? Do they all have parents who let them run the streets at night?"

"You know most of the parents from church," Jane said. "I can give you a list of their names if you want them."

"I never liked the sound of this group in the first place," her father said. "All this secret stuff and the crazy songs and things. I don't trust an organization where the members aren't allowed to talk about what goes on at meetings."

Jane finished buttoning her jacket. Then she crossed to the door to the living room.

"Mom, I'm going to hang out with some of the girls. I'll be back in about an hour."

Ellen Rheardon's eyes didn't leave the TV screen.

"Put something over your head," she said. "It's gotten windy. You don't want your ear to start acting up."

"I'll wear a hat."

For a moment Jane stood there, staring in at the woman on the sofa. The room was dark except for the flickering glow of the screen, which threw light on one side only of her mother's face and left the other dark. The effect was eerie, as though the face had somehow been sliced in two and one half discarded to leave one glistening eye, a sliver of nose, and a strange, short strip of mouth.

"You want the light on?" Jane asked. "I read an article somewhere that said it's not good to watch TV in the dark."

"That's okay," her mother said. "I like it this way."

The couple on the screen were embracing in a rose garden, arms wrapped tightly around each other, lips pressed to lips. Mrs. Rheardon drew a deep breath as though she could smell the perfume of the flowers.

Jane went back out to the entrance hall, pulling a knit hat from her jacket pocket. She pulled it down on her head and opened the front door. The crisp, clean cold of the November night came sweeping in on them.

Her father said, "About these friends —"

"Don't worry, Dad, none of us are terrorists," Jane said.

She went outside and closed the door behind her.

Chapter 10

It was a year in which there was no Indian summer. November remained November, bleak and overcast, with a cutting wind and a few surprising bursts of rain.

The maples in the school yard turned red and lost their leaves in such rapid succession that Tammy's mother, who'd planned on taking pictures to go with an article she was writing, waited one day too long and missed her chance. The Modesta football team won their grudge game against the Morenci Bulldogs, and the boys' basketball team went into regular afternoon practice. The girls' team was allotted the use of the gym to practice on weekends, and Paula Brummell and three other girls quit.

Some other items of interest to those concerned:

Erika Schneider's brother, Boyd, dropped out of college to "get his head together" and moved back into the family home to live until he could find a job. Said Mrs. Schneider: "At least he doesn't keep rats in his bedroom."

David Brewer and Ann Whitten announced their engagement in the *Modesta Tribune*. They set the wedding date for June 3.

Tammy Carncross started seeing a red-haired senior named Kevin Baker.

Kristy Grange went out on her first date; Paula's brother, Tom, took her to a movie.

Laura Snow's father and stepmother wrote asking her to spend the Christmas holidays with them at their home in Rhode Island. Laura refused the invitation.

Kelly Johnson's father moved out, and her parents announced that they were getting a divorce.

The Daughters of Eve unanimously voted to sponsor Madison Ellis as their candidate for homecoming queen and spent two evenings at Irene Stark's apartment making posters.

On the afternoon of November 7, Madison was surprised to find Peter Grange waiting for her at her locker. She was surprised, too, to feel the sudden jump her heart gave at the sight of him, lounging there in his old position, his hands in his pockets, his shoulder braced against the locker.

I thought it was over, she told herself silently, half

angry at him for being there, half angry at herself for the involuntary start of pleasure it gave her to see him. For the past several weeks, they'd passed each other in the halls without acknowledgment, she with her friends, he with his. She'd been aware, though, without ever permitting herself to focus on him, that he was never with another girl, while she, on various occasions, walked with other boys.

Boys had never been as important to Madison as they seemed to be to other girls, mainly because she'd never had to concern herself about attracting them. From kindergarten on, they had been there at her bidding, waiting to sharpen her pencils, to share the best dessert from their lunches, or to walk her back and forth to the water fountain. The only child of parents who'd been in their late thirties when she was born, she'd never lacked for affection and attention. She accepted these in the same way she did her exceptionally good looks — as natural and inevitable.

She'd started dating early, but until the spring of her sophomore year had refused to commit to one person. The truth was, in fact, that she actually enjoyed herself more with girlfriends with whom she could relax without having to be on the defensive against being fondled and fawned over. Her attraction to Peter had taken her by surprise. She'd tried unsuccessfully to analyze it, and had chalked it up finally to the fact that there were certain elements in him that duplicated those in herself. For whatever reason, on the first date she'd let him kiss her, and by the third, she'd stopped seeing other people. By the end of the school year, they'd been an acknowledged couple. Their time together during the summer had been limited because of their jobs — Peter had been up at the lake most of the time and Madison had modeled for a mall store in Adrian and other local gigs. When school resumed, however, they'd fallen back together automatically, as if they had never been separated, and Madison had thought, *Maybe this is meant to be. Maybe this is what being in love is all about.*

Now, as she approached her locker, she was aware of straightening to walk a little taller, pushing her shoulders back as she did when she was modeling and was conscious of a roomful of eyes upon her. Except that this time there was really only one pair of eyes, familiar brown ones.

"Hi, Maddie."

"Hi, Pete." She made her voice light and frosty. "Fancy meeting you here."

"How's life treating you?"

"Okay. And you?"

"Same." He moved aside so she could work the combination lock. "So I was wondering — do you have a date to the dance Saturday?"

"To homecoming? No, I'm going stag with Erika and

Paula. That's the night we have the drawings for the athletic fund. Then the queen presents the money to Mr. Shelby."

"You want to go with me?" he asked casually.

"I don't get it." Madison paused with the lock in her hand. "Why would you want to waste an evening dancing with an 'ice cube'?"

"Oh, come on, Maddie," Peter said, flushing. "I was in a bad mood the day I said that. You know I didn't mean it."

"I don't have any reason to think you didn't," Madison said. "You haven't called me since."

"I'm telling you now, aren't I? I needed time to cool down. You really got on my nerves that day."

"I'll stick by every word," Madison told him. "I'm not going to let anyone run my life for me, no matter how much I care about him."

"So you *do* care!" Peter exclaimed triumphantly. "There, you just admitted it! So you're not the ice maiden you pretend to be, now are you?"

"I never pretended to be an 'ice maiden.' I just want to control my own life, that's all. The old double standard doesn't cut it anymore, Peter." Madison opened the locker and dumped in her history book. "Why should I tie myself down when I can have the whole football team to dance with?"

"The queen is supposed to have an escort."

"I might not be the queen. The votes aren't counted yet."

"You'll get it. Who's the competition? You know you're a lock. Besides, we're a team. Like meat and potatoes."

She smiled despite herself. "Which one's the potatoes?"

"We take turns — you're a potato one day, I'm one the next. Come on, we're us, Pete and Maddie. We're the living proof that beautiful people flock together, that love can survive a fight or two."

"You said —'love,'" Madison said softly.

"I did?"

"You know you did. That's the word you use when you're trying to get something out of me. We've been down this road before."

"Maybe we have," Peter said.

"So what's different this time?" she challenged him.

"Maybe I am. Maybe I've changed."

Madison turned from the open locker to stare at him. He met her gaze directly, and their eyes locked, making it impossible for her to look away. She felt a little light-headed from the nearness of him and struggled to keep her voice light.

"That's something new for you to say."

"Wasn't it what you wanted to hear?"

"It might be. I really don't know." She closed the locker and shoved the lock together so that it snapped into place with a sharp, determined click. Slowly she turned back to the boy beside her. "So, how exactly have you changed?"

"What do you want me to say? That I'm sorry?"

"For what?"

"Stop with the questions. Just answer me, Madison. What do you want me to say?"

"I won't ask you. Just say it."

"I — care about you." His voice dropped self-consciously.

"I care — a lot."

"Since when?"

"Since I haven't been spending time with you. I've been — lonely. I've missed you. I — I really want us to get back together again."

"I've missed you, too," Madison said softly. "I've tried not to, but I have."

"So what are we going to do about it?"

"Go to the dance, I guess."

"That will work for starters. And — then?"

"We'll see. I don't know. I meant all those things I said, Pete. I've got a modeling career ahead of me, and I'm not taking any chances with it. It's not like we were going to get married or something. I've got another year of school after this one, and you'll be going off to college. We might never even see each other again."

"If my mom doesn't come through with her share of

the tuition, I'll probably be staying right here and going to state college," Peter said with a touch of bitterness. "She's got that cleaning woman coming in twice a week now, and Kristy sits around on her butt never lifting a hand."

"Hey, geek, you're talking about my sister!" Madison said. She gave in to the temptation to reach out and touch him. His hand opened and closed on hers, and suddenly it didn't matter any longer what they were saying, as the words were simply there, just a background for the electrical touching of their hands.

"Irene wants me to stop by her room a minute to talk about something," Ann Whitten said. "Want to come with me, or are you meeting Kevin?"

"He's got practice," Tammy Carncross told her, "but I'd like to try to meet up with Kelly. She's been so down these days over the divorce thing, I hate for her to have to walk home alone."

"Good idea. I'll call you later. Is she going to the dance on Saturday?"

"I don't think so," Tammy said. "Ethan Finley asked her, but she said she doesn't feel like it."

"See if you can get her to change her mind. It would be good for her to get out and do things. Maybe we could all go together?"

"Fine with me," Tammy said. "I'll talk with her and then check with Kevin. I'll call you tonight."

"Sure. Cool." Ann stood quiet for a moment as Tammy walked away from her. It was scary, she thought, how quickly changes occurred in life. She and Kelly Johnson had been close friends for years, long before either of them knew Tammy. She'd slept over so many nights at the Johnson home that the extra twin bed in Kelly's room was as familiar to her as her own. She'd gone with the Johnsons on family campouts and sat with them around campfires roasting marshmallows and singing to Mr. Johnson's guitar. It was Mrs. Johnson who'd taught her how to pluck her eyebrows one hysterical evening when she and Kelly had been twelve and experimenting with cosmetics, and Mr. Johnson who'd sat with them at the kitchen table patiently explaining the mysteries of first-year algebra. To Ann, the Johnson home had radiated the same stability as her own — more, perhaps, since the shadow of ill health had come to hang over her father and forced her to the realization that one day her mother would be alone. She'd never conceived of Kelly's mom facing such a situation.

With a sigh, Ann continued down the hall to the art room. The door was partially open, and Irene was seated behind her desk, correcting papers. She glanced up quickly when Ann came in, as though alert for her arrival, and, noting the pile of books in her arms, gestured toward the table.

"You'd better set those down before your arms snap

off. You're pretty heavily laden for a weeknight, aren't you?"

"I thought I'd better do some studying while I can. The weekend's a total loss by the time we get through decorating the gym and cleaning it up again on Sunday." Ann dropped her books on the table at which they sat for meetings and gave Irene her full attention. "You wanted to see me about something?"

"Yes, but don't look so worried. It's something pleasant. Do you remember giving me some sketches back in the early fall? There was one of crows on a fence and another of a man on a tractor?"

"Yes, of course I remember," Ann said. "You said you liked them."

"I did," Irene told her. "They were extremely well-done, considering they were the work of someone with almost no formal training. I liked them so much that I wanted to share them. I sent them to a former teacher of mine, John Griffith. He's the head of the Art Institute of Boston."

"You did?" Ann asked in bewilderment. "Why?"

"Because I wanted him to see the kind of talent young women have in Modesta, Michigan." Irene's eyes were glowing. "I have his e-mail here. Would you like to hear it?"

"He wrote back?" Ann said.

"He certainly has. Let me read it." Irene picked up a

sheet of paper from the pile in front of her. "'Dear Irene — Thank you for your note. I'd heard through the grapevine about the problems at Jefferson and am pleased to know you are now in better circumstances. I want to thank you also for submitting the sketches by your student, Ann Whitten. I see much talent here and would be very interested in having her at the Institute.

"'As you know, we have limited money available for scholarships. However, in view of what you tell me about the girl's economic situation, I would be willing to offer her tuition and dorm accommodations for the fall semester, with a full scholarship for the second semester, contingent on her performance as a student.

"'I would appreciate your putting me into direct contact with Ms. Whitten so that I may approach her about this possibility. I would also like to see more of her work.

"'I am grateful to you for having acquainted me with the work of this young artist, and I hope good things may come of this for all concerned. Sincerely, John.'"

"I don't believe it," Ann said. "He's talking about me?"

"Of course he is. Don't you recognize your own name? He mentions it twice." Irene replaced the paper on her desk and leaned back in her chair. Her eyes were twinkling. "How does it feel to be acknowledged, at seventeen, as a 'talented artist'?"

"How does it feel? It just doesn't seem possible." Ann

shook her head in amazement. "He likes my work! He really likes it! This is crazy!"

"Well, start believing it soon, my dear, because it's a fact," Irene said. "You're good, and it's time you realized it. John Griffith has seen artists come and go, and he can recognize talent as few people can. Here's your future, Ann, right in front of you. How will we celebrate?"

"I just can't wrap my head around it. He wants me to come to Boston?"

"On a full scholarship."

"But how can I?" Ann said. "I'm getting married."

"Marriage can be postponed for a little while, can't it? Is next June the only time the church is open?"

"No, but — I'm engaged, Irene. The announcement was published in the *Tribune*. I've got my ring." She lifted her left hand and looked down at the diamond in its old-fashioned setting. At the angle at which she held it, it caught the slanted afternoon light that flowed through the art-room window and threw a crazy darting pattern on the opposite wall.

"An announcement and a ring don't constitute a royal summons." The smile faded from Irene's face. "When the announcement was made, you thought your whole future was here in Modesta. Now, all of a sudden, things have changed. There's more for you, Ann, than becoming a teenage bride. You want more, don't you?"

"I — always dreamed — of painting professionally,"

Ann said. "I just never thought it could really happen. But I love Dave. I can't give him up."

"You won't have to. Dave loves you, too, doesn't he? You know he'll want what's best for you. He'll wait a little while if it's going to make a difference in your happiness."

"I think he would," Ann said, "but he's had a rough time of it lately. His mother's death really hit him hard. He was very close to her. There's that house now — so empty —"

"David is a grown man," Irene said firmly. "A grown man can manage to live for a while in an empty house."

"It's all so sudden." To her own amazement, Ann found herself blinking back tears. "You think you're set for one thing, and here's something else. You were so amazing to send in those sketches, Irene — to have thought I was good enough for them to mean something. I don't know how to thank you. I don't mean to sound ungrateful. I'm really happy. I'm just so mixed up inside."

"Talk it over with Dave," Irene told her gently. "Tell him how much this means to you. If he loves you as much as you think he does, he'll understand. He won't try to hold you back."

He wouldn't understand, of course, thought Irene.

"How do you think I'd feel," he would ask her, "getting married to a woman who earned more than I did?"

No, wait, Irene told herself in sudden confusion.

142

Those were somebody else's words. It was Bob, her Bob, who said, "I love you, Renie. I want to take care of you."

"Take care of me? By cutting me out of what I've worked toward for so long? You call that loving me?"

"Renie, baby —" He hadn't even understood what she was talking about. "It's the man's career that matters. You'll stop working, anyway, when babies start coming."

Robert Morrell or David Brewer, it made no difference. One man was like another. The stolid form that Ann had drawn on the tractor was Any-man. She hadn't even attempted to sketch in the features of the empty face.

Poor child, she faced such painful disillusionment. Still, it was better to get such things over and done with. Once she discovered for herself the shallowness of Dave's caring, she'd be able to cut herself free and move upward.

As I could have, Irene thought bitterly, *if they'd let me.*

The hatred rose within her, thick and stifling. So many long years, wasted! But, no — they didn't have to be. These girls had potential that was hers to develop.

Ann — and Kelly — and Erika — and Jane —

Irene Stark closed her eyes, and their images swam before her — leaping, soaring, carrying her with them into the shining places of her dreams.

Chapter 11

On Saturday, November 11, at 9:00 p.m., Kelly Johnson lay on her bed, fully clothed in jeans and T-shirt, listening to a CD and staring at the ceiling. The bedroom door was closed and secured with a hook that she'd purchased that afternoon at the hardware store and screwed into the door frame. Then she'd gotten a hammer from the tool chest in the garage and pounded the eyelet into the smooth polished wood of the door itself.

"Why are you doing that?" her thirteen-year-old sister, Chris, had asked in bewilderment.

"To keep you out," Kelly had told her.

"You don't have to do that," Chris said with hurt in her voice. "I don't want to come into your crappy old room."

"You're always in there. You were there in the other

bed this morning when I woke up. You sneaked in during the night without even knocking, and Mom keeps coming in all the time to check on me and see what I'm doing. I can't even do my homework in peace anymore without somebody barging in and interrupting."

"It's scary sometimes with Dad not here," Chris said. "Last night there was a funny noise like somebody was on the roof."

"You'd better get used to it," Kelly told her bluntly. "You're not going to come running in here every time the wind blows."

The cold cruelty of her own voice had pleased her, as had the look on her mother's face when she had seen the disfigured door surface. It pleased her now to lie on the bed and dig the heels of her dirty tennis shoes into the yellow quilted spread. It had pleased her a few days ago to turn down Ethan's invitation to homecoming, the invitation she'd been dreaming of for weeks and had thought he might be too shy to issue.

"No, thank you," she'd said when he'd finally gotten it stammered out in its entirety. No excuse — no apology — no explanation — just "No, thank you," as though he were the last person on earth she would want to be seen with. And later, when Tammy had called about triple dating, she'd said, "No, thank you," again with the same distant coolness.

"What was that about?" her mother had asked her as she ended the call.

"Nothing important."

"It was Tammy, wasn't it?" Mrs. Johnson had prodded. "She was inviting you to do something."

"I said it was nothing important."

"It's important for you to see your friends," her mom had objected. "I know you're upset with your dad and me, and I understand that, but you can't withdraw from the world. You need your friends more than ever now. You need people to talk to —"

"I don't need anything," Kelly had said.

And now, in the haven of the locked room, she repeated the words softly to herself —"I don't need anything. Or anybody." Not her parents, not Chris, not poor Ethan with his hopeful, cocker spaniel eyes, not Tammy, not Ann — not anyone. It was crazy to depend on other people, to let them be important to you. All it did was make you stupid and vulnerable and blind to reality.

"This isn't anything sudden, Kelly," her dad told her. "Your mom and I have been growing apart for a long time."

They had, had they? Well, it had certainly been carefully hidden from her. As far as Kelly knew, her parents had never had a fight in their lives. They were absolutely compatible; they liked the same foods, the same books, the same music. They went to church on Sundays and shared the same hymnal; they attended PTA meetings together and held hands at the movies. They even looked alike. Kelly had read somewhere that people who lived together for a long time grew to resemble each other in appearance, and her parents were living proof, with the first strands of gray appearing in their brown hair in exactly the same spots and the laugh lines crinkling at the corners of their eyes in identical fans.

What a nice, normal, congenial family they were, the Johnsons, snowmobiling together in the winter, camping together in the summer — except for this past summer, when they somehow hadn't gotten around to it. Funny, she hadn't thought much about it until now, the fact that this year there had been no camping trips. Kelly herself had been so busy, working through June as a camp counselor, going up to the lake for swimming and cookouts, playing tennis and goofing around with her friends. Fiddling around while Rome burned. Goofing away the days, while her parents' marriage disintegrated before her unseeing eyes. When exactly did her dad meet the woman he now thought he was in love with? During the summer? Before that, even? Was he seeing her, perhaps, on those sweet spring evenings when he supposedly had been working late while Kelly knelt in the cool twilight and helped her mom put in the backyard petunia beds? Had her mom suspected nothing? Wouldn't any normal, intelligent woman know when her husband was falling out of love with her? And if she'd known, why hadn't she done something? How could she just have stayed put, making meat loaves and baking cookies and quilting her daughter a lemon-colored bed-spread and pretending nothing terrible was happening?

Laura Snow's parents were divorced. That was the main reason Kelly had voted for her when she'd been proposed as a member of Daughters of Eve. She'd felt so sorry for her — in tiny Modesta there weren't a lot of broken marriages. "The poor girl," she'd said when the name had been suggested. "Her parents are divorced, you know. No wonder she's a loner, and she probably compensates by overeating."

Laura's dad lived in another state. She hardly ever saw him. He was remarried, Laura had said once, and there was a baby half brother whom she'd never even seen. Would her own dad remarry? Kelly wondered. It seemed likely that he would, since he was in love with somebody. Would there be a baby, another Johnson child living right here in Modesta? Would it look like Kelly and Chris, with a round, rosy-cheeked face and brown eyes and brows that almost met over its nose? Whose genes had produced that look? "Those Johnson girls look so much alike," people were always saying. "They're two peas in a pod." Teachers who had had Kelly in middle school kept calling Chris by her name. "I keep forgetting," they apologized. "It's like having the same student twice."

Would they now have the chance to have the "same student" three times? Or four? Or even five? Would her dad start all over again with a new life as though this first one had never existed?

And what about Mom?

What would happen to her? What did a forty-year-old housewife do when there was suddenly no man to keep house for? Get a job? If so, what? There'd been a discussion about this at one of the Daughters of Eve meetings. *When the middle-aged housewife gets forced into the workplace,* Irene had told them, *the employer isn't going to excuse her lack of experience.*

Poor old housewife, Kelly had thought. Nice, kind, stupid Kelly Johnson, always concerned about the fate of the unfortunate, but never applying the facts to herself or to anyone close to her. Poor Mom. Why couldn't she show some compassion for her mother? She loved her, didn't she? Of course she loved her. This was Mom, not some strange "other person" housewife — Mom — so why didn't she unlock this stupid door and go out into the hall and down the stairs to where her mother sat in the living room and put her arms around her and hold her and break through this terrible wall that held them both in check, so that they could cry together?

"You need your friends more than ever now," her mom had told her. Concerned about her. Loving her. Worrying over Kelly, not over herself. Wonderful, self-sacrificing Mom, and what had it gotten her? A load of crap, that's what. A load of shit, is what Madison would call it — outspoken Madison, who called a spade a spade. Kelly had never called anything by an ugly curse word

149

like that. Words like "shit" weren't used in the Johnson household. Maybe that was why Madison didn't have any hang-ups and Kelly did.

That's why I can't go downstairs, Kelly told herself now. *It's because I have a hang-up.* A hang-up about being stupid, which, in its way, was just as terrible as being cruel, because both things hurt equally in the long run. Her mom had trusted in love, and that was stupid. Her mom had built her whole life on the premise that she was half of a perfect couple, and now she wasn't anything. She was a cartoon character, walking around the house, emptying ashtrays that didn't need emptying, cooking big meals that no one could eat, changing sheets that didn't need changing, and it was all so stupid because she should've known. She should've known!

"It's the woman who gets it in the teeth," Irene had said. "Always." Calmly, she'd said it, the words cold and careful. And now Kelly understood something she hadn't picked up on before. The woman Irene had been talking about had been herself. The teacher who'd been forced out of that Chicago school hadn't been a "friend" at all — she'd been Irene. No wonder she knew — no wonder she'd been trying to warn them!

Her mother had said she needed to talk to her friends. All right, then, she would do just that. She would talk to the one friend who would really understand the situation.

Kelly got up from the bed. The music was still playing.

She'd set her iPod to shuffle songs randomly — now it was an old song by John Denver that her parents had played at their wedding. It was called "Annie's Song," and he supposedly wrote it for his wife. "Let me lay down beside you [...] let me give my life to you..." *Bullshit!*

Kelly crossed to the door and unlocked it. She opened it and went down the hall to the phone-charging station her dad had set up by the stairs. He hadn't wanted them texting when they were supposed to be doing homework, so all phones were plugged in to charge each night. The sounds of the TV drifted up the stairwell. Her mother and Chris were watching something with a laugh track.

Kelly didn't have Irene's number, but she figured it must be listed. She called information.

"Do you have a listing for Irene Stark in Modesta?"

There was a pause. Then the operator confirmed and connected her number.

"Thank you," Kelly said.

It wasn't until the phone had begun to ring that she remembered that this was the night of the homecoming dance. Irene, as the sponsor of Daughters of Eve, would be acting as one of the chaperones.

Well, so much for that, Kelly thought as the phone continued to ring with no response. Then, just as she was ready to hang up, there was a sudden rasp and Irene's voice, sounding hurried and breathless, said, "Hello?"

"Hi. This is Kelly." She couldn't believe her luck. "I thought you would've left for the dance."

"I was just going out the door," Irene explained. "I'm running a little late this evening. I'm sorry. Were you girls worried that I wasn't going to get there?"

"No, it's not that," Kelly said. "I'm not calling from the school. I'm at home. I just — just —" She didn't know exactly how to continue. What was it that she did want, anyway? Irene would think she was crazy.

"I just wanted to talk a little while," she finished lamely. "I forgot what night it was. I don't seem to have it together these days."

"Small wonder," Irene said sympathetically. "I don't really need to be at the dance until time for the presentation ceremony. Would you like me to come pick you up?"

"You don't have to do that," Kelly said hastily. "It isn't that important."

"I think it is. Needing to talk is very important." Irene spoke firmly. "You live on Third Street, don't you?"

"At one twenty-seven," Kelly said. "The big white house on the corner. Look, you don't have to —"

"I know I don't. Stop worrying, Kelly. There's no big problem. We can come back here to talk and later stop by the dance for the drawing. Put on a dress, and I'll come by for you in about ten minutes."

"I wasn't planning on going to the dance," Kelly said.

"You might change your mind. If you decide not to,

I can drop you back at your house on my way to the school." She paused. When she spoke again, it was quietly. "It's all right, Kelly. I know what you're going through. I know all too well. I've been through it, too. When I was your age exactly, my father walked out on my mother and destroyed her completely. I've never forgiven him for his callousness, and I never will."

"He — destroyed her?" Kelly said shakily.

"She had a mental breakdown. She never recovered. You see, I know —" Her voice hardened. "I do know, Kelly, what it's like to have a father incapable of giving love. You're terribly hurt, aren't you?"

"Yes," Kelly said softly.

"And you'd like to punish him, wouldn't you? To make him suffer the way he's making you and your mom suffer? That's natural, Kelly. It's nothing to be ashamed of. For men, marriage is a game, something they can walk into and out of as the mood strikes. They think they can have it all without giving anything themselves. Women have to be tough to make it in this world, Kelly. Women have to band together, because when it comes right down to it, our female friends are all we have."

At 10:30 p.m. the DJ took a break, and Mr. Shelby, the principal of Modesta High, announced the results of the elections for homecoming queen. Peter Grange proudly escorted a smiling Madison Ellis to the front of the gym to don her crown and conduct the drawing for the prizes that had been donated in support of the athletic fund.

Most of the winners weren't present for the drawing. The exception was Tammy Carncross's parents, who were chaperoning. They received a set of stainless steel steak knives.

"Now all we need are the steaks to go with them," Mrs. Carncross said lightheartedly as her husband returned from his trip to the band platform to collect the prize.

"Look on the bright side. There's no law that says we can't use them on hamburgers."

"The way I fry hamburgers, I'd say that's a good idea."

They laughed together. Lil Carncross's hamburgers were a family joke.

"It's just that hamburgers are such boring things to cook," she would explain apologetically after each disaster. "They lie there in the pan doing nothing for so long that your mind starts to wander, and the next thing you know they've taken off on you and turned to charcoal."

After twenty years of marriage, Dan Carncross accepted his wife's wandering mind in the same way that he accepted the dreamy eyes that floated soft and unfocused behind the lenses of her glasses and the disarray of curly hair that wouldn't lie in one direction. They supplied a certain winsomeness in sharp contrast with the image of the professional journalist whose witty commentaries on small-town life appeared on the pages of national magazines.

"Congratulations!" Ann Whitten called as she worked

her way toward them through the crowd. "That's what Dave and I were hoping to win, but Madison blew it. She pulled out your ticket instead!"

"You're the ones who should be congratulated," Mrs. Carncross said warmly to the bright-faced girl and the broad-shouldered young man beside her. "I haven't seen you since the announcement in the paper. Will it be a June wedding?"

"It was going to be," Ann said, "but plans have changed a little. Now we're thinking more like a year from this coming Christmas."

"Ann's won herself a scholarship to art school," Dave Brewer told them. "A real well-known one in Boston. It seemed like too good an opportunity for her to turn it down."

"That's wonderful, Ann," Dan Carncross said. "I didn't have any idea you were applying for something like that."

"Well, actually I didn't," Ann said. "Ms. Stark is the one who did it. She mailed in some of my sketches. She studied under Mr. Griffith, the head of the institute, back when she was in college. She wrote and recommended me. I almost passed out when I found out about it. I still can't believe it! It's like a miracle."

"Which reminds me, I've never seen the miracle woman," Lil Carncross said. "All you girls talk about Ms. Stark so much, I'd like to meet her. Is she here tonight?"

"She was supposed to be chaperoning, but I haven't seen her," her husband said.

"Oh, she's here now," Ann told them. "She came in just a minute ago with Kelly. That's another miracle. Tam and I tried and tried to get Kelly to come tonight, and she wouldn't even listen. Then, somehow, Irene got her here.

"There she is, Mrs. Carncross. That's Irene up there on the edge of the platform, talking to Madison. They must be getting ready for the presentation."

"The woman in green?" Lil stood on her toes, steadying herself with a hand on her husband's shoulder to get a better view. "Oh! She's certainly not what I expected."

"What did you expect?" Dan Carncross asked with interest.

"From Tammy's description, I pictured her as one of those enthusiastic young teachers right out of college, the kind the kids relate to so easily. Pretty, and very hip. Like how Madison Ellis will be five or six years from now."

"She's definitely not that!" Ann said, laughing. "But I think she's really pretty in her own way. And she understands us all so well, it's like she's one of us. If you're confused about something, Irene can sort it out so it makes sense, and all of a sudden everything falls right into place."

"What's Erika doing up there?" Mr. Carncross asked.

"As club president, she's going to be with Madison when she makes the presentation. Paula is too. She's our token athlete. It was her idea to — oh, they're going to start!"

Erika and Paula were mounting the steps at the side of the stage to join Madison at the microphone.

The queen reached up a graceful hand to adjust the weight of the crown and smiled at her audience. "Will Mr. Shelby and Coach Ferrara please come forward?"

There was a hum of friendly chatter as everyone on the dance floor parted to make a path so the two men could reach the front of the gym.

"Did you girls do well with your raffle this year?" Lil Carncross asked Ann in a low voice.

"Much better than last year."

"Ferrara will be happy about that," Mr. Carncross commented. "Those warm-up suits the basketball players have been wearing are shredded."

"Oh, but he's not —" Ann began.

"May I have your attention, please?" Madison spoke into the microphone and her light, sweet voice filled the room. "We've been having so much fun tonight, it's hard to settle down to something serious, but I promise you it won't take long. In just a minute we'll get back to the dancing.

"Erika, will you take over?"

"Thank you," Erika said a trifle stiffly. Less at home with the mic than Madison was, she leaned too close and jumped back with a start at the protesting screech from the amplifier. Drawing a deep breath, she leaned cautiously forward and began again.

"Thank you, Madison. As all of you know, Daughters of Eve is sponsoring tonight's dance. Each year our school project has been to raise money for the athletic fund.

This year, thanks to the wonderful merchants of Modesta who contributed such fine prizes and to the generous people who bought so many tickets, the raffle brought in one thousand and fifty dollars — the largest amount we've ever raised!" There was a burst of applause, and a group of boys on the left side of the gym, members of the football team, let out a roar of approval. Mr. Shelby grinned broadly. Coach Ferrara, looking very dashing in a gray-checked sport jacket, raised his fist in a victory salute.

"We're pleased, too," Erika said. "Paula Brummell will make the presentation."

Paula stepped forward. Her eyes met Erika's, and the girls exchanged a quick smile.

"Mr. Shelby and Coach Ferrara —" Paula spoke slowly and distinctly. The audience grew more attentive, aware suddenly that something different was in the offing, something apart from the ceremonies of previous years.

"On behalf of the Daughters of Eve, it gives me great pleasure to present you with this check," Paula said. "Your endorsement signifies your agreement that this money will be used only for the organization and purchase of equipment for Modesta High's first all-girl soccer team."

At 10:47 p.m. Laura Snow sat alone in the living room, her hands folded in her lap, waiting for the sound of the doorbell. She'd been waiting now for two and a half hours.

"I can't bear not being here to meet him," her mother had said when, at 8:40, Peter hadn't yet arrived. "It's just that the girls in my card club get so upset when we don't start playing on time."

"I know, Mom," Laura had told her. "You go on."

"But this is your first date! Such a big, big event! To leave you here all by yourself —"

"I don't mind, Mom." She did mind, really, but for her mother, not for herself. She couldn't remember seeing her quite so happy as she'd been during the past week. On two different occasions Laura had found her waiting in the parking lot after school to drive her to Adrian on shopping expeditions to find "the perfect dress" and "exactly the right shoes."

The shoes hadn't been difficult — Laura's short, plump feet were easy to fit — but the dress had been another matter. They had found it at last in a small, exclusive shop that specialized in "clothes for the regal figure."

A pale blue silk satin halter, the dress was cut in Empire style, fitted across the chest and falling straight to the floor, where it swirled suddenly into a light ruffle.

"Lovely," the salesgirl had murmured when Laura tried it on.

"Adorable!" Mrs. Snow had exclaimed. "You look like a fairy princess!"

Even Laura had smiled when she saw herself reflected in the elongated mirror. The dress was becoming, that

159

was indisputable; the lines were flattering and the color good with her light hair and fair skin. Better still, however, was Laura's secret knowledge that the slimming effect wasn't due entirely to the cut of the material. In the past two weeks, she'd lost almost six pounds.

It wasn't the first time she'd gone on a diet, but it was the first time she'd done so with such grim determination. Always before, she'd let her mother in on the project. Together, they'd agonized over how much mayonnaise could be spread on a slice of bread before a sandwich became "really fattening" and whether cookies made from brown or white sugar contained fewer calories. These ventures had seldom lasted longer than several days, at which time Mrs. Snow would become concerned that her daughter was "getting run-down" and "losing energy."

"You can carry these things too far," she would say worriedly. "After all, a growing girl does need to stay healthy."

This time Laura had decided to handle things herself in the simplest way possible: She'd stopped eating except for when she was in her mother's presence. The lunch that was so lovingly packed for her in the morning was deposited, unopened, in the school cafeteria garbage can. The brownies, set out for her after-school snack, were carried to her room, and from there to the adjoining bathroom, where they were flushed down the toilet. If Mrs. Snow left the table during dinner to

160

answer the phone, Laura scraped whatever was left on her plate down the disposal. She felt guilty about such subterfuge, but it seemed kinder than putting her mother through the worry that the knowledge of such curtailment of food intake would cause her.

And the diet was necessary. There were no two ways about it. Peter Grange's girlfriend couldn't embarrass him by looking like a blimp at their first public appearance together.

Except that he'd never arrived to take her.

Alone in the quiet living room, Laura examined possible reasons, turning them over and over in her mind the way she'd fingered pebbles at the lakeshore as a child. Maybe he was sick. That intestinal flu was going around. Maybe he'd gotten his dates mixed up and thought the dance was next weekend. Maybe he had car trouble on the way over and had been forced to tinker with the engine or change a tire. He couldn't do that in good clothes, so he'd have had to return home to change and, once the car was fixed, to get cleaned up and redressed. That could take a very long time.

Or there might have been a family emergency. A beloved grandparent in a distant state might have died suddenly, throwing the whole family into chaos as they scrambled to pack and rush to the airport. Or one of his parents might have been involved in a car wreck. Or his little brother could've been thrown from his bicycle.

Kristy had mentioned once how stupidly Eric rode that bike, zooming in and out of driveways and darting through stop signs as though he owned the whole road.

Or, Peter himself — no, she wouldn't let herself think about that possibility. Peter was all right. One of the other things must have happened. But which?

The answer was as far away as the phone. All she had to do was dial his home number — he'd never given her the number for his cell phone — and in another minute she would know.

In her mind she could hear his voice, embarrassed and apologetic.

"Hey, I'm sorry. We had this family emergency. I didn't think about the time until the phone rang, and right away I thought, 'Crap, I was supposed to pick up Laura a couple of hours ago!' Can you forgive me?"

She could, of course. She could understand how such a thing could happen. There would be other dances.

So why didn't she just call him? Why did she continue to sit here, staring at the wall, waiting for the doorbell to ring, when by now it was obvious that it wasn't going to? It was after eleven. The dance would be over in less than an hour. If Peter were coming at all, he would have been here before now.

The doorbell rang.

At first she thought she'd manufactured the sound within her head, willed it into existence with her wishing.

Her hands clutched each other tighter. She didn't move from her chair.

The sound came again. *Bling — blong!* The chimes that meant a visitor was at the door. Her mom maybe forgot her key? But, no — that wasn't possible. Mrs. Snow carried her house key on the same key ring with the car keys. Since she'd driven herself to her card club, she had her house key as well.

Slowly, Laura got to her feet, smoothing the folds of the blue dress so that the creases wouldn't show, shaking the ruffle into place. She was stiff from having sat in the same position for so long. One of her legs was asleep. She put her weight on it gingerly, wriggling her toes within the confines of the wedge-heeled pump to start the blood flowing. The unaccustomed height of the heels tipped her forward, and she found herself wobbling unsteadily as she crossed the room to open the door.

The boy on the front steps was wearing old cords and a gray sweatshirt with MODESTA HORNETS lettered on it in orange. He stood with his hands in his pockets, hunched slightly against the chill of the crisp night air. His dark hair tumbled over his forehead, and with his face half-lost in shadow, she thought for a moment that he was Peter.

Only for a moment. He raised his head and smiled at her, and the resemblance ended.

"What are you doing here, Niles?" Laura asked.

Chapter 12

"What am I doing? Nothing special. I was passing the house and saw the light still on. I thought you might be sitting around or something." He shivered. "Hey, it's cold out here. Can I come in?"

"Where's Peter?" They were the only words that she could utter.

"Pete? I don't know. Out somewhere. I don't try to keep track of my big bro's comings and goings. I said, is it okay if I come in for a few minutes? I'm half-frozen."

"Sure," Laura said stonily, stepping back from the door.

She didn't know why she said it. The last person she wanted sitting in the living room was Niles. She'd always felt uncomfortable with Peter's brother. There was just something about him that made her uneasy. Perhaps it was the slight but definite resemblance to Peter, which made him seem both familiar and strange. The dark good looks were there, but in Niles's case they were slightly distorted, as though viewed through a warped sheet of window glass. The fineness of Peter's features was missing. Niles's face was broader and coarser, with the brown eyes set back a trifle too far, giving an illusion of opaqueness. His mouth was wider than Peter's, but thinner-lipped, with one corner a little higher than the other, so that he always looked as though he were trying to keep from smiling. There were girls who found the odd half-smile attractive. Laura didn't.

"Are your parents in bed?" Niles asked, stepping into the room and shoving the door closed behind him.

"I live with my mom. She's out tonight."

"You look nice," Niles said, "all dressed up."

"Thanks." She'd started back toward the chair that she'd so recently vacated, but Niles seemed somehow to have gotten himself in the way of it, so she sat down on the sofa instead. To her surprise, he came over and sat down beside her.

"It's gotten really cold out," he said conversationally. "I wouldn't be surprised if there was an early snow."

"I hope not," Laura said.

"You don't like winter? Snowboarding and skiing and stuff?"

"I've never tried those things. I don't like being cold."

"You're one of those girls who likes to curl up by the fire, right?"

"I guess you could say that." She looked down at her hands. Her mom had taken her for a manicure in honor of the evening. The little pink ovals gleamed up at her against the soft material of the blue dress.

"Niles — about Peter — you're sure you don't know where he is? We were supposed to go out tonight."

"He stood you up, you mean?" Niles sounded shocked.

"I don't know what he did. I just know that he was supposed to be here at eight fifteen, and he never came." She struggled to keep the tremor from her voice. "I thought…maybe…something happened at home — some emergency —"

"You were giving him the benefit of the doubt, right? That shows what a nice person you are, Laura. Most girls would be pissed off." Niles's voice was warm, sympathetic. "So you've just been sitting here waiting?"

"It's been hours and hours." She blinked hard to keep back the tears. "When the doorbell rang, I thought it was him — that he'd come to tell me what happened — and maybe we could still go over to the dance for the final hour."

"And it was just me, the sidekick brother. No wonder you looked so disappointed. I'd take you to the dance myself, but I'm not exactly dressed for it. This is a big deal and they don't let you in without a jacket and tie."

"That's all right. It wouldn't be the same. I mean —" She realized too late the rudeness of her response. "I'm sorry, Niles. It was nice of you to think about doing that. It's just that — Peter —"

She began to cry softly.

"Hey, now, baby," Niles said. "It's not as bad as that. A dance is just a dance, huh?"

He put his arm around her shoulders and drew her over against him so that her face was pressed against his shirt. The material was thick and smelled faintly of smoke. Niles himself smelled of shaving lotion. It was the same brand Peter used, and the familiar spicy scent, combined with Niles's surprising gentleness, broke through the last shreds of her control.

"He promised!" she burst out wretchedly. "He said we were going! I got the dress and the shoes — everything — just for tonight!"

"That's rough," Niles said. "That's really rough."

"Why did he do it? Why would he hurt me like this? How can one person do something like this to another person, when they're supposed to care about each other?"

"Maybe," Niles said, "he thought it would hurt you more if he told you…" He let the sentence drift, unfinished.

"Told me what?" Laura brought her face up out of the sweatshirt. "What is it he didn't want to tell me?"

"Look, Laura, Pete's my brother. I may not approve of everything he does, but at the same time —"

"Tell me, Niles! You have to! Where is Pete now? Why didn't he come tonight?"

There was a moment's silence.

"Niles, please!"

"He's — at the dance."

"At the dance?" She couldn't believe she'd heard him correctly. "But why would he go alone to a dance when we could go together?"

"He didn't go alone," Niles said.

"You mean that he —"

"I mean, he took Madison. They got back together early this week, and he's been out with her every night since. They just weren't telling anybody yet. They wanted to get everything worked out between them first."

"But he said he hated her," Laura whispered. "He said he never wanted to see her again."

"So he changed his mind." Niles brushed her cheek with his lips. "Hey, now, baby, don't look like that. It's not the end of the world. So Pete's going out with some girl. There are lots of guys who aren't. Like me, for instance. I know how to keep a chick from being lonely. Just relax, and I'll show you that brother Peter isn't the only one who knows how to keep you warm."

"No. Stop. Don't do that." Laura stiffened as his arms came tight around her.

"Stop playing games, Laura." There was a note of irritation in Niles's voice. "Pete's told me about all the things you let him do to you when you go parking down by the creek."

"I don't believe you. Pete wouldn't talk about —"

The words were lost as his mouth closed over hers, and she twisted helplessly as he leaned against her, forcing her backward under the weight of his body. He was shorter than Peter, but stronger. His arms were locked around her, pinning her own arms at her sides, as his hands began to fumble impatiently with the zipper at the back of her dress. His mouth kept working at hers; she felt his tongue, wet and slimy, probing at her sealed lips.

In desperation, she did what seemed the only thing possible. She bit him.

He sprung back so suddenly that they both rolled off the sofa onto the floor. Laura felt a sharp jab of pain as her left shoulder hit the corner of the coffee table. She pulled herself to a sitting position, tugging frantically at her skirt, which had become twisted around the upper part of her thighs.

Niles's face was white with rage, and there was a trickle of blood at the corner of his mouth.

"Bitch!" he said hoarsely. "You freaking bitch! You took half my tongue off!"

"I'm sorry." She meant it. She hadn't wanted to hurt him. The taste of his blood in her own mouth made her nauseated.

169

"You're sorry, all right! The sorriest mess I've ever seen! You thought Pete was going to take you out in public and dance with you? He'd die first. And so would I. So would anybody."

"That's not true. Peter and I have been dating for weeks now."

"The word isn't 'dating,' it's 'screwing.' With his eyes closed. Why else would any guy in his right mind spend time with a whale?" Niles leaned toward her, enunciating each word carefully. "Pete was using you. Get used to the idea, because that's all *any* guy is ever going to do with you. You might as well take what you can get, because it's all you're going to get. You get all high-and-mighty like you just did with me, and you're going to wind up without anything at all."

"Get out!" Laura whispered. "Get out of my house!"

"With pleasure!"

When he was gone Laura got up off the floor and went over to the front door and locked it. Then she went upstairs and took off the blue dress. She stood staring at it for a long moment; then she wadded it into a ball and stuffed it into the back of her closet. She took off the pumps and threw them in after it.

Then she went into her mother's bedroom and opened the bottle of sleeping pills she kept on her bedside table. She didn't bother to count them. She took them all.

* * *

The dance was over at midnight.

Holly Underwood arrived home at 12:14 a.m. Her date, Steve Penrose, walked her to her door. This had been their first date, and neither one had particularly enjoyed it. They said a polite good night, keeping a careful distance between them. Holly went into the house, and Steve went back to his car.

Irene Stark dropped Kelly Johnson at her home at 12:20 a.m. and then drove several blocks farther to let off Erika Schneider and Paula Brummell. Erika was spending the night at Paula's.

Tammy Carncross and Kevin Baker went to the coffee shop before calling it a night.

Tammy's parents pulled into their driveway at 12:23 a.m.

"That was quite an evening," Mrs. Carncross commented.

"You can say that again," her husband said. "Did you see the look on Ferrara's face when Paula dropped her bombshell?"

"How could I miss it?! Do you think they'll really do it — use the money for a girls' soccer team?"

"Not if they can help it. Ferrara has his heart set on those warm-up suits."

"Mr. Shelby was laughing."

"He probably thought it was a joke."

"There's nothing wrong with starting a soccer team," Lil Carncross said. "It's a popular girls' sport in lots of towns."

"I can't imagine the school organizing a soccer team for the girls when the boys don't even have one yet." Mr. Carncross opened the car door. "Hey, does that dancing we saw tonight remind you of disco?"

"Nothing can replace disco," Mrs. Carncross said. "It was also sort of nice dancing cheek to cheek."

Peter Grange took Madison Ellis home at 12:30 a.m. They took a long time saying good night.

At about the same time, David Brewer and Ann Whitten were parked in the Whittens' driveway. The porch light, which Mrs. Whitten had left on for them, illuminated the porch steps and a strip of lawn, but stopped short of the front of Dave's pickup truck. In the darkened interior of the cab they sat close together with their arms around each other.

"I felt kind of funny tonight," Dave said. "A graduated guy at a high-school dance."

"It was fun, though, wasn't it?" Ann asked.

"It was fun because you were having fun. It's just that when I'm around a bunch of your school friends like that, I realize I'm robbing the cradle. They all seem like such kids."

"You're not *that* much of an old man," Ann said. "It's only been three years since you were in high school yourself."

"It's been a long three years. Tonight, looking around at those boys — Tammy's boyfriend with the red hair, and the guy Peter, that Madison goes with — I felt like they were living in a whole different world. They're thinking about partying, sports, scouting out each other's girlfriends; I'm thinking about the farm, getting the leak in the barn roof fixed before the first snow, getting married."

"You're not happy, are you, about my going to art school?" Ann asked him softly.

"I think it's what you've got to do. If you don't, you'll always feel like you missed out on something."

"That's what I feel," Ann said. "It's like it was meant to be, the way it fell out of the sky right into my lap like that."

"That's not how it happened," Dave said. "Your teacher friend arranged it."

"Well, still —"

"She knew what she was doing. She knew we were engaged, the wedding date was set, everything was planned. Nothing 'fell into your lap,' Annie. A lot of strings were pulled."

"You sound as though Irene did something mean and sneaky," Ann said in astonishment. "That she was trying to hurt us instead of help us."

173

"I wouldn't go that far," Dave said. "It's just hard to like somebody when you know they don't like you."

"Irene likes you!"

"No, she doesn't. When you introduced us tonight, I could feel the vibes coming out of her like cold air from a freezer. There's a lot of bitterness in that woman, and I don't like the idea that you're around her so much."

"You're wrong," Ann said. "Irene's the warmest, most understanding person in the world. She wants me to get this training because she thinks I have real talent. She takes my painting seriously."

"So do I. I told you, I'd make you a little studio room to paint in."

"But you think of it as a hobby, not as a career."

"I think of it as something you need to do to be happy," Dave told her. "If you mean by a 'career' that I expect you to sell paintings and make money to pay the expenses around the place, then you're right, I don't think of it that way. That's my job. If I couldn't support us, I wouldn't get married."

"That's an old-fashioned point of view," Ann said.

"And I'm an old-fashioned guy. What do you want me to do? I'm letting you go off to Boston. I'm going to sit here and wait for you. What more do you want?"

"But you want me to feel guilty, like you're doing me a big favor!"

"I've never tried to make you feel like that. It's just" —

his voice grew husky — "it's just that I'm going to miss you."

"Oh, Dave, I'll miss you, too." She turned and pressed her face against his shoulder. "I'm so confused that sometimes I'm not sure how I feel about everything myself. I love you so much. I don't want you to be unhappy."

"I love you, too, my gentle Annie," Dave said quietly. "I know that things are different now than they used to be when my dad and mom were married. I know girls want different things now, and I guess that's how it should be. It's just that I've grown up a certain way. I can't change the whole way I think and feel about things like that overnight. I'm trying. That's the best I can do. I'm trying."

Jane Rheardon hadn't gone to the dance. She went to bed early, and then, as she often did, woke around midnight. At 12:32 a.m. she was lying in bed, reading.

She heard the siren when it was still a long way off and got up and went to the window. All the houses along the street were dark.

Somewhere, someone is hurt, she thought. *In a car accident, or a fire. But that person isn't Mom.*

It had been a pleasant Saturday. Her father had left the night before to go hunting in the northern part of the state. She and her mother had gone shopping for material and then had spent most of the day sewing.

Jane was trying to make her own dress for the first time ever — her mom made it look so easy — and that night they had gone to Brummell's Café for dinner. Her mom had been chatty, giggly, like a young girl. They had ordered fried chicken, and for dessert they had both had chocolate sundaes with whipped cream and nuts piled on top.

Her mom was sleeping now, safe and alone in the queen-size bed in the next room. The sirens were not for her.

Kristy Grange heard the siren when she stood on the porch steps, kissing Tom Brummell good night. She stiffened, turning her head to listen.

"A fire engine?" she said.

"Or an ambulance. It's close, isn't it? It sounds as though it's only a couple of blocks away."

"I hate sirens," Kristy said with a shudder. "They freak me out."

On his way home, Tom passed the ambulance. It was parked with its lights flashing in front of the Snow house.

Chapter 13

At breakfast the next morning, Tom told his sister and her overnight houseguest about the ambulance.

"It was on Locust, just a block or so from the Granges'. That white house with the little fence around it."

"Not the one with the oak tree in the side yard?"

"That's it," Tom said. "Do you know who lives there?"

"Laura Snow. I've picked her up a couple of times to go out to the nursing home." Paula turned to Erika worriedly. "Something bad must've happened. Do you think we should call?"

"Yes, definitely," Erika said. "You know, she's all alone there except for her mom. If Mrs. Snow's had a heart attack or something, Laura's going to need us."

"Should I call her cell or the hospital?" Paula asked, getting up from the table.

"The house."

The phone was answered on the first ring. The conversation was short.

When Paula returned to the table, she looked more worried than ever.

"It's Laura, not her mom," she said. "One of their neighbors is over there and answered the phone. She wouldn't tell me anything except that the 'crisis is over,' but Laura's going to be in the hospital for a few days. Mrs. Snow was there with her most of the night, but she's home now, sleeping."

"She didn't say what happened?" Erika asked. "Was it her appendix or something like that?"

"She wouldn't say. In fact, when I asked her, she basically hung up on me. Should I try the hospital?"

"Tell them you're her sister," Erika advised. "You might be able to learn more that way."

This second call provided no more information than the first. Laura Snow was, indeed, a patient at Modesta Hospital. She was "in fair condition" and "resting comfortably." There was no phone in her room, and she wasn't allowed to have visitors.

By noon all the members of Daughters of Eve had been given the news, and Erika had called Irene Stark.

"Can you find out what happened?" she asked her. "They'll talk to you. You're her teacher."

"I'll try," Irene said. "I've never met Mrs. Snow, though, and I don't know that my name will mean anything to her."

"She didn't show up at the dance," Erika said. "From something she said, I thought she was going to come."

There was a pause. Then Irene asked slowly, "With a date?"

"I don't think so. Laura doesn't have a boyfriend."

"I think she does," Irene said.

"You're kidding! I've never seen her with anybody. That kind of news gets around fast. Modesta High is one big gossip factory."

"Think carefully," Irene said. "What was it she said that made you think she would be at the dance last night?"

"I don't remember. Oh — wait — yes, I do! She was telling somebody, maybe it was Holly, that her mom had bought her a dress. It was a little tight, but she thought she would fit in it by homecoming. She was on a diet; I know, because she and Paula and I share the same lunch period. Laura used to eat with us, but recently she hasn't even been coming into the cafeteria. She said watching us eat made her too hungry."

"I'll call Mrs. Snow tonight," Irene told her. "Meanwhile, I think it would be best not to make too much of this. I wish you'd tell the girls not to talk about it at school tomorrow."

"But when Laura is absent, won't people be curious?"

"I don't see why. Students are absent all the time. Whatever the reason for Laura's hospitalization, it's obvious her mother would prefer to keep it quiet. So until we know more about this, let's keep it between us. All right?"

"All right," Erika agreed readily. "But you will tell the Daughters of Eve, won't you? That is, if you find out anything?"

"Of course," Irene said. "You're her sisters."

The November 13 meeting of the Modesta chapter of Daughters of Eve was called to order by Erika. The pledge was repeated.

Ann Whitten read the minutes from the previous meeting:

"Irene Stark brought up the possibility of making a special designation as to how the money collected through the raffle will be used. After much discussion, Paula Brummell moved that the money be spent to start a girls' soccer team. Jane Rheardon seconded the motion, which was passed unanimously."

"It shook up a few people, too," Kelly Johnson commented wryly.

"A few people!" Holly Underwood exclaimed. "That's the understatement of the century! You should've heard Steve on the way home from the dance! He was so mad he could hardly talk. You know, he's on the basketball team, and they'd been counting on those warm-up suits."

"My dad doesn't think Mr. Shelby will go along with us," Tammy said. "Dad thinks he's taking it as a kind of joke."

"He has to go along with us if he endorses the check," Paula said. "We have it printed right there on the back. When he signs his name, that's his agreement."

"Please, everybody, I think this comes under the heading of 'old business,'" Erika broke in. "Let's do things in order. Are there any additions or corrections to Ann's minutes? No? Then they stand approved as read. Madison, could we have the treasurer's report?"

"We took in five hundred and fifty dollars through dance admissions. Materials for decorating the gym were one hundred and twenty-three dollars; drinks were donated; and the DJ — meaning Brad Tully and his laptop — cost one hundred dollars. After writing a check for the girls' soccer team, that gives us a personal balance of three hundred forty-seven dollars, even before we collect December dues. In other words, we're rich," Madison announced with satisfaction. "Let's have a party."

"We just had a dance. That should last us awhile," Holly said. "I think we ought to order some flowers to be sent to Laura in the hospital."

"Yes, let's do that," Tammy said. "Do we know how long she's going to be there? Has anybody heard anything?"

"Irene was going to try to find out for us," Erika said.

"I talked to Mrs. Snow last night." Irene was silent for a moment. Then she said, "I saw Laura this morning."

"I thought she wasn't supposed to have visitors," Paula said in surprise.

"She asked especially to see me. She'd written a letter she wanted me to read at today's meeting." Irene withdrew a folded sheet of notebook paper from her purse. She spread it flat on the table in front of her. "I'd better tell you first that Laura won't be coming back to Modesta High. She's being discharged from the hospital later today, and she'll fly immediately to her father's home in Rhode Island. She's going to finish the school year there."

"But why?" Jane Rheardon asked in bewilderment. The question was echoed in eight other faces.

"Let me read you the letter," Irene said, leaning forward over the paper.

"'Dear Sisters — I am sorry to be going away like this without saying good-bye. I just don't feel that I can face anybody right now. I don't think I can come back to school and face certain people ever. I want to go to a new place and start all over. I wish I could forget my whole life except for you, my sisters. You are the only kind people I know in the world. I want you to know how grateful I am that you let me be one of you. My homecoming dress is in the back of my closet if one of you has a use for it. I sure never will. I love you all — Laura.'"

For a moment no one spoke.

Finally, Jane said, "I don't understand. That doesn't explain anything."

"Somebody did something terrible to her," Kelly said.

"What happened, Irene?" Erika asked. "Did Laura tell you?"

"Yes, she did," Irene said. "I think it's right that I share this with you, but first I want your promise that it will never go any further. What I'm going to tell you must not be repeated outside of the sisterhood."

"That's part of the pledge," Kelly reminded her.

"That's right, it is. 'We pledge ourselves to divulge to no one words spoken in confidence within this sacred circle.' I just want to be sure that everyone understands how important it is that this pledge be kept." Irene glanced about the circle of solemn faces.

"When Mrs. Snow returned last night from a card party, she found that Laura had taken sleeping pills. The empty bottle was lying on the bedside table. Luckily, Laura's mother found her in time. She called 911, and the ambulance was able to get to her before the bulk of the medication got into the bloodstream. If she'd been a few minutes later, or if she hadn't noticed the bottle and realized what had happened, Laura would have died."

There was a collective gasp.

183

"Did she mean to take them?" Ann asked in horror. "I mean, was she trying to — to —"

"To commit suicide? I don't know, Ann. Laura herself doesn't seem sure. She told me this morning that she was in such a state of shock and pain she just wanted to 'sleep and forget everything.' As Kelly said, somebody did something terrible to her. She wasn't tough enough to handle that."

"Who was it?" Kelly demanded. "What did they do?"

"I think I know," Kristy Grange said. "It was my brother, Peter."

"Peter?" Madison exclaimed incredulously. "But Pete wasn't anywhere near Laura! He was with me all evening. Besides, they hardly know each other."

"Yes, they do," Kristy said. "When I went up to bed after the dance, there wasn't a glass in the bathroom. I wanted to brush my teeth, so I went down to the kitchen to get one. Niles and Peter were there talking. They didn't see me in the doorway, and I heard them — heard them talking about —"

"About what?" Madison said. "Stop stalling, Kristy!"

"The way they were talking, I guess...Pete's been hooking up with Laura," Kristy said miserably. "That's how it sounded. You know the way guys talk, though. They like to brag and blow things up bigger than they really are."

"It figures," Madison said slowly. "I kind of

wondered — all that time after we stopped going out and he didn't seem to be seeing anybody else — it didn't seem like his style. Pete doesn't sit around and lick his wounds. But — Laura! No, Kristy — you must have heard wrong. They were kidding around or something."

"No, they weren't." Kristy shook her head. "Laura thought Pete was going to take her to homecoming."

"And then when he and I got back together again he canceled the date?"

"No. He just — just didn't show."

"He stood her up?" Madison's face was pale with anger. "Of all the shitty things to do! To both of us! You should have heard the line of crap he gave me. How he'd missed me. How lonely he'd been. And all the time he had Laura waiting in the wings! I wonder what he was telling her that whole time. How far do you think it went?"

"I think — pretty far."

"That bastard! Freaking bastard!" Madison brought her clenched fist crashing down on the surface of the table. "And I thought he'd changed, that he really cared about me and about our relationship! How could I have been such an idiot!"

"You're not an idiot," Tammy said, trying to soothe her. "You believed what he said, and why shouldn't you? There was no way you could've guessed this was going on with Laura."

"I believed him because I wanted to, that's what was

stupid. And Laura — well, at least she had the excuse of not having a lot of experience. I can see where she might fall for his crap, but with me — I've been going out with guys since middle school! I should've known better!"

"So should Laura," Kelly said coldly. "Maybe she hasn't had dating experience, but she had a dad who walked out on her and on her mom. That should be enough right there to teach her that you can't trust men."

"We don't really know —" Ann began.

"Of course we do! Irene and I had a long talk about that very thing the other night. All of us know a whole lot of things down deep inside, but we close our eyes and our minds to them. Like Madison just said. We believe what we want to believe. It's easier than standing up for ourselves."

"Like with my mom," Jane said. "She keeps telling herself that it's her own fault Dad beats up on her because she's dumb and irritates him and things like that."

"What would happen if she faced the truth, Jane?" Irene asked quietly. "What if she acknowledged the fact that she is married to a cruel and brutal man who hates all women and is taking this hatred out on her?"

"She'd have to leave him," Jane said.

"And if she did that —?"

"She'd have to be by herself and that scares her. She doesn't know how to do that."

"And so she stays where she is and lets herself be beaten?"

"You're making it sound as if I should be doing something," Jane said. "What can I do? I've talked to Mom. I've told her to leave him. She says she will someday, after I'm grown. That's just an excuse. She'll never leave, no matter what he does to her.

"I don't understand it. I only know I'm never going to get into anything like that, ever."

"Not all men are like that," Ann said. "My dad would die before he'd do anything to hurt my mom. And Dave is the same way."

"You may think that now," Kelly said. "Jane's mother probably felt like that, too, in the beginning."

"Cruelty isn't always physical, either," Irene said. "In many cases it's quite subtle, an undermining of a woman's self-confidence, a draining of her self-esteem so that she's forced to channel her energy in nonproductive directions."

"That's what happened to my mom with her music," Holly said.

"But not to mine," Tammy announced adamantly. "She's doing her own thing, and she's happy. My dad's really proud of her, too."

"What about last summer when she was offered that lecture job at the writers' conference in California?"

Kelly said. "She turned that down because your dad had to stay here and teach summer school."

"He didn't make her turn it down. She made her own decision. She doesn't like to take trips without him."

"How does she know she doesn't when she's never tried it?" Kelly asked. "Face it, Tam, she's afraid that if she leaves for a month your dad might find somebody else. Every woman is scared of that, or, if she isn't, she should be."

"That's a nasty thing to say," Tammy said. "My dad would never think —"

"Sure, he would! Why should he be any different from my dad?"

"Girls, let's not fight among ourselves," Irene said. "We need our strength and unity for the larger fight. We have to work together. Our strength is in our sisterhood."

"But you're making it sound like all men in the world are enemies," Tammy said. "Just because Kelly's dad fell in love with somebody else doesn't mean my dad is going to. There are people who stay together because they love each other, and they try to make each other happy. It may not always work out perfectly but they try."

"You live in a dream world, Tammy," Irene said coldly. Her voice was low and controlled. "Little sisters of mine, wake up! You must open your eyes! You are not like your mothers and grandmothers! You are a whole new generation. You don't have to let yourselves be ground under-foot, as they have been. You can rise — fight back — show the world that you know your own worth!"

"The way we did by forcing them to use the raffle money for a girls' team?" Paula said.

"That was a beginning."

"If that creep, Peter, thinks I'm ever going to go out with him again, he's got another think coming," Madison said. "As far as I'm concerned, it's over, and I mean forever."

"Is that all?" Irene asked her.

"All?"

"That seems like mild retribution. This is a man who drove a trusting and loving girl into an attempt to take her own life. Does your refusal to date Peter in the future seem like sufficient punishment?"

"It's a beginning." Madison smiled slightly as she repeated the teacher's words. Her sharp blue gaze flickered around the table. "If it's going to be more than that, I'm going to need help."

"You've got plenty of that right here," Kelly said.

"Then we'll plan something. Something he won't forget for a long while. Is that what you meant, Irene?"

"This decision must be made by all of you. This is a club, after all. Motions must be voted on. It's appropriate, I think, for you to present a proposal for group consideration."

"What about Kristy?" Madison glanced across at the younger girl. "Pete's her brother."

"If Kristy doesn't want to be involved, she's free to leave."

"What exactly is it that you're going to do?" Kristy asked nervously.

"That hasn't been decided." Madison regarded her thoughtfully. "If you're going to leave, you should probably do it now before this goes any further."

"I don't want to leave."

"Then you'll have to remember, you're bound by the pledge."

"I'll remember. Don't worry," Kristy said solemnly. "Pete may be my brother, but Laura's more than that. She's my sister and my friend."

"Are you going to take part in it?" Tammy asked.

"I guess so," Ann said slowly. "We don't have much choice, do we? We voted."

"We could drop out."

"Leave the group?" Ann shook her head. "We can't do that. You tried it once and it didn't work, remember? No, we're all together in this. We have to do our share."

The late afternoon light was thin and gray, and the wind was beginning to pick up intensity as they walked. Tammy dug her hands into her jacket pockets for warmth and her mind slid back to another day, two months ago — was it only two months? Yes, unbelievably, it was — when she'd run out of the school building into the bright warmth of the September afternoon. But she hadn't been warm. She'd been shivering, in the grip of some cold, strange thing that chilled her through, despite the golden sweetness of the day.

It chilled her now. Her spine was like ice, and her teeth were chattering with a cold that didn't come from the November wind.

"Madison was so angry," she said. "I've never seen her like that. She's always been the laid-back one, who didn't get upset about anything."

"She has reason to be mad," Ann said. "She trusted Pete. She thought he loved her. And then there's Laura. It makes me want to cry when I think about her."

"Kelly's the one who scares me," Tammy said. "She's changed so much, so fast. She's become so bitter."

"Who can blame her? I'd be bitter, too, if my dad walked out on Mom and me. Wouldn't you — if it was your dad?"

"Yes." She couldn't deny that.

"And think about Jane."

"Yeah — Jane. That's a bad situation." Tammy shuddered. "I never believed people could really be that way. You see her parents at church, and they look so happy together."

"It's like Irene says, we've had our eyes shut," Ann said. "You and I are luckier than most people. We've been sheltered. But the real world is out there, and you never know when it's going to reach out and grab you. It can happen so suddenly."

"How did you vote?"

"I voted to punish Peter."

"That doesn't sound much like 'gentle Annie,'" Tammy said wryly.

Her friend gave her a surprised glance. "How did you know Dave calls me that?"

"I didn't. It just came to me, the way things do sometimes. I told you once that something was going to happen this semester. I saw a candle — with blood —"

"Tammy, don't," Ann interrupted curtly. "I don't want to worry about your seeing things. I've got problems of my own."

"I'm sorry," Tammy said contritely. "Do you want to talk about them?"

"No. But I really don't want to talk about bleeding candles. Sometimes, Tam, you're so weird it creeps me out."

It was the first cruel thing Ann had ever said to her. Or, as far as Tammy knew, to anyone.

Chapter 14

November 29 was a Wednesday.

Two days short of December, the final month of the year. Something happens at that break point between November and December. There is a quickening, a shift in movement; days that formerly shuffled along as though in bedroom slippers begin to sharpen their pace into a measured clip like the staccato rap of boots on asphalt. Soon the end, and then a new beginning. Hurry, hurry along and wind the old year up so that the new one may begin.

November 29 in Modesta broke through a week of overcast skies as a bright, blue day, as blue as the shade of David Brewer's eyes. A sharp, whining wind arrived with the dawn; it dropped to a lull in the middle of the day and rose again toward evening. People built fires. Along Locust

Street and Elm Street and Maple Street, along First Street and Second and Third, rows of chimneys emptied columns of smoke into the skies, and the wind caught them and twirled them and sent them riding upward in a soft, gray haze, which hung like a blanket over the town.

Mrs. Rheardon cooked venison for dinner that night. Bart Rheardon had killed a deer on his hunting trip. The meat was stringy and tough with an odd, wild taste that made Jane gag, but she ate it anyway, washing it down with water. Her father was in a good mood. She wanted to keep him that way.

"I have to go over to Kristy's tonight to study for a history test," she told him.

Tammy Carncross's mother fried hamburgers.

Paula Brummell's mother served spaghetti with canned sauce. She'd done eight heads of hair that day, one of them a frosting. She was tired.

Paula excused herself early to get started on cleaning up the kitchen so she could go next door to Erika's and get some help with her math homework.

Erika Schneider announced at dinner that she'd need to use the car to drive over to Barnards' Pet Emporium to pick up a new breeding cage.

"They aren't open at night, are they?" her father asked her.

"They are until nine. After I leave there I have to stop at the Carncrosses' to get the application forms for the science fair. I need to get those filled out before the end of the week."

The dinner hour ended. Here and there throughout the town, doors opened to let young girls step through them, out into the early winter darkness.

Holly Underwood had to go to church to practice the new organ pieces for Sunday's recessional.

Ann Whitten and Madison Ellis were going to the apartment of one of their teachers to work on an art project.

Kelly Johnson and Tammy Carncross and Kristy Grange all had work to do at the library.

Parental voices. "You're not going to try to walk, are you?"

"No — no — of course not. I've got a ride with Erika" —"with Kelly" —"with Holly."

"Did you get your note, Pete?" Kristy called back as she left. "I left it on your dresser."

"Who's it from?" Niles asked. "Another hot admirer?"

"Madison."

"Oh, well, there's no difference. Love note?"

"Nope. It's weird. I don't get it," Peter said. "It doesn't sound like her. Even the handwriting's different. Scrawly. As if she were in a hurry or mad or something." He held out the paper for his brother to read. "What do you make of it?"

"'*Meet me at the creek. Seven thirty. Very important. M.E.*'" Niles grinned. "It sounds to me like she's finally coming around."

"Not Maddie. Not like this, anyway." Peter frowned. "She never wants to meet me anywhere. I always pick her up."

"Maybe she wants her own set of wheels so she can take off when she feels like it."

"That's what worries me. Do you think she knows about Laura?"

"No way," Niles said. "How could she? That fat bag isn't going to go around telling people. You should have seen her Saturday night. She was a basket case."

"You shouldn't have gone over there."

"Why not? It was worth a try."

"She's not like that."

"How was I supposed to know that? If she'd put out for one guy, she might for another."

"You could've asked me first," Peter said. "You'd have saved yourself a bloody mouth."

"Win a few, lose a few. I'll admit I was pissed, but hell, that's life." Niles shrugged. "The point is, she's got nothing to brag about. You're back with Madison, and Laura's out. That's not the kind of thing a girl broadcasts around school."

"No kidding," Peter agreed. "Besides, I don't think she's been to school this week at all. So where does that leave us? That damned Maddie, always finding some way to keep me off-balance!"

"Well, you'd better get a move on if you want to find out what's up," Niles said. "She wants you to meet her at seven thirty. It's past that now."

"Damn," Peter snorted in frustration. "Trust Kristy to wait till the last minute. I bet that note was sitting there for hours."

Pointer's Creek ran along the southern edge of the town. Pointer's Creek Road followed it along its north shore, then crossed by means of a narrow bridge and continued along the wooded south shore, winding as the creek did in a series of gentle dips and curves. At one point west of town, where the creek cut across the southeast corner of Dave Brewer's property, the road swerved away for a time, returning again a mile or so later to reunite with the strip of moving water.

The creek was many things to many people. To farmers like Dave, it was a source of irrigation. To fishermen, it was a fly caster's paradise. To the children of Modesta, it was a foaming highway for canvas rafts and inner tubes, and to their worried mothers, a summertime ogre waiting with dripping jaws to devour their young.

Dan and Lil Carncross, Tammy's parents, had courted on the shore of Pointer's Creek. Holly Underwood's parents had become engaged there. It was on a footpath along the creek's edge that Kristy Grange's mother had walked and dreamed during the lonely months when her husband-to-be was overseas fighting a war. As a toddler, Kelly Johnson's sister, Chris, had almost drowned in the creek when she wandered away during a family outing, and a few years later, Paula Brummell had broken her foot there jumping on rocks. As this new generation grew to young adulthood, they, like their parents before them, began to come as couples to the sweet, dark privacy of the wooded banks. It was during a summer picnic there that David Brewer had looked at the slim, brown-haired girl beside him, bent in concentration over her sketchpad, and thought — *This is my love.*

Peter Grange was no stranger to Pointer's Creek Road. He drove it this night with the ease of long familiarity, anticipating each curve before it appeared in the glare of his headlights. Nor had he been confused by the brevity of the message. "At the creek" could've meant any spot along a ten-mile stretch of water, but to Peter it meant only one. There was a particular place where the road jogged abruptly south and the creek was lost to view behind a curtain of trees. Here, with the entrance half-hidden by branches, there were dirt tire ruts that led a hundred yards through the underbrush to a clearing.

"Our place," he and Madison called it. He had taken her there on their third date. It had been springtime then, and the creek had been full to the brim, splashing and frothing in a silver rage as it tumbled over roots and rocks and leaped wildly at tree limbs.

Madison had been beautiful in the moonlight, more beautiful even than she was at school. The long, bright hair had felt like damp corn silk beneath his fingers as he turned her head in his hands to look down into the small, exquisite face.

He had told her he loved her. It was the first time he'd said this to any girl, and the sound of his voice speaking the words had filled him with terror. It was as if with one statement he had been stripped naked, leaving himself vulnerable to any blow she might wish to give.

But she hadn't laughed or done anything to hurt him. Her face had gone soft, and whatever words she murmured had been lost against his mouth.

Later, Niles had asked, "How did you hook that chick when every guy in school was after her?"

"With pretty words," Peter had told him. "Girls are like Google — enter in the right search criteria at the right time, and *click!* — you get back what you want."

Niles had liked that, and for weeks he'd gone around repeating it. Each time he did so, he'd throw Peter a conspirator's grin. Peter would smile back, cool and superior, bestowing the benefits of his advanced experience on an admiring younger brother. Never did he admit to Niles — or to himself, for that matter — that those words spoken by the stream might have been true.

As soon as they started going out, he knew he was out of his element. He couldn't handle Madison; he couldn't control their relationship. She kept him continually off-balance with her combination of sensual femininity and hard-core toughness. Her self-centeredness matched his own; her self-confidence was awesome. She was smarter academically, getting A's in subjects in which, the year before, he had struggled for C's. Her career aspirations were concrete and attainable; she didn't need him to direct her future or to give it meaning.

When he walked through the halls with Madison on his arm, he felt like the King of the World. Two minutes later he might find himself deserted, left staring at the back of her bobbing blond head as she went racing off to speak to one of her many girlfriends or to participate in some activity that didn't include him. She wouldn't go all the way with him. She teased and kissed and cuddled until he was weak with excitement, then left him feeling sick with longing and frustration.

The worst part was keeping up a front before his friends. All of them thought they were doing it. He couldn't admit the truth, even to his brother; Niles had been screwing around with girls since he was fourteen.

Twice, he'd attempted to break up with her. When they parted for the summer, he'd determinedly shoved her from his mind and set out to hook up with every pretty girl at the lake. For a while, he'd thought it was working. His days and evenings were always full, and he slept too soundly at night to dream. Then school had started. On the first day, he'd passed Madison's locker, and there she was, wearing one of those skintight T-shirts, flipping that shining hair back over her shoulders in that familiar way. All the air had gone out of his lungs, and his legs had gotten weak, and a moment later he had been beside her saying, "Hey, Maddie, which way is your next class?" And they'd been walking together. And his hand had found hers. And it was all back the way it had been, as though there'd been no interruption.

The second breakup had been the recent one. This time, he'd tried to fill the gap with Laura. He wasn't particularly proud of this. He would never even have started it if he hadn't been in such a rage at Madison and if Laura hadn't appeared suddenly right in front of him. Seeing her there on the sidewalk, he had pulled his car to the curb and called, "Hey, need a ride?"

"No, thank you," she'd started to respond. Then she'd turned enough to see who it was. Her mouth had fallen open. It had been funny to see her expression.

"Oh..." she'd murmured. "Peter!"

"Hop in," he'd said. "I'm headed in your direction. By the way, are you busy tonight? What about seeing a movie?"

He had taken her to the theater over in Adrian, and then, out of spite for Madison, to "their place" at the creek. And it had happened — the thing he had wanted for so long. At first he couldn't believe that she wasn't going to stop him. Later he wondered if perhaps she didn't fully understand how fast things were moving and what the ultimate outcome would be. When it was over she'd cried a little, but she hadn't meant it, because when he asked, "Can I see you again?" she immediately said, "Yes."

From then on he saw her several times a week. There were times when he felt a pinch of guilt about the situation, but then he would tell himself, what the hell, she didn't have to continue going out with him if she didn't want to. When she began to pressure him for a public relationship, he had known it was time to end it. He'd told Niles and a few of his friends what was happening, making a kind of joke of it, but he certainly wasn't ready to start appearing at parties with a girl who almost matched him pound for pound.

At about that same time, Madison was nominated for homecoming queen. A poster with her picture was up in the hall at school. Each time he passed it, he found himself turning to look. The eyes in the picture seemed to be waiting to catch his with a provocative, teasing glance that sped his heartbeat.

He began to have dreams about how she would look that night, wearing a crown, smiling and nodding to a room of adoring subjects. As far as he knew, she hadn't been seeing anybody since their breakup, but if she were to start, that was sure to be the night. There wasn't a guy in Modesta who wouldn't kill to be her date. Rumor had it that Craig Dieckhoner, the captain of the football team, was going to ask her. So was Brad Tully. So was Trevor Hatchell.

One day he waited after school and caught her by

her locker. He said some more pretty words. He meant them all. He had been lonely. He did want to get things back the way they used to be.

With Madison in his life again there was, of course, no more room for Laura. He knew that if he broke the news in any formal way there would be tears and recriminations. Peter hated scenes. He could see no reason for putting himself and Laura through this one. It wasn't as though she had any real reason to expect anything of him other than what he had already given her. They'd shared an experience that had been fun for both of them. How many chances did a girl like Laura have to be romantically involved with someone like himself? A face-to-face breakup would be degrading for her and painful for him. It was far better, he decided, simply to stop seeing her and to let his absence speak for itself. That way she could invent her own explanations, kinder ones than he would be able to provide for her, and perhaps pretend that she was the one who'd made the decision that the affair was over.

And now, more than two weeks later, he still felt he'd handled things in the best way possible. Laura had been angry, Niles said, but that was inevitable and couldn't have been avoided. At least she'd had the gumption to send Niles sailing out the door when he made a pass at her. Peter respected her for that and had no sympathy for his brother, who was a first-rate opportunist.

But what about Madison? What was this note about?

It was out of character. They had a great time together at homecoming and had sat parked in Madison's drive-way for a long time after the dance was over, talking and really communicating in a way they never had before. The next day, her parents had invited him for dinner. The Ellises had always liked him and seemed happy to have him back on the scene. Then for the next two weeks, between Madison's club meetings and schoolwork and his own basketball practices, he hadn't seen much of her. When he stopped to think about it, she'd been act-ing a little weird in school, distant, as though she had something on her mind.

Maybe Laura called her? No — as Niles said — why should she? The only reason would be to hurt him, and Laura wasn't a spiteful person. Besides, to hurt him would be to hurt Madison as well, and she and Madison were friends.

Peter's mind had been working at such a fast clip that he'd hardly thought about where he was. The curve loomed ahead. His foot came down hard on the brake. He brought the car to a complete stop before twisting the wheel to the right so he could inch his way through the thicket of brambles onto the dirt trail that led to the creek. The wheels rotated slowly on the hard, dry earth, and branches were clutching fingers against the wind-shield. Then moonlight, silver and sparkling, struck his face, and he was in the clearing.

It was empty.

He was here, as summoned, but where in the world was Madison? Was that a car parked far back from the stream in a pocket of shadows? Why would Madison park there, so far over? Or *was* it a car? He turned the key in the ignition, shutting off the engine. The silence of the wooded creek side seemed to close in on him. He pressed the switch to turn off the headlights and sat, quiet, waiting for his eyes to adjust to the pale world of darkness and moonlight.

In the brush to the left he caught a rustling movement. Madison?

He strained to see, but the bushes were still again. What was it there, concealed by dry leafy branches? A person? A girl? If it was Madison, what was she doing crouched so low to the ground, making no effort to rise and come to greet him? Was something the matter? Could she be injured? Could someone have followed her as she drove out from town, a beautiful girl alone in a car, headed down a deserted road, a girl who turned onto a lonely trail, its entrance half-concealed by foliage?

She'd wanted him to meet her at seven thirty. It was now almost eight. That meant she could've been here by herself for half an hour, defenseless against attack.

The thought made him sick to his stomach.

"Madison?" he called out softly. "Is that you?"

He opened the car door. The hinges squeaked; the sound sliced through the heavy stillness like a shriek of warning.

Peter stepped out onto a withered carpet of decaying leaves and into the dead, brown smell of winter before it was softened and purified by snow. The clearing had become an alien place, a hundred years from springtime, a million years from the time that the creek had been running full and wild and he had fallen suddenly, violently, in love.

"Madison?"

Silence.

He took a step away from the car. Another.

"Maddie?"

She'd said she would be here, that it was "important." Where was she? What could've happened?

Peter began to shiver. It was cold, of course, but not so cold that he should be trembling like this. The wind moved the higher branches, and the shafts of moonlight danced and darted in dizzying patterns on the ground. Peter's pupils narrowed...widened...narrowed once more with the shifting light. His eyes couldn't seem to focus. Tree limbs twisted and tangled, throwing strange, writhing shadows.

She wasn't here. He was sure of that now. But something was, something that moved silently around him the way the wind moved above him. He couldn't see it or hear it, but he could feel its presence, and his heart began to pound as it had when he was a small child and woke in the night to find that the door to the lighted hallway had blown closed.

"Madison?" He called the name one final time before turning back to the car.

Over in the shadows, something moved.

Peter stiffened, caught by the whisper of sound. And then he saw it, a human figure, black against the lighter darkness.

"Maddie, is that you? What the hell are you —?"

He started toward her and then, in disbelief, felt the strap around his throat. It caught him so suddenly that his feet went out from under him and he fell backward, held momentarily suspended by the neck. Immediately something came tight around him, binding his arms to his sides, and hands were on him, dragging him to the ground.

Somewhere a voice cried, "Peter!" High and shrill, cutting through the night like the screech of an owl. "Peter! Peter! Peeeeeee-ter!" The voice was filled with hatred. The voice — no, not one voice: two, six, a dozen! A chorus of piercing voices cried out his name as the strap around his throat cut off his breathing and he sank, sick with terror, into the rotting leaves.

"Peeeeeee-ter!"

He couldn't get air into his lungs; he couldn't move his limbs. The terrible fear froze him and deadened his senses. The silence was gone now, and the night was filled with voices — a chirp, a growl, a twitter — a burst of high-pitched laughter. How could he have thought that the clearing was empty! It was alive with frenzied movement, as the faceless shapes milled about him, crazed creatures from some evil other alien universe.

A blast of white light struck him full in the face, and he recoiled, blinded by the suddenness and the intensity of the glare. He tried to raise his hands to cover his eyes, but they were anchored to his sides. His head was being forced forward, and the pressure at his throat lessened, only slightly, allowing a stream of icy air to enter his bursting lungs. His gratitude was so great that he felt hot tears welling behind his closed lids, and he dragged in small breath after frantic breath, oblivious to the clicking sound at the back of his head.

Snip — snip — snip.

His breathing slowed and his mind began to clear as he tried to piece together what was happening to him. Cold metal brushed his ear. Then a buzzing insect attacked his head and began to trace a jagged path back and forth, across his entire scalp. He felt a sting of pain as something pierced his flesh.

And then — he knew! Peter let out a horrified shout that emerged as a whimper. He began to throw his head back and forth from side to side, struggling and straining against his bonds. The contents of his stomach rose into his mouth and he gagged on it as, in response to his flailing, the pressure at his throat grew tighter. The world began to spin around him, so that he was no longer sure about the reality of this dream.

Because it was a dream, wasn't it? What else could it be? Something like this couldn't be happening to Peter Grange!

Chapter 15

PETER! PEEEEEEE-TER!

No, I don't hear it. I won't let myself hear it.

Tammy Carncross turned restlessly on her bed, pressing her head into her pillow in a vain attempt to shut out the voices.

I wasn't there, not really. Well, yes — yes, I was — but it wasn't because I wanted to be. It was the vote. The majority ruled. I had to go along with that, didn't I? But I didn't do anything; I wasn't really part of it. I just stood in the background and watched what the others did.

Watched the hatred — so much hatred.

A series of pictures flickered relentlessly across the screen of her sleeping mind, of faces illuminated by moonlight or impaled for an instant by the flashlight beam. Familiar faces, gone suddenly strange, as though distorted by a fun-house mirror. Kelly, laughing. Had she really been laughing? Yes, she had. Madison, self-contained, almost expressionless, standing a little apart from the others and staring down at the boy who lay thrashing on the ground. Jane, so earnest, that fine, soft hair a pale halo around her solemn face. It was Jane who had held his head. And the rest of them — they had all been there: Erika, Holly, Paula, Ann, even Kristy. Kristy had brought the razor, Peter's own razor.

"That's a very appropriate gesture," Irene had said.

The other faces faded before the strong image; there on Tammy's mind's screen there glowed the face of Irene Stark. How young she'd looked, as young as any one of them, with her thick hair flying loose and her black eyes shining! She'd seemed to be surrounded by a field of electric energy; an invisible current radiated from her in waves.

"Now!" she'd whispered to them excitedly. "Now! Get him — now!" as the car had come crunching toward them through the night.

"For Laura — for our sister, Laura!"

But, it won't help Laura now!

"He must be punished! Peter must be punished! When people hurt our sisters, it is we who must punish them!"

It's horrible! I hate it! Please, Irene, stop them!

Why hadn't she shouted the words aloud? How could she have stood there, motionless, conducting the whole exchange within her mind? But she had. She hadn't opened her mouth as they ripped off his clothes, hadn't made a single move to stop them. Even when he screamed. When he realized what it was they were doing, he had screamed, a high, shrill bleat of horror, not the cry of a man, but the wail of an animal!

She couldn't hear that sound again, not even in memory. If she did, she would break apart. The part of the mind that protects the soul while the body is sleeping gave her a mighty wrench, and she came awake, sweating and shaking.

Thin, sweet sunlight was streaming through the bedroom window.

The room was oddly bright, as though lit by some ethereal source. The blue painted walls were like slabs of sky. Each object in the room stood out from its background, outlined in brilliance. The oval mirror over the dresser snatched at the sunbeams and sent them out in all directions in a blinding shower.

I must still be dreaming, Tammy told herself groggily. Then, as she lifted her head from the pillow, she saw that the branches of the trees outside her window were layered with snow.

"Was it snowing last night when you got home from the church?" Mrs. Underwood asked at breakfast.

"No," Holly said. "In fact, the sky was clear. There was lots of moonlight."

"How did the practice go?"

"What? Oh — fine. Just fine."

"How else would it go?" her dad asked as he helped himself to the bacon. "She spends half her life banging away at that organ over at the church and the other half at the piano here. It would be a wonder if she wasn't able to hit the right notes by this time."

"I don't 'bang away,'" Holly said.

"Oh, you don't, huh?" Mr. Underwood said in amusement. "I'll tell you, Miss Hollyhock, when I come home from work at night this house is shaking like there's an earthquake going on. I'm thinking of selling that blasted instrument just to get some peace and quiet."

"You can't sell the piano," Holly said. "It belongs to Mom."

"What's hers is mine as long as she lives in my house."

"No, it isn't," Holly told him coldly. "Not if it's something she owned before you were married. That's not the way the community property law works."

"Well, aren't you the *smart* one," her father said. "'Smart' meaning 'sassy.' What are they teaching you over at that school, anyway, how to be a lawyer?"

"I don't like to hear you talk back to your father like that, Holly," Mrs. Underwood said. "You know he's just kidding around."

"No, he's not, Mom. He really thinks he has a right to own everything in this house just because he makes the mortgage payment." Holly shoved her chair back from the table. "Excuse me. I've got to go find my library book. It's due back today."

"What's with her these days?" Mr. Underwood asked when his daughter had left the room. "She's grown quills like a porcupine. You can't joke with her about anything without getting a face full of stickers."

"Maybe she's coming down with something," his wife said. "She looks sort of flushed and funny." She paused. "Or maybe it's just the age. I was talking to Jean Brummell the other day, and she was saying it's the same with Paula. She was always such a sweet, well-adjusted girl, and all of a sudden this year, she's just gone haywire."

Mr. Schneider left for work at 7:35 a.m.

At 7:38 he was back in the house again, the snow on his shoes dripping rivulets onto the kitchen linoleum, shouting, "Erika, come down here! What the hell have you been doing with my car?!"

"Harry, please," Mrs. Schneider protested. "Boyd is still sleeping."

"I don't give a damn who's sleeping, I want to know where that girl went last night." He crossed to the middle of the kitchen and raised his voice in a bellow that caused his wife to cover her ears. "Erika, do you hear me? I want you downstairs right now!"

"I'm here, Dad," Erika said, appearing in the doorway. "I was feeding the rats. What's the matter?"

"The matter is that half the paint is scraped off my car," Mr. Schneider said angrily. "Where did you take it last night? That sure didn't happen over at the pet store."

"I'm sorry," Erika said. "I don't know what could've scratched it."

"Well, you'd better start thinking. This isn't the sort of damage caused by some car clipping you in a parking lot. It looks as though you went driving through a patch of thornbushes."

"There's a bush of some kind by the side of the Carncrosses' driveway," Erika told him. "I guess I could've pulled in too close when I stopped for the forms for the science fair."

"It's not one side that's scratched up, it's both!"

"Well, maybe there were two bushes."

"And maybe there weren't any. You can't make me believe that happened by pulling into somebody's driveway. You had that car out in the woods, now, didn't you?"

"In the woods!" Erika exclaimed. "Why would I go there?"

"That's a good question. Why would you?"

"I didn't."

"Then where did you go?"

"I already told you. To the Pet Emporium and then to the Carncrosses'."

"Would you like me to phone Mr. Carncross and check on that?"

"You can if you want to. I don't care." Erika took off

her glasses and breathed on them and began to polish them with the front of her blouse. Without the rims to give emphasis, her eyes looked suddenly very small and pale, overpowered by the length and sharpness of her nose.

Mrs. Schneider said, "Why won't you ever wear mascara? It would make such a difference in your looks, Erika."

"We're not discussing Erika's looks, we're discussing my car," Mr. Schneider said.

"Well, if she says she took it to Carncrosses', that's where she took it." Mrs. Schneider regarded her husband reprovingly. "It's a terrible thing to accuse your own daughter of lying. Erika's never given us any cause to doubt her. If she doesn't know how the scratches got there, then she doesn't know, and all the yelling in the world isn't going to make her suddenly come up with an answer."

"I'm really sorry, Dad," Erika said. "I'll save up and have the car repainted."

"I never asked you to do that."

"But I want to do it. It's your car, and I got it scratched up and I owe you a paint job. Now, can I go up and clean those cages before I have to leave for school?"

"Oh, go ahead. I don't have time to go into this any further. Tonight, when I get home, I'm going to ask you about it again. You think about that during the day, all right? See if you can't revise the story so that it rings true."

"There won't be anything different to tell you," Erika said, putting her glasses back on.

215

She left the room, and her parents could hear her footsteps as she ascended the stairs. The footsteps went down the upstairs hall, and they heard the door of her bedroom close.

"She was lying," Mr. Schneider said bluntly.

"I imagine she was."

"You imagine — what?" Harry Schneider turned to his wife in amazement. "Then why the hell did you give me that speech about how Erika's word is to be trusted? Do you know something about this situation that I don't?"

"No, nothing. It's just that, Harry, you know as well as I do that no girl drives out and parks in the woods by herself."

"You mean, you think —"

"She was with a boy. It has to be that. Eighteen years old, and she's finally got a boyfriend! If you do one thing, one single thing, to mess this up, I swear, I'll never speak to you again as long as I live."

"Our daughter's sneaking out on a school night, lying to her parents, and parking with some creep who doesn't even have his own car, and you're happy about it?" Harry Schneider shook his head in bewilderment. "You've got to be crazy."

"She's a normal young girl who's fallen in love."

"You don't know a thing about who this guy is or what he might be doing to her."

"Erika isn't stupid, dear. She's waited a long time for this. She isn't about to go out and pick somebody awful." Mrs.

216

Schneider put a hand on her husband's arm. "We've worried about her for so long, about this thing of hers about wanting to be a scientist. That bedroom full of rats! I have nightmares about it. I wake up at night, and I'm afraid to walk to the bathroom for fear one of them has gotten out and is running around in the hall somewhere. You've kept telling me it was just a stage and she'd outgrow it. Well, maybe she has. Wouldn't that be wonderful!"

"But why can't she tell us about him? Why can't she bring him home and introduce us to him?"

"She will when she's ready. She's probably shy about it. Erika's awfully young for her age in a lot of ways. When I was eighteen, you and I were already engaged!"

"We were?" Mr. Schneider's voice softened. "Were you really that young, Barb?"

"Of course I was. Don't you even remember?" Barbara Schneider sighed. "All I want for Erika is for her to find somebody like you and marry him and be as happy as I've been. Is that too much to ask for your only daughter?"

"Mom!" Niles said. "You've got to come quick! Something's happened to Pete!"

"What do you mean, 'something's happened' to him?" Edna Grange pried open her eyes to gaze groggily up into the face of her second-oldest son. There were fifteen minutes left before her alarm went off and it was her habit to luxuriate in every one of them. George was up and out of the house at 5 a.m. and picked up breakfast at a truck stop, but Edna was accustomed to sleeping in for an extra hour and a half before facing the hectic ritual of feeding three teenagers and a nine-year-old and getting dressed to prepare for her own day at work.

"Is he sick?" she asked Niles.

"It's worse than that! He just got home and he's — he's —" Niles choked on the words as if his throat were constricted.

"He *just got home*?" She was wide awake now and was throwing back the sheets. "How could that be? It's almost six thirty in the morning!"

"He was out all night. But, Mom, that's not what's so scary! *He doesn't have hair, and something happened to his head!*"

"What?! What do you mean something happened to his head?" Leaping up from the bed, she shoved her way past Niles as if he were the size of a toddler and took off at a run down the hall to her older sons' bedroom.

"Peter? Peter, where are you?"

"He's in bed," Niles told her, racing along in her wake. "He's got his head wrapped in a bath towel, and he won't talk to me. He's lying there shaking. He's freezing. He didn't have a jacket on. Just — um — a dress."

The room that the two boys shared was dimmer than their parents' room. The blinds had been lowered against the glare of the morning light. There was one empty bed with blankets draped to the floor. The other contained a figure.

"Peter, what happened?"

"Go away."

"Petey?" She went over to the foot of the bed and stood gazing helplessly down at the blanket-covered form. "What's wrong with your head? Have you been injured?"

"I told you, go away! Get out of here!"

"Unwrap that towel." Edna went around and sat down on the bed and put her hands on the sides of his head, turning it gently so that she could see his face. She caught her breath. "You've been crying! Look, sweetie, I want to know what happened. I'm not leaving for work until I find out what this is all about."

"Okay, okay, so you want to see it — take a look." Peter shoved her hands away and sat up. Reaching up, he unwound the towel and let it drop to his lap. "Okay. Now you know. Are you satisfied?"

"Good god!" Edna Grange had never used the Lord's name in vain in her entire life. Now, she did so without even realizing it. "My god, what happened?" There was blood on the towel.

"I got mugged."

"Somebody jumped you?"

"It wasn't just one guy, it was a bunch of them. If it had been just one or even two I could've defended myself, but this was a mob."

"I can't believe it! How could anybody be so horrible?!" She reached instinctively once more for his head, and he jerked quickly back from her touch. "Honey, I just want to help. Does it hurt?"

"Goddamn it, of course, it hurts! It makes me want to puke!" His voice was shaking. "The bastards shaved off my hair, all of it, even my eyebrows and chest hair and my...you know. And...and..." he broke off with a hiccup and turned so she could see the back of his head. Scratched into his skull was a word: SLUT. Niles balled his hands into fists so tight that they turned white. "And they left me out in the woods in my underwear. I couldn't even drive home because my keys were in my jacket pocket. I had to walk all the way. I nearly froze my ass off."

"You didn't come upstairs in your underwear," Niles said. "You had a dress on. Where did you get a *dress*?! Mom, it's there on the floor. That blue thing over there."

"They left it for me. Some sick sort of joke. They must've gotten it out of a trash can. It was lying beside me when I managed to get my hands free. They had me tied up, but loose. And there was that dress, and I was naked, and I had to walk back into town. I had to put it on."

"Did anybody see you?" Niles asked.

"Of course people saw me. Ann Whitten's farmer boyfriend was out slopping his pigs and I had to run past the corner of his farm. And once I got into town, the joggers were out. Steve Penrose was out on his paper route, and he drove by. I could see him leering out the window, but he sure didn't offer me a lift. By this time tomorrow everybody in town will know about it!"

"Oh, honey! Oh, Petey!" Edna had to restrain herself from putting her arms around him as she had when he was a child. "Who did this to you?"

"I don't know. I never saw them before."

"Where did it happen?" Niles asked him. "Was it down at the creek?"

"Yeah."

"Where you went to meet Madison?"

"Madison wasn't there. It was these guys instead."

"But she wrote the note."

"I said it wasn't her!" His voice rose sharply. "I told you back when I got it that it didn't look like Maddie's handwriting. Somebody forged it. Somebody pretended to be Madison so they could get me to go down there where they could jump me with nobody around."

"Why would anybody do that?" Niles asked matter-of-factly. "Did they take your wallet?"

"I don't know." Peter lifted the towel and began to wrap it again around his head. "It was in my pants pocket. I guess they must have."

"What did they look like? Were they young guys, like in high school?"

"It was dark. I couldn't see them well. I just know they were big. They had arms and shoulders like gorillas. One of them got a rope around my neck and choked me with it while another one grabbed me and pulled me down and sat on me. I must have blacked out, because the next thing I knew I was lying there alone in the clearing, and I didn't have clothes on. Everybody was gone. My head felt funny. I reached up and felt it — and — I didn't have hair. They'd left me a baggy dress, like from a costume party. I put it on because I didn't have any choice."

"Thank god they didn't kill you," his mother said softly. "Money is such a small thing to part with. It could've been your life."

"You're sure Madison wasn't in on it?" Niles asked.

"Madison!" Edna Grange exclaimed in astonishment. "But she's Pete's girlfriend!"

"She's the one he went out to meet. She knew where the place was."

"Madison didn't have a damned thing to do with this," Peter exploded. "Even if she got mad at me about something, can you picture a skinny girl like that attacking a full-grown man?"

"She could've gotten some guys to help her."

"Well, she didn't." Peter turned to his mother. "You better just deal with it — I'm not leaving this house until my hair grows back. And you'd better tell Kristy that if she dares to breathe a word, and I mean one single word, about this to those loudmouthed bitches she runs with, she'll be sorry."

"Dear, you're being ridiculous," Edna said. "This is

your senior year. You can't drop out of school. First, though, we need to call the police."

"No way," Peter told her.

"Those men are monsters. They were probably on drugs or something. If they could do this to you, they could do something even worse to somebody else."

"I'm not going to call the cops and get all written up in the paper."

"We've got to report it —"

"Mom, lay off." Niles moved over to stand beside her. "Pete knows what he's talking about. You don't know what it would do to him if this got around school. I'll go talk to his teachers and get his homework. I'll say he's got mono and the doctor won't let him come back until after Christmas."

"But that's ridiculous," Edna began in bewilderment. "He could wear a hat, or say he did it himself."

Peter snorted in hysterical laughter. "Yeah, like I would call *myself* a slut!"

"You don't understand," Niles said. "Pete's not just anybody. He's got an image. And Pete's image is *my* image. We're the Granges." His eyes were smoldering and his wide, thin mouth was tight with fury. "If I ever find the dudes who did this to Pete, I'll kill them."

"You shouldn't say such a thing, Niles," his mother said. "You know you don't mean it."

She turned quickly away before she could see in his face that she was wrong.

223

Chapter 16

The first December meeting of Daughters of Eve was called to order by the vice president, Kelly Johnson, in the absence of the president, Erika Schneider. The pledge was repeated.

Ann Whitten presented the minutes of the previous meeting, which were approved as read.

Madison Ellis gave the treasurer's report.

"We carried a balance of three hundred forty-seven dollars from last time, and I'm collecting December dues today, so if everybody forks over, that's three hundred ninety-seven dollars," she said. "No, wait a minute — without Laura, it will be three hundred ninety-two dollars. The only expense since the dance was a get-well card for Laura, which was five dollars."

"How is Laura, anyway?" Ann asked. "Has anybody heard from her?"

"I talked to Mrs. Snow at church yesterday," Holly Underwood said. "She said she called Laura on Saturday and she sounded okay. She isn't going to start school there until next semester."

"With Laura gone, are we going to vote in another member?" Kristy Grange asked. "Weren't we supposed to keep a membership of ten?"

"I'd like to propose Jennifer Deline," Tammy Carncross volunteered.

"Why her?"

"Well, she's really nice, and she's into things around school. And she's a junior. That means she would still be here next year to help get things going when a bunch of us have graduated."

There was a moment's silence. Then Madison said slowly, "Do we really want another member?"

"Like Kristy said, we're supposed to keep it at ten."

"According to the rules, we can't go over that, but I don't know that there's anything that says we can't go under." She paused. "What do you think, Irene?"

"We need to think this over carefully," Irene Stark said. "We do have such a congenial, close-knit group here that it might be difficult to introduce a new member at this particular point in the year."

"We'd have to tell her about Peter," Jane Rheardon said.

"That would be all right, once she took the oath."

"I don't think we should take in anybody right now," Holly said. "She'd be so far behind on things, she might never catch up with us. I move we leave the membership at nine for the rest of the school year and start over with ten again in the fall."

"I second the motion," Jane said.

"I don't think we should vote on it," Kelly said, frowning, "Erika and Paula ought to be in on the decision."

"Does anyone know where those two are?" Irene asked. "I know they were both in school today. I saw them in the hall together just before last period."

"Didn't Erika have her meeting with my dad today about her science project?" Tammy said. "She came by our house last Thursday to pick up the entry forms."

"That's right — and Paula's probably waiting for her. They'll be along." Madison turned to Kristy. "How's your baldheaded brother? I notice he hasn't been coming to school."

"He's not going to till his hair grows back," Kristy said. "He stays in his room all the time. Mom takes his meals up to him. Niles is going around to all his teachers and getting his assignments for him. He's telling everybody Pete has mono."

"The 'kissing disease' for the slut!" Madison gave a snort of bitter laughter. "That's a good one. Niles gives me the creeps. We should've gotten him the same time we did Peter. Do you know he came up to me in the hall on Thursday and asked me where I was Wednesday night?"

"I hope you remembered what to tell him," Irene said.

"Of course. That I was at your place working on an art project. He asked me if anybody else was there, and I told him Ann was."

"I'm glad we synchronized our stories," Ann said. "He got me cornered in the cafeteria the other day to double-check."

"Do you think he really suspects anything?" Holly asked Kristy.

"He might've recognized Laura's homecoming dress," Kelly said. "That's what she was wearing when he made his move on her. But he has no way of knowing that Laura dumped it in her closet and Kristy and I snagged it when we went over to help Mrs. Snow pack up Laura's clothes."

"Peter told him he got jumped by a bunch of guys," Kristy said. "I think Niles wondered at first if Madison put them up to it, but he doesn't anymore. Her being with a teacher is an unbeatable alibi."

"Why did Peter lie to him?" Jane asked, puzzled. "He must've known we weren't men. He couldn't see our faces through the masks, but he could hear our voices."

"You don't know Pete," Madison said. "He'd die before he'd admit he was attacked by women."

"But he has to realize —"

"He won't let himself. It would be too humiliating.

He'd have to give up the whole macho thing he's so good at, and if he did that, what would he have left?"

The door at the back of the classroom opened and Paula Brummell came in. She gave the door a hard shove, so that it closed with a bang, and came over to the table.

"Sorry I'm late," she said to the group in general. "I went down to the office to talk to Mr. Shelby about organizing the soccer team. He kept me sitting there waiting for twenty minutes, and then he had his assistant tell me he was busy. He said to check back with him next week."

"What's with him?" Madison said. "That's the second time he's done that. Our check was cashed. That means he's got the money for equipment right there in his hand."

"Did Erika go with you?" Irene asked Paula. "We thought the two of you might be together."

"Nope. She had that meeting with Mr. Carncross. I saw her in the hall, though, as I was coming back from the office. She said she was going home."

"Going home!" Kelly exclaimed. "You mean, she's not coming to the meeting?"

"She's bummed," Paula explained. "She just found out she won't be taking her science project to state."

"She won't?" Ann exclaimed. "I can't believe it! She's been working on it for what seems like forever. I don't know exactly what it is she's been doing with those rats, but whatever it is, she's been so excited about it."

"She's had a right to be," Paula said. "She's been conducting a study on alcoholism. She was sure Mr. Carncross would be impressed out of his mind with all her research."

"So what happened?"

"He told her the project was unacceptable and he wanted Modesta High to be represented by Gordon Pellet."

"Gordon Pellet, with his solar energy experiment?" Holly asked incredulously. "I was in class when he put that together. It was just a demonstration to go along with one of Mr. Carncross's lectures. Gordon had this solar collector he ordered from a magazine, and he put a lightbulb in front of it. Then he built this little pump to put water through it. When the water came out the other end, it was hot."

"Well, duh! That sounds like a real winner," Madison said sarcastically. "Why wouldn't it be hot?"

"And that's what beat out Erika's year of original research?" Paula turned to Tammy accusingly. "Why would your father choose that over Erika's experiment?"

"How should I know?" Tammy said. "He must have his reasons. He knows what he's doing. Dad's had students participating in these fairs for years."

"Have any of them been winners?" Irene Stark asked her.

"Sure they have! A lot of them have gone on to the regionals. In fact, there was a boy a year or so ago who went all the way to the nationals and took second prize. Dad was really proud about that."

"It was a boy who did that?" Irene asked quietly.

"Yes."

"And the ones who made it to regionals, were they boys, also?"

"I don't know — I guess so," Tammy said reluctantly. "Not too many girls enter science competitions."

"So the judges at state level are used to thinking in terms of having male winners? And your father is aware of that fact?" Irene glanced around the table. "Perhaps we have an answer to Paula's question."

"Mr. Carncross vetoed Erika because she's a girl?" Ann didn't sound convinced. "I don't think he'd do a thing like that. He's a very fair person."

"The fairest person can be influenced by the expectations of society," Irene said firmly. "It means a lot to teachers to have their students achieve at a high level. It reflects on their abilities as instructors. Science has long been considered a 'man's field,' and the judges award the majority of the scholarships to boys. Mr. Carncross undoubtedly feels that he has a better chance of sponsoring a winner if he sends a male student to compete."

"But that's not fair!" Kristy said angrily. "Erika did the work! She deserves to have her chance!"

"My dad isn't like that," Tammy objected. "He must have thought Gordon's project was better than Erika's, or he wouldn't have picked it."

"The lightbulb and the pump?" Holly said. "Oh, come on, Tam."

"You're just guessing that's what Gordon's entering. He

might have come up with something else. He might have invented something to dispose of nuclear waste or found a way to use salt water for irrigating food crops or — or —"

"Or found a way to jump over the moon without a spaceship?" Paula was regarding her with disgust. "You're just sticking up for him because he's your dad's protégé. You don't want to face the fact that you're related to a male chauvinist."

"My dad's not a chauvinist," Tammy said angrily. "Take that back!"

"I'm not taking back anything. Why can't you be objective? Look at Kristy. She didn't try to think up excuses for Peter just because he's her brother."

"Well, maybe she should have," Tammy said. "There is such a thing as loyalty to people you care about."

"Don't you care about Erika?" Paula challenged.

"Of course I care about her!"

"If I were to choose between my dad and my 'sisters,' there's no question which way I'd go," Jane said. "My sisters come first."

"If I had a dad like yours, I'd probably feel the same way. But, thank god, I don't."

"Until we compare the projects, there isn't any way we can say Mr. Carncross didn't make the right choice," Ann said. "Maybe Gordon really did work up something special."

"Okay, let's compare them," Kelly suggested. "Where are they?"

"Down in the science room," Paula told her. "Oh, not the cages with the rats — Erika was afraid to bring them out in the cold air — but all her notes and records that relate to the experiment."

"And Gordon's project?"

"That's down there, too. Erika said Mr. Carncross wanted to keep both of them on display for a week so the students in his various classes could examine them."

"Now, would he do that if everything wasn't on the up-and-up?" Tammy asked triumphantly.

"I want to see them," Kelly said.

"You're in his second-period class. You'll get to see them tomorrow."

"I want to see them now." Kelly's voice was flat and hard. Staring across at her, Tammy could hardly believe this person was one of her two closest friends. There was something about this face she'd never seen before. The softness was gone from it, and so was the warmth. The eyes that challenged hers were a stranger's eyes, cold and distant and outraged.

Outraged at what? At me? At my father? What has Dad ever done to Kelly? Dad likes her. He's always liked her. The very first day she came over, he told me afterward, "That's a really sweet girl."

What's happened to Kelly? What's happened to us all?

"I want to see them now," said the stranger with Kelly's face.

"I don't think we can get into the science room," Kristy told her. "The janitor probably locked it already."

232

"I have a skeleton key," Irene said. "It works for all the classrooms."

"Then you think we should go look?" Jane asked her.

"Of course, you must look. Did any good ever come from hiding one's head in the sand? That's what women in this town have been doing for far too long, girls, hiding their heads, closing their eyes, because they've been unwilling to face the fact of discrimination."

"My mom's one of those," Holly said.

"My mom created the role," Kelly said bitterly.

"But your generation is different," Irene said fiercely. "You're our hope! You can't be afraid to open your eyes and see things for what they are. Only then will you be able to begin correcting them! Poor Erika! In her own way, she's been as badly hurt as Laura. Erika's future has been taken away from her."

"She'll have other chances for college," Tammy objected. "There are all sorts of academic scholarships she can apply for. Erika's GPA is so high, she'll be in the running for a lot of things."

"But nothing this big," Paula said. "Besides, she has a right to this!"

"But maybe Gordon —"

"Shut the hell up, Tammy," Kelly said viciously. "We don't need to listen to that shit."

For a moment, there was silence. The words, and the

233

vicious tone in which they had been uttered, stunned them all.

Then Madison said slowly, "Kelly's right, Tam. If you're for Gordon, then you're not for Erika. And if you're not for Erika, then you don't belong here. This is a sisterhood. We support each other. Either you're one of us or you're not."

"Then I guess I'm not," Tammy said.

"Oh, Tammy, of course you are!" Ann said in distress. "Kelly's upset. She didn't mean to say what she did. And Madison, too. We're all worried about Erika, and so are you."

"But I can't be part of — the thing you're going to do," Tammy said.

"What do you mean?"

"It was bad enough — the thing with Peter — but at least we knew he deserved it. With this, we don't know anything! It's just feelings! Everybody's so angry, but it's not really Gordon —" She left the sentence unfinished before the blank expressions that surrounded her.

Even Ann was regarding her with bewilderment.

"What do you mean, 'the thing we're going to do'? Nobody's suggested doing anything except going down to the science room and looking at the projects. How is that going to hurt anything?"

"Girls, Tammy must make her own decision," Irene said. "We mustn't pressure her to remain a member of Daughters of Eve if she doesn't want to. Perhaps we shouldn't have coaxed her to return when she rejected us the last time."

"You're right, Irene. I should never have come back." Tammy shoved her chair back from the table and stood up. "I won't be coming to meetings anymore. You can take my name off the membership list."

"You're still bound by the oath," Kelly reminded her. "You can't get out of that. You swore that you would reveal nothing sacred to the sisterhood."

"I know. I won't say anything to anybody about — about — anything."

"That includes Peter Grange."

"Yes — and — the other." Suddenly she couldn't wait to get out of the room, to leave them all behind her. "The thing that's going to happen today."

"Hey, Erika! Wait up a minute, will you?" The tall boy with the wheat-colored hair was shouting to her from half a block away.

Erika's first reaction was to quicken her pace as though she hadn't heard him. Then, when he continued shouting, she stopped walking to allow him to catch up with her. He did so at an awkward lope that reminded her absurdly of an adolescent giraffe.

"I didn't know you were going home," Gordon Pellet panted. "I thought you had some sort of club meeting on Mondays."

"I do, but I decided not to go." Erika began walking again, and he fell into step beside her. "I felt like being alone for a while."

He ignored the hint. "I don't blame you. I bet you're really mad. I know I would be if I were you."

"It's my fault," Erika said. "I should've discussed the project with Mr. Carncross right at the beginning. I was so unsure of what the results would be that I wanted to work through it all myself before I talked about it to anybody. And then, when I realized the way it was turning out, I wanted to surprise him."

"You surprised him, all right."

"Yeah," Erika said ruefully. "But not as much as I surprised myself."

"Look, Erika — I'm sorry. That's the truth. I'm really sorry. You deserve to go to state. Your experiment is incredible. You've got something that's way beyond the projects that usually show up in competitions like this." He paused. When she didn't answer, he continued, "If I could do something to make your project go through, I'd do it. I know how mine compares. I feel like a fraud even going to state, much less participating."

"It's okay," Erika said. "Like I said, it's my own fault."

"But it's not right."

"Yes, it is. Like, we all have to learn to live in the real world, right? So I should've talked it over with Mr. C. If I didn't want to do that, I should've read all the small print in the regulations. I should've known the rules about using animals."

"You didn't hurt those rats."

"In a way I did. Nobody turns into an alcoholic without being hurt, does he? Human or rat? It does stuff to your liver."

"An alcoholic is an alcoholic. You didn't make those rats that way. That was what your experiment was all about. You were proving that they were that way to begin with because of heredity."

"But an alcoholic with no access to liquor is a dry alcoholic. I made those rats wet alcoholics. There's no way they'd have gotten liquor if I hadn't given it to them. So the 'cruelty to animal' regulations do really apply."

"Your experiment was cool. Really incredible."

"Thanks, Gordon."

"I mean it. If I could I'd switch places. Do you believe that?"

"I — yes. Yes, I do." Erika turned to look at him, really look at him, for the first time since they'd begun to walk together. What she saw was a young man who was too tall and too thin and who had a shock of hair so blond that it was almost white. He wore glasses, just as she did. His Adam's apple was too big. When he talked, it bobbed up and down so fast that it seemed to vibrate. Behind the lenses of his glasses, his eyes were a clear, clean gray, like snow clouds. They were quiet eyes, intelligent eyes. He had acne on his chin. Not a lot. Just enough to show that his chin was real. It wasn't a weak chin; in fact, it was surprisingly strong, considering the narrow lines of his face.

"You could've put together a real project," Erika said. "Why didn't you? That solar system was a cop-out."

"I know. I didn't realize I had any competition."

"That's no excuse."

"You're right. Next time I'll know better. I'll know people like you are waiting in the wings." He cleared his throat. "Erika — are you mad?"

"Not at you or Mr. C. At myself."

"I'd like to see your experiment setup. When we were talking with Mr. Carncross this afternoon, all you had there were the records and notebooks. I'd really like to see a demonstration with the rats and the bottles and everything. Would it be all right if I came over sometime? Like, when you're feeding them or something?"

"I feed them mornings and evenings," Erika told him.

"Could I come over tonight?"

"I'll be feeding them around eight."

"That would be great." He drew a deep breath and let it out slowly. "After you feed them, maybe you and I could go out for some food or something. Okay?"

"I guess so," Erika said. "I mean — sure. Why not?"

She wasn't smiling. When you saw a year's worth of research go down the drain, smiles didn't come easily. But — quite suddenly — she didn't feel quite as terrible as she had a few minutes before.

Chapter 17

The next morning, Tammy Carncross didn't get up to go to school. She lay in bed with her eyes closed until her mother stuck her head in through the doorway to check on her.

"I have cramps," Tammy told her.

"Bad ones? Do you need some Midol?"

"I already took some, thanks."

She hated having to lie to her mom. It was far too easy. Lilly Carncross always accepted everything Tammy told her at face value, so deception was no challenge. Still, there was no way this morning that she could tell her the truth — that she simply couldn't face the day.

So Tammy lay guiltily in her bed, listening to the usual morning sounds of a house coming alive — water running, toilets flushing, her dad's electric razor buzzing from the bathroom across the hall, the clank of pans in the kitchen. Eventually there was the sound of the front door opening and closing and the car engine turning over in the driveway beneath her bedroom window.

That receded, and almost immediately it was replaced by the clicking of her mother's computer.

Huddled beneath the covers, Tammy could picture her father parking his car in the faculty lot and entering the school building. Stopping by the office to check his mailbox. Walking down the hall to his classroom. Inserting his key in the lock. Turning the knob.

I should have prepared him, she thought miserably. *But how could I? I did take the oath. I can't go back on that. Besides, it's not as though I really know anything. Like Ann said, all anybody talked about doing was going in to look. Maybe that's all that happened. Maybe —*

She sighed and closed her eyes, trying to block out the unwanted certainty.

She did know.

"My, God, Dan, I've never seen such a mess in my life! And the smell — the stink — what the hell did they do to the walls?"

The principal stood in the doorway of the science room, looking as though he'd been struck in the face.

"Neither have I, Shel. That's why I called you down

here. I couldn't possibly describe it. You had to see it for yourself to have any idea of what must have gone on." Dan Carncross glanced helplessly about him, his eyes moving from one disaster area to another as though desperate for a place to light. "If a bomb had gone off in here, it couldn't have done more damage. And like you say, that stuff on the walls. It's got to be animal feces of some kind. Not cows or horses — something else."

"Do you have any idea who's responsible?"

"None at all. I was here a good half hour after school yesterday talking with a couple of students about their science fair projects. The three of us left the room together. The building was pretty much empty by then except for a club meeting going on in one of the classrooms down at the end of the hall. Nobody seemed to be hanging around. There wasn't any indication that... *this* would happen."

"Did you lock up?"

"Of course, but Mr. Moore hadn't been in to clean yet. He must have forgotten to relock after he swept up. The room was open when I got here this morning."

"Is there anything that can be salvaged?" the principal asked.

"Not much, I'm afraid. They destroyed almost everything of value — the lab equipment, the test tubes, even the burners. Gordon Pellet had his project set up over there on the table. That's smashed. Everything on my desktop was dumped on the floor, and — and the feces — smeared on top of it. All the papers were set on fire in the sink. The drawers were pulled out and emptied. I had a photograph of my wife and daughters in the middle one; somebody ripped that to shreds and poured chemicals on it." Dan shook his head in disbelief. "And what's on the board — it's crazy. What more can I say?" Someone had used a permanent marker to write the word PIG in large, sprawling letters on the whiteboard.

"This isn't the sort of thing that comes out of nowhere," Mr. Shelby said slowly. "Something must have triggered it. Have you had any run-ins with students recently?"

"No. Absolutely not. This has been a good semester."

"What about the kids you saw after school yesterday?"

"Gordon Pellet and Erika Schneider? There's no way one of them was involved in this."

"You were only able to select one to represent Modesta High at state, weren't you? That must have caused a few hard feelings."

"I don't think it did. Erika's an intelligent girl. She understood the problem. She was disappointed, of course, but certainly not vindictive."

"What 'problem' was it she understood?" Mr. Shelby asked.

"She had a project that would've been disqualified by the judges at state. There's a special committee that certifies all experiments involving live animals. There's a strict list of requirements, and Erika's project doesn't meet them."

"So Gordon's going to state?"

"Well, he was." Dan Carncross nodded ruefully at the splintered remains of the solar collector. "There's no chance of that now."

"I guess the first thing to do is call the police," the principal said. "Maybe they can get some fingerprints. This vandalism represents several thousand dollars' worth of damage to school property. Beyond that, though, there's the psychological aspect. As you say, it's sick."

"Because of the club meeting, the building must have been open until after five," Dan said. "That means anybody who wanted to could've walked in through the south door and hidden out someplace — maybe in one of the restrooms — until the place was empty."

"It would have to have been done that way," Mr. Shelby agreed. "Otherwise the students down in that end room would have heard it. You don't smash up a roomful of furniture and equipment without making a lot of noise."

"It was some outsider, I'm sure of that," Dan said. "None of our students would do a thing like this."

"I'm inclined to agree with you," Mr. Shelby told him. "This sort of mindless destruction is the work of a maniac."

"Irene, can I talk with you a minute?"

"Why, certainly, Ann." Irene Stark glanced up at the girl in the doorway. "This is my free period. But don't you have a class?"

"I do, but I'm cutting it. I really need to see you. May I close the door?"

"Of course." Irene frowned slightly as she watched Ann shove the door shut and turn to approach her desk. There was something about the look of her that was disturbing. In fact, when she thought about it, Ann hadn't been looking like herself for a week or more. She appeared thinner than she had been, and there were shadows beneath her eyes, as though she weren't sleeping.

"Sit down," Irene said. "You look tired. Are you worried about Tammy? I know she's always been a close friend of yours. It must be distressing to have her resign as she did."

"That's her own business," Ann said, pulling a chair out from the art-room table and turning it so that it faced the teacher. "Tam hasn't been happy in the group for a while now. It's probably just as well for her to drop out."

"It was better, if it had to happen, that it was before we went to the science room. Tammy is a great girl in many ways, but she's having problems working out her loyalties. The warning we felt we had to issue yesterday

244

might not have been something she'd have felt comfortable with."

"I'm not comfortable with it either. Not the part about what the girls did — with what I said about Dave."

"Your sisters felt Mr. Carncross was a 'male chauvinist pig.' You agreed with them."

"That's true. And when they started brainstorming about who around here owned pigs, I told them Dave did. But I didn't realize they'd go to his farm and shovel that nasty stuff out of the bottom of the sty and use it like they did. Dave would be horrified if he knew about that. I'm kind of horrified myself."

"But that's not what you came here to talk about, is it?" Irene said.

"No," Ann said. "And it isn't about Tammy either. It's me. Irene — I'm — I'm not going to Boston."

"You can't mean that!" Irene said sharply. "Everything is all set."

"No, it isn't. Something's happened to change things. Dave and I have decided — we're going to get married at Christmas."

"*Next* Christmas. That's what you've been planning on. I've always been sure, though, that once you got established at the institute you would decide to continue there longer than one semester."

"*This* Christmas. We thought, maybe, on Christmas Eve."

"But, you won't even graduate until the end of May!"

"Don't you think I know that?" Ann's voice went suddenly shrill. "I'll drop out and get my GED. Lots of people do that. It works out fine."

"That's ridiculous!"

"No, it's not. And even if it was, I wouldn't have a choice. I'm — I'm pregnant."

Irene was silent for a moment. Then she reached across the desk and covered Ann's hand with hers.

"Oh, my dear," she said quietly. "What you must be going through!"

"It's been — really hard," Ann said shakily, unnerved by the unexpected sympathy. "I couldn't believe it. I kept thinking I was wrong — that if I just waited and pretended it wasn't true — that it would turn out to be a bad dream or something."

"You're certain?"

"Yes. I'm sure. I haven't been to a doctor yet, but I took a home test. So yes, I'm sure."

"Do your parents know?"

"Not yet. I only told Dave last night. He was wonderful about it. In fact, I almost think he was happy. He said he's always wanted to have a big family, and he doesn't mind starting one right away."

"Well, he's managed to accomplish that very nicely, hasn't he?" Irene said dryly. "And to finish off your chance for an art career in the process."

"That's not fair," Ann objected. "Dave was very understanding when I told him I'd been offered a scholarship. He encouraged me to take it. He said he'd wait for me until I came back from Boston and was ready to settle down."

"And he then saw to it that you couldn't go."

"No, it wasn't like that," Ann insisted. "Dave's never pressured me into anything. This was just as much my fault as his. It happened the night his mom died. That was such a shock, Irene, you have no idea! Dave had just come in from doing the evening chores, and there she was, lying on the bed. He went over to lay a blanket on her, and he saw she wasn't breathing. He called me — and I went over, Kelly drove me — and an ambulance came — and they took her away." Her eyes filled at the memory. "After they left, the house seemed so quiet, so empty. I looked over at Dave, and he was crying. He wasn't making any sound, just sitting there on the sofa, staring at nothing, and the tears were sliding down his face. There's something so heartbreaking about seeing a man crying, especially a strong man like Dave. I went over and put my arms around him, and we hung on to each other, and he said, 'Annie, stay with me. Don't leave me alone.'"

"So you stayed."

"I had to! He needed me! I guess we weren't thinking straight. I know we should have...you know, used something...but it didn't seem to matter right then. All that mattered was being together completely. I love him, Irene. If I had it to do over again, I'd do the same thing."

"Would you really?" Irene asked, withdrawing her hand. "Even knowing what the outcome would be, knowing the sacrifice you would have to make, you can still say that?"

"Yes — I think so. Maybe not. Oh, I don't know. It's too late now to even think about that."

"How late is it, exactly?" Irene asked her. "When did you become pregnant?"

"Seven weeks ago, or thereabouts. It was the night Holly had her birthday party."

"And you say you haven't told your parents?"

"No. Dave and I are going to do that together. We thought we'd get our plans all worked out first so we could tell them when the wedding would be and everything," Ann said miserably. "That's going to be the hardest part of all. My dad's not well. I don't know how he'll take this. He and Mom really like Dave, and they've always trusted us so completely."

"Why do they ever have to know?" Irene asked her quietly.

"It'll be pretty obvious, won't it, when the baby comes early? My parents aren't stupid."

"And neither are you, my dear," Irene said. "Though at the moment you're acting that way. It's perfectly safe to terminate a seven-week pregnancy. There's no reason in this day and age for any woman to bear a child unless she wants to."

"If you're talking about abortion, I couldn't," Ann said. "Dave would never agree to it. I couldn't even suggest it."

"I hardly think Dave has a right to make this decision for you. You're the person who has to carry this baby and bear it and raise it. You're the one who has to give up your dreams and opportunities in order to spend your days alone in a farmhouse changing diapers. Dave would be getting exactly what he wants — a substitute for his mother, a woman tied at home to cook and clean and do laundry, and god knows what else a farmwife is expected to do these days. I suppose he'd have you canning vegetables."

"I don't mind canning. And I love babies."

"You could still have babies. You have thirty good childbearing years ahead of you, Ann. The question is one of timing. When do you want those babies? Right now, when you have so much exciting living to do, so much to learn and achieve — or later — when you're ready?"

"I want them later, of course," Ann said. "But we've already got one started, and it's growing inside me right now. And Dave would never let me abort it. He doesn't believe in abortion."

"Why would you have to tell him?"

"I'd have to. He knows I'm pregnant. If I suddenly tell him I'm not pregnant he's going to want an explanation."

"Which could simply be that you were mistaken to start with," Irene said. "You haven't been to a doctor. Those home tests aren't always accurate. It's possible that you really will start your period tomorrow. This could turn out to be the bad dream you'd like it to be. Suppose you could wake up in the morning and find everything back the way it was. How would Dave react to that?"

"He'd be happy for me."

"And sorry for himself?"

"Maybe. Or maybe he'd be relieved for both of us. I don't know. I'm so confused about everything. Abortion is such an ugly thing to think about. It's like murder."

"It isn't like murder," Irene said. "It's like stopping something before it has a chance to begin. Consider this, Ann: Every single month a woman's body produces an egg which has the potential to become a human being. Every month that this egg is produced and not fertilized, it dies. Yet I've never heard anyone refer to abstinence as murder. Have you?"

"Of course not."

"What's the difference?"

"I don't know. When you put it that way, there doesn't seem to be much of a difference," Ann said. "I just feel like abortion is wrong. I've been raised to think that way."

"That's because you live in a town that's a hundred years behind the times. I still can't believe that a place like this still exists. Pregnancy and motherhood are the ultimate weapons men use to keep women helpless and 'in their place.' In this case, you're going to be robbed of a

250

wonderful future. In its way, that itself is a form of murder, isn't it? It's the murder of Ann Whitten, the artist."

"I — I know what you're saying," Ann admitted. "Yesterday, in the science room, when I saw that stupid experiment of Gordon's set up on the table as though it was so important — and I thought about Erika, missing out on her chance, just because she's a woman — I got so angry."

"Your anger wasn't just for Erika, was it?" Irene prodded gently.

"It was for me, too. I'm missing my chance, too, because I'm a woman."

"The baby won't hold Dave down," Irene said. "His life will keep on rolling along the way it always has."

"It's just not fair!"

"Gordon's experiment no longer exists," Irene reminded her.

"I watched Kelly smash it. At first I couldn't believe what she was doing. Then when I heard the crash and saw the glass flying all over the place, it was like something was exploding inside of me."

"You weren't afraid then," Irene said.

"No, I wasn't. I grabbed up a rack with test tubes in it, and I started banging it against one of the tables. And the others — they were doing it, too — just banging and yelling! It was all so crazy! It wasn't just for Erika — it was for me, for Laura, for Jane — for all of us!"

251

"That's what sisterhood means," Irene said. "We are all one. Your sisters' pain is yours, and your pain is mine. That's why I cannot bear to see you destroyed in this insidious way. Ann, listen to me — you cannot have this child!"

"I wouldn't know how to go about — having it — taken care of."

"You don't worry about that. I can find out for you."

"It wouldn't have to be done here in Modesta, would it?" Ann asked nervously. "My mom knows so many people who work at the hospital."

"There's a clinic in Adrian. I'll drive you. You can come back to my place afterward."

"You sound like it's all decided."

"I think it is, isn't it?" Irene said.

"No, not yet. I have to think about it. It's too big to decide so quickly."

"Fine, but you realize there isn't much time," Irene told her. "The sooner this can be done, the easier it will be. Every day that goes by increases the chances of problems. In another few weeks most doctors will refuse to help you at all."

"I understand that, but I need to talk to Dave."

"That is what you absolutely should *not* do," Irene said firmly. "You're under enough emotional pressure right now without giving him the chance to influence you further."

"But it's his baby, too!"

"It isn't a baby at all." Irene spoke slowly. "There will only be a baby if you permit there to be one. And that decision must be yours, not David's."

"It's the most important decision I'll ever make," Ann said in a half whisper. "I don't think I can make it alone."

"You're one of my girls, Ann," Irene said gently. "As long as I'm here, you will never be alone."

As she left the art room, Ann walked straight into Kristy Grange, who was hurrying down the hall. The two girls stumbled and clutched at each other for balance, and Kristy's books tumbled to the floor.

"I'm sorry," Ann said, stooping to help gather them up. "I wasn't looking where I was going."

"Neither was I," Kristy said. "Have you heard about what Mr. Shelby did?"

"No."

"Niles told me just a couple of minutes ago. Coach Ferrara called a special meeting of the basketball team this morning. Mr. Shelby's giving them money for new warm-up suits."

"Where did it come from?" Ann asked.

"Where do you think? From our check! Not only that, but they're getting new practice balls!" Kristy paused, and when there was no immediate response, said, "Don't you get what I'm saying? He's taken the money from the raffle and ignored the stipulation. There's not going to be any girls' soccer team — or any girls' anything! The boys are getting every penny, just like they always have."

"He can't do that, can he?"

"He can't, but he has. No wonder he wouldn't talk to Paula yesterday. I'm going in to tell Irene about it now. We want to call a special meeting to discuss what we can do. We can't let him get away with this, Ann!"

"I guess not," Ann said.

"You guess not? What's the matter with you?" Kristy said angrily. "Don't you care?"

"I care," Ann said. "I've just got something else on my mind right now."

"You'll be at the meeting?"

"No, I can't. I've got to be by myself for a while and think."

"I don't get it," Kristy said. "Don't tell me you're going to pull a Tammy and bail on us."

"I'm not like Tammy," Ann told her. "I wish I were. Tammy has feelings she can trust."

She turned and started off down the hall, leaving Kristy staring after her.

Chapter 18

The first snow of the winter had arrived early and melted away quickly. Within twenty-four hours it had turned to slush and run off down the gutters, leaving children resentful and frustrated and adults relieved.

When it snowed again, things were different. Cell phones leaped into action as the children of Modesta called each other to spread the joyful tidings: "It's sticking! It's going to last!" Mr. Johnson arrived at his former home with shovel in hand to clear the front walk and driveway; Chris went outdoors to help her father, and Mrs. Johnson served them hot chocolate and homemade cookies. Eric Grange and his friends hauled out the sleds that had been stored in their garages since early springtime and sanded the rusted runners.

It was a wild, white world.

At a special meeting, the Daughters of Eve voted to send a letter to Mr. Shelby requesting that, if their contribution to the school athletic fund wasn't going to be used as designated, it be returned to the club. Since the secretary, Ann Whitten, wasn't at the meeting, Madison Ellis volunteered to write the letter.

She delivered it by hand to his box in the office.

Suddenly, with the second snowfall, Modesta came alive with the anticipation of Christmas. Colored lights appeared as if by magic in blinking strings down Main Street, and stores throbbed with the strains of "Silent Night" and "It Came Upon a Midnight Clear." Salvation Army Santas materialized on street corners, tinkling their silver bells, and Mrs. Underwood hung a massive wreath of holly on her front door, explaining for the eighteenth season in a row, "This wreath means a lot to us! We named our own daughter after it."

The Senior Honor Society was sponsoring the winter formal, which was to be held on Friday, December 15, the last day of school before the holidays.

"It's such a shame Peter is sick," Mrs. Ellis remarked sympathetically to her daughter. "It'll be hard going to all the holiday parties without a date."

"Don't worry about me," Madison told her. "I'm going to the dance with Craig Dieckhoner."

Tom Brummell invited Kristy Grange.

Gordon Pellet invited Erika Schneider.

On Friday, December 8, the Daughters of Eve had a group dinner and early gift exchange. The get-together was held at Irene Stark's apartment.

When Jane Rheardon returned home at 10:20 p.m., she found Mrs. Geiger, the woman who lived next door, waiting in the living room.

"Don't take your coat off, Janie," her neighbor told her. "You're going to be going right out again. Your mom's had an accident. She's at the hospital."

Jane froze, her hands poised over the second button of her jacket.

"What happened?"

"She was carrying dinner in from the kitchen and slipped on a spill," Mrs. Geiger said. "She fell and hurt her hip."

"Where's my dad?" Jane asked.

"He's already over there. They let him ride with your mom in the ambulance. He wanted to get hold of you, but he didn't know where you were. He asked me to wait and bring you over to the hospital when you got home."

"He knows my cell phone number," Jane said.

"People get confused when they're upset. Your poor daddy is about out of his mind, he's so worried over your mom."

"Yeah, I bet," Jane said shortly.

Mrs. Geiger drove her to the hospital and went in with her. Mrs. Rheardon was in surgery when they got there. Jane's father was in the waiting room, leafing through a magazine.

"It's a fractured hip," he told them. "They're operating now to remove some bone chips that got wedged down into the joint socket." He addressed himself to Jane. "She fell in the kitchen. There was grease spilled on the linoleum floor."

She didn't look at him.

"You know how careless your mother can be about things like that," Bart Rheardon continued. "She never cleans things up when she ought to. It's a wonder something like this hasn't happened before now."

They sat in the waiting room, Jane in silence, her father and Mrs. Geiger making stilted conversation, until a white-clad doctor came in to inform them that Ellen Rheardon was out of surgery and was being transferred to the recovery room.

Jane got up from her chair and went out into the hall. When her mother was wheeled past her, she stepped in close and stood, gazing down at the slack face.

The eyes were closed, the lashes a sooty fringe against the pale cheeks. The mouth hung open. The left side of the jaw was puffy and purple.

"Mom?" Jane said tentatively.

"She won't be out from under for a while yet, honey," one of the nurses said. "You'd best go on home and get some sleep and come back in the morning."

Jane walked outside to use her cell phone.

"It's Jane," she said when a woman's voice answered. "Irene, could I please come back to your place? My dad almost killed my mom, and I need somewhere to spend the night."

Saturday, December 9, was a gray day, and cold. The snow, which had softened slightly the day before, had refrozen during the night, and the roads were slick and icy. Few people ventured out unless they had to.

Mrs. Schneider spent the morning happily snipping and stitching as she made adjustments to a formal dress they'd purchased for Erika to wear to the dance.

"I told you she had a boyfriend," she told her husband with satisfaction.

At the Johnson home, Mrs. Johnson sat at the dining-room table, addressing Christmas cards. Kelly came and stood behind her, reading over her shoulder.

"Are you writing notes in all of them?"

"I thought I should. It's one way to let out-of-town people know about your dad and me."

"What about our tree?" asked Chris, who was sprawled on the sofa with a book. "Is Dad going to take us out to the woods to cut it?"

"What do you mean, 'it'?" Kelly said. "You mean 'them,' don't you? He'll have to cut two trees. He's got his own place to decorate."

"Okay —'them,'" Chris said mildly. "Is he, Mom?"

"I don't know," their mother said. "I was thinking about getting an artificial tree this year. There wouldn't be those needles all over the rug, and after Christmas we could just collapse it and store it in the attic."

"Sounds sensible," Kelly said. "An artificial tree for an artificial family."

"Kelly —" Mrs. Johnson lowered her pen and turned to look at her older daughter. Her brow furrowed as she struggled to find the right words.

"What is it?"

"I think — after Christmas —" Mrs. Johnson said slowly, "it might be good for us to get some professional counseling. All three of us, you and Chris and me. We're not adjusting the way we should be."

"You don't mean 'we,'" Kelly said. "You mean, *I'm* not adjusting. You and Chris are doing fine. You're having a good time playing the martyr, and Chris is milking it to get more from both of you. If you think I'm going to go to some shrink so I can be more like you guys, forget it, Mom. I don't want to be 'adjusted.'"

"I just can't bear to see you so bitter," her mother said. "Other children seem to survive a divorce in the family and still keep on loving their parents and feeling good about their lives."

"Other 'children' may not realize how terrible the world is," Kelly said.

Late in the evening, more snow began to fall. Ann Whitten's mother went out to the woodpile at the side of the house and brought in some logs and built a fire in the fireplace in the den. Mr. Whitten sat in front of it with his stocking feet propped up on a footstool, letting the flames warm his toes.

After a while, Ann, who'd been resting in her bedroom, came into the den, drawn by the scent of the burning wood. She dropped a light kiss on her father's scratchy cheek and settled herself on the floor beside his chair.

"Feeling better now, baby?" he asked her fondly.

"Yes, a little, thanks. I must have eaten something weird at the potluck last night."

"The stomach flu's going around, I hear."

"I guess it is."

"David called twice already this morning," Ann's mother said. "He said he's been trying your cell and just getting voice mail. I told him you weren't feeling so good and were lying down awhile. He said for you to call back when you could."

"I don't feel up to it now," Ann said. "I'll call him later."

"Is there something wrong between the two of you?" Mrs. Whitten asked her. "You haven't been spending much time together lately. I thought winter was when farm people always had plenty of time free."

"Lovers' spat?" Ann's father suggested playfully.

"No, nothing like that."

Ann leaned her head against her dad's side, and he slipped an arm around her shoulders. The flames in the fireplace leaped and fell, and the orange light danced.

Mrs. Whitten was knitting, and the click of the needles seemed to keep time with the crackle of the logs.

"This is going to be a sweater for your cousin Debbie's baby, if I ever get it finished," she said. "I'd forgotten how long it takes to make something with these little needles."

"When's Deb due?"

"Sometime in January."

"Is she happy about it, do you think?"

"Your Aunt Bonnie writes she's been in maternity clothes since her second month. So everybody would know. You know how Debbie was when she was little, always fussing over a cradle full of dolls. That girl's never had a dream in her head except to be a mother."

They were quiet for a moment.

Then Ann said, "You lost a baby, didn't you, when I was around three? Do you think about it much?"

"I used to," her mother said. "Not anymore, though. It's been so long now."

"Was it a girl or a boy?"

"I wouldn't let them tell me. I thought if I knew I'd start seeing its face in my mind, looking in carriages and strollers at other people's babies, thinking 'That's the way it would have looked if it had lived.' It was easier not knowing. That way it didn't seem so much like a real person."

"Why did it die?"

"Who knows?" Mrs. Whitten said. "Doctors didn't know as much about such things back then. I always figured God just didn't mean for it to get born. His plan was to take it back with Him, and that's how it was." The knitting needles stopped clicking. "Is anybody ready for some lunch yet?"

"I'm not hungry, thanks," Ann said.

"Is there any of last night's stew sitting around out there?" Mr. Whitten asked.

"There sure is. Would you like me to heat you up a dish?"

"You don't have to ask me twice to get a 'yes' to that one."

The couple smiled at each other, and Mrs. Whitten set the knitting carefully down on the arm of her chair and got to her feet. A moment later they could hear the clank of pans in the kitchen.

Mr. Whitten tightened his arm around his daughter's shoulders.

"Annie," he said softly, "this is your own life you're leading. Nobody else can live it for you. You've got to decide things the way you think they'll be best."

Ann looked up at him in disbelief. "What do you mean?"

"I mean exactly what you think I mean."

"How did you — know?"

"I'm your daddy. I've been around you a long time. I'm not likely to sit here blind when my daughter gets sick every morning and goes around looking like the world's coming to an end."

"Mom —?"

"She doesn't want to know. That's all right. Your mom has enough to worry about with me sick without taking on an extra other thing right now. She'll stand by you, though. She'll always be here to help you. The thing is, she can't face it now to talk about."

"What do you think I should do?" Ann asked him.

"I can't tell you, Annie, and nobody else can either."

"There's a friend who thinks I ought to have an abortion."

She expected a violent reaction, but she didn't receive one.

"That's one answer, I suppose," her father said. "They're safer these days. You can even go home the same day."

"Do you think it would be wrong?"

"What I think doesn't matter," Mr. Whitten said. "It doesn't matter what your mom thinks either, or what this friend of yours thinks. I don't know about Dave. I guess what he thinks ought to matter some, but then again, maybe it shouldn't. It all comes down to you. You've got to make a decision you can live with, and once you've done that, you've got to accept it and go on from there."

"It's not fair," Ann said miserably. "Why do I even have to decide this? It's because I'm a girl, that's why! Look at all the guys out there, sleeping around, and not one of them ever has to worry about who ought to live and who shouldn't get born."

"Of course it's not fair," her father said. "Why should it be? Whoever said life is fair was a moron."

"What?" Ann said in bewilderment.

"Nothing's fair," Mr. Whitten said briskly. "It isn't fair for a man of forty-six to have a heart attack. There I was with everything — a good job, a happy marriage, all the makings for a great life — and what happens? Clunk! The old pump goes out on me. Suddenly I'm an old man whose feet are always cold. There's half a lifetime that somebody owes me, and I'm never going to get to use it."

"Daddy, you are!" Ann protested.

"Don't give me that guff. I've got months left, a year maybe. I've been cheated out of what's due me, and it's not right. Do you know how many nights I've laid awake in my bed and cursed at God and asked Him, 'Why? Why me? Why John Whitten who's always tried to do good and live by Your holy laws? What have I ever done to deserve a blow like this?' A thousand times, at least, that's how many. And do you know what He's told me?"

"What?"

"Not one word, that's what. Whatever the answer is, it's not for me to know it on this earth."

"I love you, Daddy," Ann said.

"And I love you. More than anything else in my life."

"And you'll be okay — whatever happens? Whatever I decide to do?"

"Whatever you decide."

They sat, staring into the fire, his arm still around her. The dry wood snapped, and the sparks flew, and the logs resettled themselves. Outside the den window the flakes of snow continued to fall.

After a while, Mrs. Whitten came in with a bowl of stew and set up a TV tray so her husband could eat by the fire.

"Well, Tammy, this visit is certainly unexpected," Irene Stark said.

"I'm sure it is."

Tammy had been in Irene's apartment only the month before, when the Daughters of Eve had gathered there to work on posters for Madison's campaign. At that time it had seemed like a pleasant place, warm and inviting and humming with happy activity.

Today it was different, quiet and empty. The furniture looked as though it had never been sat on. Glancing around her, Tammy became acutely aware of the oil paintings that covered the walls. All were abstracts, done in dark, intense colors against a background of white. The size of the pictures and the starkness of the sharp, strong images crowded so close upon one another in the confinement of the small room made her oddly uncomfortable.

"Won't you sit down?" Irene asked politely.

"Thank you." She seated herself on the edge of the sofa and then hesitated, caught by the sight of a familiar jacket thrown across the back of a chair. "Do you have company?"

266

"It's only Jane. She's asleep in the bedroom. The poor girl was at the hospital most of the night waiting for her mother to come through surgery."

"Oh, I'm sorry," Tammy said awkwardly. "I didn't know. Is Mrs. Rheardon going to be okay?"

"They can't say yet. Her husband hurt her badly."

"That's horrible," Tammy said. "Jane can stay at our house if she needs to. I know my parents would be glad to have her, and we've got an extra room, with Marnie away at college."

"That won't be necessary," Irene said.

"I wish you'd tell her —"

"Jane is taken care of, Tammy." Irene paused. "You wanted to see me about something? It must be important if it brought you out in this weather."

"It's about what happened in my dad's classroom."

"The Pellet boy's experiment —" Irene began slowly.

"It wasn't just Gordon's demonstration," Tammy interrupted. "It was everything! All the lab equipment! All Dad's personal things! And the manure they plastered on his desk and on the walls! I knew something was going to happen when I left the meeting, but I never guessed it would be so bad — you called him a sexist pig!"

"Peter was punished. Why shouldn't your father be?"

"My dad isn't like Peter! He doesn't go around hurting people! He had a good reason for rejecting Erika's experiment —"

"Don't shout, Tammy," Irene said quietly. "You'll wake Jane."

"You can't go on doing these things," Tammy said, fighting to get control of her voice. "I have a terrible feeling about what's going to happen. You're making people do things that are wrong."

"I hardly think it's up to you to pass judgment," Irene said. "I have never forced anyone to do anything. Daughters of Eve is a democratic organization. Every issue is decided by a vote of the members. As sponsor, I don't even participate in the voting."

"Maybe you don't exactly force people," Tammy conceded, "but — you do something. You make things happen. I've known most of these girls for years. They've changed. You've changed them."

"By helping them face reality? By giving them courage to stand up for their rights?" There was satisfaction in Irene's voice. "If I've brought about those changes, then I'm delighted. Men have to learn that we are a force to be reckoned with. I've lived longer than you have, and I know what I'm talking about. Men don't know the meaning of words like 'loyalty' and 'love.' They care about nothing and no one except themselves. They view women as servants to be exploited. We have to rise up and overthrow them if we are to survive!"

"Maybe there are a few like that, but —"

"All of them! All of them!"

"You can't really believe that," Tammy said incredulously. "If you do, you're as prejudiced as you think they are."

"You truly can't see the difference?"

"No, I can't."

"Then I think this conversation is over." Irene regarded her coldly. "You are no longer one of us. You have disassociated yourself from the sisterhood. Our goals are not yours. There is really nothing more for us to discuss."

"Yes, there is," Tammy said. "There's my dad's classroom. You led the girls into doing what they did there."

"There's no way for you to have any idea of what went on that afternoon," Irene said. "You weren't even with us."

"It can't go on, Irene! If it does, something terrible will happen! I feel it — I know it!"

"You took an oath," Irene reminded her.

"I know that, and I'll live by it. I will 'divulge to no one words spoken in confidence within the sacred circle.' But that doesn't apply to anything else that might happen. From now on, I'm not a member of Daughters of Eve. I'm just me, Tammy Carncross, on my own, and I'll do whatever I think is right."

"Are you threatening us, Tammy?" Irene asked quietly.

"I guess you could say that."

"Then I think I should warn you that threats have a way of boomeranging. It makes people very angry when they're threatened. Emotions get out of hand, and regrettable things can happen."

"What do you mean?"

"Do you remember what I told you about Robert Morrell?"

"No. Yes — I mean, I think so." Tammy was confused by the turn of the conversation. "Was he that PE coach at the school in Chicago?"

"That's right. He blocked my friend from her new position. Well, I may have told you, some students staged a demonstration. Emotions ran high, and somebody threw a bottle."

"Threw it at him?"

"It undoubtedly was an accident, but the result was very sad." She paused. "Your father isn't as handsome as Morrell was, Tammy. Still, it would be a shame —" She let the sentence dwindle off, unfinished.

Tammy sat staring at her, too stunned to speak.

The telephone on the end table jangled shrilly. Irene leaned over and picked up the receiver.

"Hello? Oh — Madison." There was a moment's silence. Then she said, "I see. Can you hold a moment?" She turned to Tammy. "I think we're done, aren't we?"

"You're insane," Tammy said hoarsely.

"Oh, no, my dear," Irene said softly. "It's just that I refuse to be intimidated — not by the men in this world, and not by you. And I won't let my girls be threatened either. We are a sisterhood, and we take care of our own. Do you understand me?"

Silently, Tammy nodded.

"Then don't you think you should be leaving? You have a long walk home through the snow."

Numbly, Tammy got to her feet. When she was standing, her eyes were even with the painting on the wall directly across from her. The images swam before her — black and purple and red — the red, thick and dark like blood; the black, like a heavy metallic object — strong, brutal shapes that were a silent cry of fury.

"That picture —" She blinked, and the forms seemed to shift. There was no recognizable object there at all, only hatred. A canvas full of hatred.

"That day — at the initiation," Tammy said haltingly, "something was wrong. I knew it — but I didn't know what. I got scared — I ran — but I didn't know what it was I was running away from.

"I know now. It was you. I was running from *you*."

The snow delayed the delivery of the day's mail. It was 2:45 p.m. by the time the mail carrier had made it along the slippery roads as far as the Ellis house on Fourth Street. He brought an assortment of cards in square envelopes bedecked with Christmas seals, and a letter for Madison.

The letter read:

Dear Miss Ellis:

It is my understanding that those citizens of Modesta who contributed so generously to the school athletic fund through the November raffle

271

did so out of a desire to support the program as it currently exists. To use these funds for another purpose would, I believe, be unfair to the contributors.

I appreciate your group's concern for the future of the Modesta athletic program. Your desire for the development of a girls' soccer team will be kept very much in mind in the future. However, at this particular time, I feel the donations from the community will be best used to further the sports activities the school already sponsors.

I am grateful for the continued support and help of the Daughters of Eve.

Sincerely yours,

J. Douglas Shelby, Principal
Modesta High School

"That self-satisfied bastard!" Madison said softly when she'd finished reading the letter. "The nerve!"

She took out her cell phone and made several short calls.

Then she told her mother, "I'm going out for a while."

Hurriedly, before her mother could question her further, Madison put on her ski jacket and left the house.

Throughout the town of Modesta, the doors of other homes were opening to spill an assortment of teenage girls out into the blowing snow. Some were on foot. Others borrowed cars from their parents. The ones with the cars collected those without.

Paula Brummell stopped at the Schneider house to pick up Erika.

To her surprise, she found her upstairs in her bedroom, doing homework.

"I'm not going," Erika told her. "I don't think this is the way to handle things."

"We did it for you when you got screwed over," Paula reminded her.

"I know, and I wish you hadn't. If I'd been at the meeting that day, I'd never have let you. You can't go around destroying people's property because you're mad at them for doing things you don't want them to."

"You think we should sit still for discrimination?" Paula demanded.

"It wasn't discrimination that kept me from going to state. Mr. Carncross knew my project would be disqualified. He told me about a student two years ago who trained a rat to run a maze by rewarding it with food. To get it hungry enough to perform well, the student didn't feed it for twenty-four hours. The decision committee banned the project because they thought it showed cruelty to animals. If they'd do that, you can imagine how they'd react to a bunch of rats crawling around with the d.t.'s."

"He probably made that story up," Paula said.

"I don't think so. I believe him."

"You can't know it's true."

"And you can't know it isn't true," Erika said. "But if it wasn't, if he was deliberately trying to keep me from going to state because he liked Gordon better, that still wouldn't have been reason to smash up all that expensive stuff. I saw that place the next day. It looked like a bunch of animals went crazy in there."

"So what about punishing Peter? Do you think that was wrong, too? You were part of that as much as the rest of us."

"It didn't seem wrong at the time," Erika admitted. "Now, though, I think it might have been. I did take part in that, but I thought it was going to be a one-time thing because of Laura. I didn't know it was just the beginning."

"We have to stand up for our rights!"

"You sound like Irene."

"So what's wrong with that? Are you turning on Irene now?" Paula regarded her incredulously. "I'll tell you, Erika, you and I have been friends for a long time, but if you dare say one thing against Irene, our friendship's over. Look at all she's done for us, at all she's taught us. How many teachers give their all for their students the way she's done? If it wasn't for Irene, we'd still be the same bunch of spineless nothings we were a year ago, rolling along without any real direction, doing do-gooder projects and having our little parties. It's Irene who's shown us what sisterhood can be."

"It's gotten out of hand," Erika said. "It's gone too far. The basic premise is fine, but there's so much hate, we can't see anything clearly anymore."

"Of course there's hate! It's normal to hate people who hurt you!"

"I don't hate Mr. Carncross, and I don't hate Gordon. I like Gordon. He's a cool guy."

"And I suppose you 'like' Mr. Shelby? Did Madison read you that letter?"

"Yes, and I don't like it, and I don't like him. I think the letter was insulting, and there's got to be something we can do about it. But not this. This isn't going to get us anywhere. What good will it do?" Behind the thick lenses of her glasses, Erika's eyes were solemn and worried. "Paula, this scares me. If things go on like this, somebody's going to get hurt. Badly hurt."

"Mr. Shelby, you mean?"

"I don't know who, but somebody. Violence leads to more violence. You know Tammy's 'candle with the blood on it'? I don't want to be there to see it burn."

"That's your problem, then," Paula said.

"I guess it is."

Erika didn't bother to go downstairs and walk Paula to the door. It wouldn't have mattered. Despite the years of closeness between them, they were no longer friends.

Chapter 19

On Saturday, December 9, at 5:50 p.m., Jane Rheardon entered her home by the front door and went through the entrance hall to the stairway leading to the second floor.

As she passed the door to the living room, her father called out to her, "Jane, is that you? Come in here."

Jane hesitated at the foot of the stairs, torn as to whether to obey the command or continue to her room. Finally, she turned and came slowly back to stand in the entryway.

Bart Rheardon was seated in his accustomed chair with the evening paper lying open on his lap and a martini already in his hand.

"Well, look who's decided to come home," he said,

lifting the glass in a sardonic toast. "The wanderer has returned at last. Where've you been?"

"If you'd been really worried, you would've called the police," Jane said.

"I wasn't 'really worried,' as you put it. I was sure you'd taken off to the home of one of those girlfriends of yours. I wasn't about to go calling all over town to find out which one. The question is, why are you here now?"

"To get my clothes," Jane said.

"Oh, really? You mean you girls don't share each other's clothing? They're your soul sisters, aren't they? I thought you passed around everything like you were one big family."

"I'm not staying with one of the girls. I spent the night with Ms. Stark. And you wouldn't have had to 'call over town' if you'd wanted to find me. You know the number of my cell phone. You could've reached me that way when Mom had her 'accident,' too."

"Why should I? One more hysterical voice wouldn't have added much to the occasion."

"Well, now you won't have to listen to any voices at all," Jane said. "You can have the whole place to yourself. I'm moving out."

"This teacher friend is planning to put you up indefinitely?"

"At least until Mom gets out of the hospital."

"And then where will you be going?"

"With Mom," Jane said. "Wherever she wants to be."

"She'll be here, with me, the way she's always been," Bart Rheardon told her. "Your mother wouldn't know what to do with herself if she wasn't here. The doctors think she'll have to be in a wheelchair for a while. That means she won't be able to do all the things she used to do. You'll have to pitch in and help out a lot more than you've been doing."

Jane stared at him in amazement.

"Dad," she said softly, "sometimes I simply can't believe you."

When he spoke like this, acted like this, he seemed so normal. He was a handsome man — heavy-jowled and beginning to gray a little at the temples, but still far better-looking than the fathers of most of her classmates. He had honest eyes with a direct, straightforward gaze — a strong, square chin — a wide, pleasant mouth. His was the kind of face that people liked and trusted. If you ran into someone with a face like that on a street corner and he asked you for directions, you wouldn't think twice about standing there and giving them to him. If you found yourself sitting next to him at a lunch counter and he smiled at you, you'd chat a little. He was well-known in the community. People respected him. Her mother loved him. That was the ultimate mystery — the fact that

her mom, who knew him at his worst as well as his best —
continued to love him.

That morning at the hospital Jane had asked her,
"How did it happen?"

Her mother had looked up at her and lied.

"I slipped on some grease," she'd said.

"No, you didn't." Jane hadn't even tried to pretend to
believe her. "You know that isn't true. It was a Friday
night. Dad came home in one of his tempers like he
always does. You must have said something he didn't like,
and he hit you."

"It was an accident."

"It's never an accident." Jane bent closer to study the
swollen face, trying to judge it objectively despite the
nausea rising within her. "He must have hit you on the left
side of the jaw and knocked you down. You hurt your
hip when you landed. I can't believe none of the doctors have wondered about those bruises and all that
swelling."

"I hit the table." Ellen Rheardon spoke so softly that
at first Jane couldn't be sure of what she was saying.

"I can't hear you, Mom."

"I fell into the table," her mother said more loudly. "I
slipped and fell, and my face went into the edge of the
kitchen table."

"You couldn't have fallen forward. If you had, you'd

never have broken your hip. You had to fall backward to do that."

"I tell you, that's how it happened." The woman on the bed gazed up at her with pleading eyes. "I told that to the doctors, and they didn't question it. Why are you trying to hurt us, Jane?"

"Trying to hurt you?!"

"It's between your dad and me, so you just stay out of it. It's not for you to pass judgment. He's sorry. He's living in hell, he's so sorry. See those flowers over there by the TV? Those roses? Aren't they beautiful? He must have gone out to a flower shop in the middle of the night and made them open up special so those would be waiting for me when I woke up this morning." She grimaced as the effort to talk became too much for her. "I need — to rest a little."

"Yes, you rest, Mom. I'll come back when you're feeling better."

Her mother's eyelids fluttered, and she gave a deep sigh. They had given her a shot of something to control the pain. She was struggling against it, trying to keep her thoughts in order so that she could convey them.

"And — Janie?"

"Yes, Mom?"

"He can't help what he is, you know. Dad's father — he used to use a horse whip. Your daddy told me about it once. When he and his brother were naughty, his father used to go out to the garage and get that whip."

"That has nothing to do with you and me," Jane said.

"Maybe — it could help you — understand better."

"I will never understand him," Jane said softly, "and I never want to."

And now, staring at the man in the easy chair, she said again, "I simply can't believe you. You're — unreal."

"I seem to be real enough when it comes to paying the bills around here," Bart Rheardon said. "I'm 'real' when you want a new dress or curtains for your room or a movie ticket. How many kids do you know who get an allowance the size of yours?"

"You're an asshole."

Jane spoke the words slowly and clearly, enunciating each syllable. They shot into the air between them and hung there, so sharp and strident that they could almost be seen. Her father's eyes widened with shocked surprise.

"An asshole," Jane repeated with satisfaction. "Mom won't say it, but I will, I'll say it for both of us. And when she gets out of the hospital, she's not coming back here. I'm not going to let her."

"I don't think you'll have much to say about that," Mr. Rheardon said.

"I think I will, Dad."

"I say you won't. End of story."

"This isn't the Dark Ages," Jane said. "Women don't have to let themselves get beaten up, and they don't have to watch other women get beaten. I'm going to the police."

"And accomplish what, Jane? It will be your word against mine and your mother's. She's not going to back you up."

"She doesn't have to. There'll be the doctors at the hospital. They've seen her bruises. Not just her face right now, which is bad enough, but the others. She's got them all over her."

"Your mother has had several unfortunate falls," Mr. Rheardon said in a tight, controlled voice. "She herself will testify to that if she is forced to. Nobody is going to listen to a kid like you, especially when the person you're supposedly defending calls you a liar."

"They *will* listen to me! I'll make them listen!"

"You can't make anybody do anything," Bart Rheardon said with a short laugh. "A little piece of chicken fluff like you has about as much clout as peach fuzz."

"You'd better think twice before you say something like that, Daddy," Jane said in a burst of anger. "You know what your sweet little 'chicken fluff, peach fuzz' daughter was doing this afternoon? She was chopping up office furniture with an ax!"

"You don't even own an ax."

"It came from Paula's house. Her brother Tom takes

282

it with him when he goes hunting. We all got to use it! We chopped up the desk! You should've seen it!" The words came pouring out of her in an uncontrollable rush. "Mr. Shelby's desk was this big, mahogany thing; now it's like firewood! And the cabinets and the bookshelves, we did the same to them! We burned all the books! That was Kelly's idea. We had to rip them up to start with because they were too thick, but that didn't matter. We had the whole afternoon!"

"You're making this up."

"I'm not making up anything! Every bit of it's true!" His refusal to believe her drove her to greater fury. "I'm nobody's 'chicken.' I'm a woman, and women are powerful! We can do whatever we want when we band together! You lay a hand on my mom again and you'll find out how strong we are! We'll make you sorry — even sorrier than Peter!"

Her voice was rising higher and higher, a shriek of desperation. Far and shrill, she could hear it screaming out words she never meant to say. *Stop,* she cried to it silently. *Stop! Please, be quiet!* But it wouldn't obey her.

"We'll get you! We'll punish you!" the voice screamed.

Jane saw her father rise from his chair and come toward her, but she didn't take in his full intent until she felt the blow. His fist struck her on the left ear and sent her reeling backward across the room into the bookcase. The wooden shelves behind her kept her from falling, and she stood, leaning against them, stunned into silence.

Her father said, "Come here."

No! Jane mouthed the word, but no sound came. Terror drained all strength from her body. She lifted her left hand and pressed it against the side of her face.

"I said, come here!" Bart Rheardon said hoarsely. "Do you hear me, daughter?"

Numbly, Jane nodded. She managed to get her feet aligned under her and took a tentative step forward. The world spun dizzily around her. She took another step, and her father's hand closed hard on her shoulder.

"Now, you listen to me," he said, "and you listen good. Number one, you're resigning from that Daughters of Eve club. I don't know what's going on there, but whatever it is, it's turned you into a vicious, smart-mouthed troublemaker in just a couple of months. Number two, you're not moving out of here until you graduate. This town would have a heyday gossiping about 'that Rheardon girl who left home to live with one of her teachers.'

"Number three, you're going to shape up and behave yourself. You raise your voice to me one more time, and you're going to find yourself sharing a hospital room with your mother. Do you understand me?"

Jane made a second painful attempt to nod her head.

"You tell me, 'Yes, Dad.'"

"Yes, Dad." She brought the words out in a whisper.

He released her shoulder, and she took a quick step backward.

"You're not leaving this house. You're here to stay awhile." Bart Rheardon went back to his chair and seated himself. He picked up the glass, which he had set down on the coffee table, raised it to his lips and took a long swallow. "That teacher was with you, right?"

"What do you mean?"

"When you girls were in Shelby's office axing up his furniture, your friend Ms. Stark was right there with you. She had to have been or you'd never have been able to get into the building."

"I thought you didn't believe me," Jane said in a cracked voice.

"Maybe I do, maybe I don't. We'll see. If it really happened, it's all going to be in the papers. And let me tell you, if it did happen the way you said it did, that Stark woman isn't just going to be out a teaching job — she's going to find herself behind bars. We've got enough trouble with our kids today without having people like that around to influence them."

"You won't say anything?" Jane asked wretchedly. "Please, Dad, you can't! Irene's been so good to me!"

"Don't you try telling me what I can and can't do." He picked up the newspaper, which had fallen to the floor beside his chair, and opened it to the sports section. "Go fix us some dinner."

Jane stood, staring at him. "You want me to cook for you now?"

"Damned right, I do. With your mother out of commission, you're the woman of the house. You might as well start learning what woman's work is all about."

Jane didn't move for a moment, and then she slowly crossed the room.

In the kitchen, her mother's heavy iron skillet stood in the drying rack. Jane picked it up and held it a moment, testing the weight of it. Then she went back into the living room, moving quietly, and stood behind her father's chair.

She lifted the skillet as high above her head as she was able. She closed her eyes. The smell of lemon-scented hair tonic filled her nostrils, and beneath it there was the faint, lingering odor of pipe tobacco. There was nothing of her mother. Nothing at all.

The left side of her face twitched violently.

With her eyes still closed, Jane braced herself and brought the skillet down with all her strength onto the top of her father's head.

FOR THE RECORD

Three years later.

Erika Schneider is a first-semester senior at the University of Michigan at Ann Arbor, working toward a Bachelor of Science degree in biochemistry.

Ann Whitten Brewer is a housewife in Modesta, Michigan. She is the mother of two sons, David Jr., two-and-a-half years, and John, seven months. Her watercolor paintings have won prizes in two state fairs, and she has started selling them online.

Tammy Carncross is a junior, majoring in English at Hillsdale College, Hillsdale, Michigan.

Kelly Johnson is a junior, prelaw, at the University of Michigan at Ann Arbor.

Holly Underwood was killed in an automobile

accident the summer following her high school graduation. She was returning from a party celebrating her scholarship to New England Conservatory in Boston.

Paula Brummell is a saleswoman for JCPenney in Adrian, Michigan.

Madison Ellis is a fashion model who works for a prominent agency based in New York City.

Kristy Grange Brummell is a housewife, and works as an administrative assistant for an insurance agency in Modesta, Michigan.

Laura Snow Keller is a housewife in Cumberland, Rhode Island. She is the wife of an insurance salesman and the mother of a daughter, Mona Irene, four months. Her mother lives in a condo two blocks away.

Jane Rheardon is a patient at the Forest View Psychiatric Hospital in Grand Rapids, Michigan.

Irene Stark is the assistant principal at Modesta High School. For the fourth consecutive year she is sponsor of the Modesta chapter of a national sorority called Daughters of Eve.

Q&A WITH THE AUTHOR

Young adult author Malinda Lo sat down with

Lois Duncan to ask her all about

Daughters of Eve

Malinda: First, I just want to say, Lois, I'm such a big fan of yours. I read all of your books that I could find when I was a teen!

Lois: Thank you.

Malinda: DAUGHTERS OF EVE is an incredible book. When I read the original version I thought it was really an amazing portrait of a specific time in U.S. history: the late 1970s, when the women's movement was pushing so many boundaries everywhere in our culture. I don't believe that sexism has been totally vanquished today, but now it's often a lot more subtle than it was back then. So when you were updating this story, how did you deal with the differences in sexism between now and then?

Lois: This was the hardest one of my novels to revise. As you say, the original version has to be viewed in the context of the time in which it was written. DAUGHTERS OF EVE was published in 1979 when the feminist movement was just taking hold, and girls of that generation, including my own teenage daughters, were very confused about what was expected of them, and what their rights were, and what they really wanted out of life. Men and boys were equally confused about the new social roles that women were trying out. Everything was in chaos and people were acting out their fears and resentments in sometimes inappropriate ways. That's what the story portrayed; it was a slice of social history. In revising it I had to keep making reference to the fact that this little rural town was sort of a throwback. In the words of Irene Stark, it was a town that was "stuck in a time warp." That's the only way I could handle the situation.

Malinda: Everybody's actions in this book are so complicated, and nothing is black or white, not even the ending. I'm really curious to know what inspired you to write this book, since it's really quite different than the other suspense novels you've written.

Lois: It is very different, and I was inspired to write it because I wanted to write something different. I don't like to write the same book over and over again. The idea I got was that I would have a fanatical, charismatic adult exerting influence upon vulnerable kids who looked up to and respected that adult. I wanted it to be in a setting where other adults, such as parents, wouldn't be aware of what was happening. So my first idea was to have it be a church youth group with a charismatic, male Sunday school teacher. I actually wrote five chapters and it was going pretty well, and then I thought, *Oh, my lord, this will be banned everywhere. School librarians* *will be afraid to put it on the shelves because all the fundamentalist parents will be furious.* You have just got to stay away from things having to do with religion. So I started over and I used the same theme, but I made the adult a vehement feminist female.

Malinda: It's funny that you say it would be banned everywhere. Did this book get any sort of push back like that when it was published?

Lois: Oh, yes. I keep being informed by kids that it was banned here and there. But the author is the last to know when a book is banned.

Malinda: Did they tell you why it was banned?

Lois: I think all the feminists think it's antifeminist, and all the antifeminists think it's feminist. I was trying to walk a nice gray line, but people who feel very strongly about a subject don't want a nice gray line. They want it to be all black or all white.

Malinda: I felt that in the original edition, Irene Stark really did walk that gray line, but for some reason setting it in 2011 seemed to turn her into more of a caricature of a feminist—like a feminazi. Do you think changing the setting changed Irene's character a little bit?

Lois: I think it might have, yes. I can't pinpoint how. But I think it did and I think she became nastier in the second version. But also, I think her cause was justified; she had been misused by a man she trusted and by an employer she trusted. But she took it too far and went over the edge.

Malinda: How do you feel about Irene as a character?

Lois: I think Irene is a very bitter woman and has reason to be, but is also probably unstable. And when she becomes a fanatic, she goes all the way.

Malinda: Well, another one of the really interesting changes you made when updating this book was that you really intensified the actions the girls take when they assault Peter and when they break into the science lab. The things they do in the newer version are much more violent, I think. Why did you choose to do that?

Lois: My editor wanted me to do it. Today's teens are so conditioned to violence from movies and video games that she thought they would find the acts of vengeance in the earlier version of the book ridiculously tame. So I made those changes reluctantly, and then I realized she was right. But I didn't go so far as to have real physical violence. What was done to Peter was worse than what happened in the first book, but nobody did him any real physical harm.

Malinda: It was really chilling, though, to see these acts intensified.

Lois: There's a mob mentality here, too, and that applies to women as well as men.

Malinda: In one particular instance you changed one word that I thought was very, very telling. You changed the word "communist" to "terrorist," and it really made me think that the more things change, the more things stay the same.

Lois: I think you hit it. That's exactly what it is. You can always find villains in any era—or people who are regarded as villains. One group might be regarded that way in one era, but somebody else takes their place in the next one.

Malinda: How do you think women's roles have changed, or not changed, since you first wrote DAUGHTERS OF EVE?

Lois: I think women today have a lot more opportunities than women did at the time I wrote DAUGHTERS OF EVE, as far as careers go, but there has been a painful trade-off. There is one indisputable fact that can never be changed, and that is that women are the ones who have babies. That triggers women to want to build nests and to see to it that those babies are well cared for and happy. So women are torn, because they have only so much energy to give, and to invest yourself full-time in a demanding career and at the same time be a fully devoted mother is very hard. So in some ways women's lives have changed for the better, and in other ways they haven't, because so much more is now expected of them than used to be expected of them.

Malinda: That's true. There is one line in your book where one of the girls is talking to her mother and her mother did say that the reason men do things is because they can't have babies. I thought that was really poignant and a very deep moment in the book. Thinking about teen girls today reading DAUGHTERS OF EVE now, why do you think girls will still identify with this story?

Lois: I think the characters are believable in whatever era they're presented. I don't think that the personality of those girls would be any different back when I wrote the book than they would be today; it's just that the pressures upon them might be different. I think that if you look at this many girls, you're going to relate to somebody.

Malinda: Well, I know that every girl in this book had a certain aspect of her personality that I definitely related to. Is there any one character in the book whom you felt most like when you were growing up?

Lois: No, I don't think so. Not one particular one. I think aspects of myself are in every one of them, except perhaps Jane. Because it's very hard to write about a character without some part of yourself creeping into that character, just out of your subconscious, because that's what's familiar to you. And that's what makes characters real.

Malinda: Unlike some of your other books, there isn't just one central female protagonist — there are ten girls here. Why did you decide to write the book from each of their perspectives instead of just focusing on one?

Lois: I wanted the challenge of trying to write from that many viewpoints, and it was hard, because I think perhaps I had too many characters. But you can't have a club with only three characters in it, so some of the characters I used just as foils, while I let the stronger characters — or the more dramatic characters — carry the brunt of the story. But I wanted to at least show glimpses of the others, to fill it out.

Malinda: Let's talk a little bit about this idea you had of a charismatic person leading these teens into dangerous fanaticism. You said your original idea was the charismatic Sunday school teacher, which is so fascinating. And then you have Ms. Stark here, who is really making a huge impression on the girls she teaches — they're so susceptible to her teaching. Just as a teacher has a responsibility to guide his or her students in their education, do you feel any similar responsibility as an author?

Lois: Yes, I do. That's one reason that I have set some standards for myself that I try to stick to. My novels don't contain sensationalized violence or graphic descriptions of gore and horror, and they don't contain explicit sex scenes. In this book, Ann does get pregnant, but that happens offstage. The reader doesn't watch it happen like a voyeur. And Jane's act of violence at the end is very played down. She commits the act, and it's shocking, not entertaining, and then it stops and the reader doesn't wallow in a vivid description of the aftermath of it.

Malinda: Do you think that's part of the reason you decided to write for a young audience? To tell these kinds of stories without resorting to more graphic language?

Lois: I started writing for a young audience because I was so young myself. Teen issues were all I knew about, and when I got one book published, the publisher optioned my next book, whatever it would be—but it had to be a young adult book. So I wrote another one and they optioned my next one. I got into the genre because of my own age. I was writing pretty much for my peers. And then later, when people kept trying to get me to write for adults, I realized that I didn't want to have to go into sensationalized violence and explicit sex. This way, writing for teens, I could still write about all of the subjects that interested me, and I still could write with suspense and write an exciting story, but I would not have to write about things that made me uncomfortable. So I was happier staying there, and although I have written in many other genres as well, this is the genre that I've had the most success with.

Malinda: Even if you don't describe them in detail, the violence and sex, I feel like your books have scared me more than a lot of YA books.

Lois: I think some of the gory scenes are totally unnecessary. The book actually can be scarier without them, because the readers have to use their imagination.

Malinda Lo, a former entertainment reporter, is the author of *Ash* and *Huntress*, two young adult fantasy novels. She lives in Northern California with her partner and their dog. Her website is www.malindalo.com.

LOIS DUNCAN

Lois Duncan is the author of over fifty books, ranging from children's picture books to poetry to adult nonfiction, but is best known for her young adult suspense novels, which have received Young Readers Awards in sixteen states and three foreign countries. In 1992, Lois was presented the Margaret A. Edwards Award by the *School Library Journal* and the ALA Young Adult Library Services Association for "a distinguished body of adolescent literature." In 2009, she received the St. Katharine Drexel Award, given by the Catholic Library Association "to recognize an outstanding contribution by an individual to the growth of high school and young adult librarianship and literature."

Lois was born in Philadelphia, Pennsylvania, and grew up in Sarasota, Florida. She knew from early childhood that she wanted to be a writer. She submitted her first story to a magazine at age ten and became published at thirteen. Throughout her high school years she wrote regularly for young people's publications, particularly *Seventeen*.

As an adult, Lois moved to Albuquerque, New Mexico, where she taught magazine writing for the Journalism Department at the University of New Mexico and continued to write for magazines. Over three hundred of her articles and stories appeared in such publications as *Ladies' Home Journal*, *Redbook*,

McCall's, *Good Housekeeping* and *Reader's Digest*, and for many years she was a contributing editor for *Woman's Day*.

Six of her novels—SUMMER OF FEAR, KILLING MR. GRIFFIN, GALLOWS HILL, RANSOM, DON'T LOOK BEHIND YOU and STRANGER WITH MY FACE—were made-for-TV movies. I KNOW WHAT YOU DID LAST SUMMER and HOTEL FOR DOGS were box office hits.

Although young people are most familiar with Lois Duncan's fictional suspense novels, adults may know her best as the author of WHO KILLED MY DAUGHTER?, the true story of the murder of Kaitlyn Arquette, the youngest of Lois's children. Kait's heartbreaking story has been featured on such TV shows as *Unsolved Mysteries*, *Good Morning America*, *Larry King Live*, *Sally Jessy Raphael* and *Inside Edition*. A full account of the family's ongoing personal investigation of this still unsolved homicide can be found on the Internet at http://kaitarquette .arquettes.com.

Lois and her husband, Don Arquette, currently live in Sarasota, Florida. They are the parents of five children.

You can visit Lois at http://loisduncan.arquettes.com.

DISCOVER THE

Thrills

AND Chills

I KNOW WHAT YOU DID LAST SUMMER

They didn't mean to kill him

LOIS DUNCAN

THE BESTSELLING AUTHOR OF *KILLING MR. GRIFFIN*

Revenge is a dangerous lesson.

KILLING MR. GRIFFIN

LOIS DUNCAN

THE BESTSELLING AUTHOR OF *I KNOW WHAT YOU DID LAST SUMMER*

DON'T LOOK BEHIND YOU

The chase is on.

LOIS DUNCAN

THE BESTSELLING AUTHOR OF *I KNOW WHAT YOU DID LAST SUMMER*

LOIS DUNCAN

Available wherever books are sold.

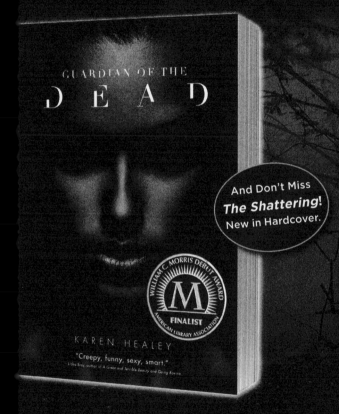